7

EXPERT WITNESS: A TESTIMONY

Volume Two

Awakenings

By

J. Richardson

To my Dad, who was my rock in the storm; to my Mum who, even in her final illness, shone a light for me; to Richard, who understood before I did; to Esme, who gave me shelter and kept me sane; to Amy, of Women's Aid, who helped me plan a future; to Lynn, who listened and helped me look at things more positively; to Marianne for her support and cool detective work; to Hilary, who took time to share her kindness and wisdom with this un-believer; to Sharon, who showed me how to fight back; to Joe, who never, ever gave up on me and to Anna, who carried me.

I would further like to dedicate this book to everyone out there, in the courts or in their private lives, who are struggling against domestic abuse and all other injustices and oppression, against all the odds.

I would like to acknowledge the many acts of compassion from many friends, family and strangers who helped me when I needed it – without any one of whom I might have gone under, leaving this story untold; also the help and support from 'Women's Aid' and their material I have reproduced here, from memory, in the hope it will help others; I would also like to acknowledge the support and insight from my trade union, *Unison*, in the fight to tell the truth about domestic abuse.

I would further like to acknowledge the insights I gained into the function and fallibility of expert witness evidence from reading 'Memoirs of a Radical Lawyer' by Michael Mansfield.

Also, thanks to Graham Norton for his insight into the human heart, which I found helpful and have quoted in this book; and also to the great rock-band 10CC, for their song-lyrics, likewise quoted herein.

CONTENTS

Chapter 1

Obviously the police wanted to check what had happened and see if everything was okay. I moved Joe from my lap onto his cushion; he was engrossed in the Postman Pat drama which was unfolding on the screen, and I went to answer the door. A police woman and a police man stood there.

I said, "Hello?"

She said, "We're here to arrest you on suspicion of assault." It sounded strange in the crisp spring sunshine.

I invited them in.

She said, "You'll need to come down to the office for a couple of hours, is there somewhere you can leave your little boy?"

Joe came through and I said the nice police were here to make sure we're okay. I kept my hands out of sight so he wouldn't see they were shaking.

The police officer offered Joe his cap and Joe put it on, laughing as it fell over his eyes; I laughed with him. Everything had to be normal so as not to scare him.

The police woman asked me if I wanted to sit down. I did and she sat with me and then asked me what had happened. The police man went into the back room, Jay's bedroom, and Joe toddled after him. I saw the policeman partly close the door and look at what he saw on the wall behind it. I saw Joe, standing next to the policeman, also look up and heard him say, "What's that?" as he also looked at the bloodstain on the wall.

As Joe was out of hearing I started to tell her in a whisper – then suddenly choking as long suppressed stress rose up in my throat and I had to speak around it. I started crying. I realised I was shaking as I remembered the scenes of that morning, of thinking I was going to get killed. It all seemed surreal, as if it had happened to somebody else, as if this was happening to somebody else. I explained about Jay losing his temper and my trying to get out of his way and then realising I'd actually hit him with the pan, I hadn't meant to, I'd just wanted him to not start hitting me – in case he wouldn't then be able to stop.

She asked if there was somewhere Joe could go while I came down to the station to sort things out.

Of course, I realised, they would have to talk to Jay so he could tell them about his anger rages and how he sometimes went out of control and hit things – so then they'd understand.

I thought of Joe's various friends – there were two parents I could ask to look after him – I chose Esme: she would be at home, she already had four children and Joe could just fit in as he did when we visited normally. We were not confidantes, I didn't confide in anybody after all, but she was kind and I liked the way she looked after her kids – Joe would be fine there for a couple of hours. Also, she was not alone – she had her mother and her partner living with her while Marianne was alone. For some reason, I felt Marianne might be vulnerable if Jay turned up. He didn't like any of my friends after all.

Esme and I knew each other because Joe and her youngest, Ed, had become friends in the nursery and we'd sought each other out at the nursery door. Joe had been to her house several times; for glorious Easter Egg hunts around her farm and to Ed's birthday party: Jay had even come along that time and met with she and her husband on one of the rare occasions he'd come out with us. They had later offered him some work around the farm but he'd declined.

Esme and her son had even visited our house for the children to play – together with Marianne and her little boy. I hadn't repeated this experiment as Jay had found it too stressful. He had snarled at me upstairs that he didn't like Joe having food in his room when I'd taken the children a picnic plate of sandwiches to eat as they played. I'd then hurriedly persuaded the children, keeping my voice low below the music so the other parents wouldn't hear this odd change of plan, to come downstairs, setting up a little tent with blankets on the furniture to maintain the 'treat' and hide the real reason they couldn't eat in his room, terrified the whole time that Jay would 'lose it' – and then Joe's friends' mothers would leave and Joe would lose his friends. It hadn't been worth the risk of inviting them again so we always went to their houses except when Jay was away. But neither Esme nor Marianne knew anything about that. I'd kept quiet about my real home-life for fear of driving people like them away. They didn't know it but they had long been my lifelines.

I rang her. She came on the phone and I explained – it was difficult to put into words on this sunny Sunday morning. "Sorry to bother you – but the police are here – it's because I've hit Jay over the head with a frying pan – he was going for me – and now I'm being arrested and I need someone to look after Joe for a couple of hours?"

I waited for her to be silent for a moment and then for the change in her voice as she said, "Oh, sorry, we're really busy today." But instead she said, "Of course, yes, he can stay as long as wanted. No problem. Are you okay?"

I said 'thank you' and it was arranged.

I told Joe, all cheerfully and happy for his sake, that he was invited to go and play over at Ed's and he was delighted. I got together what he'd need in his rucksack – sunhat, sun-cream, change of clothes. I switched off the television. We went to get in the police car.

I made it fun for Joe. "We're going in a real police car!" We were sat in the back of the car together and Joe still had the police hat on. We drove the few miles to the farm where Esme lived and pulled up. Joe got out of the car and ran down to where we could see Ed and his brothers, playing in the sandpit in the garden. Esme came out to see me and I started to explain again but she hugged me, waved me away, took the rucksack and told me Joe'd be fine.

The police car pulled out and I could see the top of Joe's favourite pink sunhat among the hats and heads of his friends as we reversed out of the drive.

Then the floodwave came. That dark cloud I'd kept pressed down for so long, until it had grown and spread to hide in every corner of my life, welled up and overwhelmed me at last. I sat in the back of the police car racked with sobs which hurt my throat and would not be stopped. I had never left Joe anywhere before except at crèche.

After the first storm, I struggled to become coherent again and told it all, blurted it all out; all about Jay, all about what had happened, all about what he had threatened, what annoyed him, the endless list of what annoyed him, what irritated, what upset, what hurt; what I tried to do to help, to avoid making him angry; what had gone wrong that morning, how I usually managed to keep out of his way, how angry he would get, how it had got worse since I'd told him I wanted to leave, how he wasn't always like that but you could never tell when he was going to 'blow'…

I didn't seem to be able to stop talking, and crying and my voice choked and cracked, high-pitched, breaking, not like my voice at all. I struggled to control it and sound normal. My throat hurt. The police officers didn't interrupt. The radio crackled intermittently.

They were also talking on the radio to someone else as we travelled the long twenty-five miles into town. The police man asked me if I had a solicitor. Why would I need a solicitor?

At the police station, I had to stand behind a line painted on the floor in front of the desk and tell them my name, my date of birth and give them the belt off my jeans and the laces out of my trainers. I realised that was to stop me hanging myself and was routine.

The officer said, looking at the screen on his computer, "You've never been in trouble before, have you?"

Then I was allowed to make one phone call. I rang Esme to give her the number of the police station so she could ring if there was any problem with Joe or if he wanted to speak to me. I'd never left him anywhere before except at nursery. It might be strange for him to be at Ed's house without me being there. Silly really, as the officers had said it would only be for a couple of hours and he was used to me being away for eight.

Another police woman took DNA samples from inside my cheek and from under my nails. There was blood on my fingers. She took samples off my clothes. She asked if these were the clothes I'd been wearing 'during the incident'. I explained they weren't as I'd been in my pyjamas and had wet myself so I had changed. She asked what had happened so I told her about it. It sounded surreal. It had all happened so fast – one minute I'd been making breakfast, doing usual things to try and keep the atmosphere alright and not annoy Jay – and the next minute I was here in the police station with blood on my hands.

She asked if my partner had a military background and nodded when I said 'yes' – it was a pattern they'd seen before. I wanted to explain that Jay wasn't like that – he was no bully; he couldn't help his rages and didn't know what he was doing, anything could trigger him, I wanted her to understand and not think badly of him – but it was time for my photograph and then to wait in a cell.

The cell had its own metal toilet and a CCTV camera and a wooden bench-bed with a blanket. I'd been in police cells before, keeping youngsters company, as their key-worker from the children's home or as a social worker, when they had been arrested. I'd ask to wait with them to keep them company rather than sit outside in the police station office – but I'd not been in a cell on my own before or on my own account.

I didn't know what else to do so I asked God or gods or the universe – anyone really – to look after Joe and keep him safe. In my mind's eye, I could see Jay leaving the hospital and, in a temper, going to snatch Joe. Jay was still at the hospital, an officer told me – but the ambulance paramedic had said that he was okay and that he was only going in for some routine tests so he'd probably be out later that day.

What would he do? Would he lose his temper with the staff in the hospital? He hated hospitals – and then they might spot he needed help. He might listen to them more than to me as they were professionals, in uniform. He had had therapy before. He had had anger-management therapy. Would he realise at last he couldn't carry on like this – terrifying people, attacking people, even people who loved him? Would he at last accept we couldn't carry on?

The time ticked by. An hour, then two went by. Then another. I used the toilet in the cell. I lay down on the bench. Esme rang and left a message that Joe was okay and had his sun-cream and hat on this bright spring day and a police officer brought me this message. I was so grateful to him and to Esme for knowing I needed to know this.

Lunchtime came and they brought me lunch. They told me Jay was still in the hospital waiting for tests. This was routine as they had to do this with any head injury. At least he wasn't yet on his way back to the house. Would the police tell him where Joe was? Would he go to Esme's house? Would he snatch Joe? He had threatened to snatch him a few times after all. Did Esme guess what he was like and that she might be in danger?

The police had to wait for a solicitor before interviewing me and they had to wait to hear from the hospital too. I knew it was always best to have a solicitor with you when being interviewed by the police from working with youngsters but it seemed a bit over the top in this case as it had all been a terrible mistake on my part.

I should never have gone into his room when he was already in a bad mood – although I'd thought turning the television down, not off, might have helped that – but my going into his 'space' must have been the last straw when he was in that kind of mood. Stupid of me. I usually avoided invading his space when he was edgy. But then he would get angry and 'kick off' about children's television in general and adverts in particular when the mood took him. At other times, he'd find them amusing. It was always difficult to know what was best to do as what set him off changed so much from day to day.

And the reflex action of hitting out behind me when I heard him losing his temper so close behind me, feeling the frying pan I was holding connect with something solid and the tide of fear that had then risen, realising I had actually hit him, whirling round to fend off his fists which always hit out at whatever was in reach when he 'blew' – and hitting him for real, his stumbling back against the edge of the door, it slamming, Jay sliding down its width into the corner, pushing himself up, leaving a blood stain on the wall and coming towards me, blank-eyed, me thinking these were the last moments of my life and Joe was upstairs and what would happen to him?

Then Jay, stepping towards me, stumbling on the mattress on the floor and falling sideways, landing hard with the edge of his head on the wooden bench under the window and lying still, me standing frozen with the pan still in my hand, unable to move except shaking with fear, *Stay down, don't touch me! Stay down, don't touch me!* or something in desperation. Seeing the edge of his head on the hard edge of the bench, realising he wasn't going to get up and attack me and that he was hurt, handing him a cloth from off the bed to fold and put between his head and the bench to soften it. He took up the cloth and wrapped it around his head. Then he'd said, "I'm bleeding. I need an ambulance."

Then hearing Joe running back down the stairs, banging on the door, shouting, "Mummy! Mummy!" and coming in. "What happened?"

Following me out as I said, "Daddy's had an accident – I need to ring the hospital – to get an ambulance."

"Is that your work?" he'd said, coming to the telephone with me. Joe knew I worked in a hospital.

Then Jay suddenly walking past us and out of the house, draped in the duvet which was stained with blood. "I'm going next door to get a lift."

I told the man on the phone he had just walked out and the man said he would stop the ambulance coming if he had left the area. Totally confused, I told the man yes, he would be here, no problem, and ran out after giving Joe one of his toys to sit with at the table, saying, "I'll be back in a minute."

Jay was standing in the road, waving his phone to get a signal, me grabbing his phone and rushing back into the garden to get him to follow me or at least get off the road, the ambulance already on its way. He came towards me, cursing and I stepped quickly out of his way, the phone dropping on the grass verge. At least he was off the road. I ran back in the house but he headed off down the road.

This played through my head over and over again as I lay on the bench in the cell. I couldn't remember the order of things as it was all jumbled up but the pieces kept replaying. What had Joe seen? He'd come into the room, Jay had been lying down, his head wrapped in the pillowcase and himself covered in the duvet. He'd heard 'the incident' from upstairs – shouting, yelling. He'd seen the bloodstain on the wall. He hadn't known what it was though. He had heard Jay shouting before. He hadn't seemed distressed this morning. It had all been over a lot quicker than some of Jay's rages we had both lived through.

I lay on the bed-bench. Jay would want to separate now, surely, but how could I keep Joe safe? I knew Jay would be okay as the ambulance paramedic had told me he was okay – but what would he do now? Surely he wouldn't really want to take Joe – he didn't really enjoy looking after him after all so why would he? For revenge, came the answer. I'd stepped way out of line. I should have let him hit me. This was the second time I'd fended him off. But when he lost his temper he didn't know what he was doing – I knew that much. Once he'd started hitting me – when would he have stopped? If I'd done a bad thing or reminded him of his dad he may well not stop until I was dead – he hadn't stopped with that young man until he'd been pulled off him. Would he take out his anger on Joe? Would his attachment to his child be enough to protect Joe?

Jay couldn't cope when I crossed him even just verbally or even when I didn't wholeheartedly agree with something he said – and I'd just clouted him with a frying pan. He'd probably 'triggered' about the television being left on too loud and had still been angry with me about the day before – but as soon as the frying pan touched him he had gone over the edge with rage. Thank God Joe had been upstairs – what if I'd been carrying him?

About 6pm that evening, the police were ready to interview me. There was a duty solicitor and I was called out of the cell to meet with him. His name was Richard. I'd met duty solicitors before when they met with the youngsters who had been arrested for taking and driving away without consent or caught burglaring or causing criminal damage of some kind. It felt surreal to be meeting with a solicitor for myself as if someone else, an errant teenager, was missing from the scene.

I started to explain what had happened that morning but he seemed to know what had happened and cut across me with the following:

"What was it like at home – did you used to be treading on eggshells?"

The question seemed to cut straight to a tender, delicate, painful point I never looked at. Treading on eggshells?

I'd heard the phrase before but had never applied it to myself. But it summed up exactly how I behaved around Jay – trying to be careful, not to make a noise or break anything. Tense all the time. Anxious all the time. Fearful of what might happen next.

But it wasn't like that. It wasn't as if I wasn't coping. Tense all the time, but careful not to act as if I was tense – as that would also trigger Jay. He would get really angry if he sensed I was anxious about anything. He hated me to look anything other than cheerful and quiet – he said it reminded him of how his mother had looked if I looked anxious or nervous or unhappy – and that annoyed him too.

I said yes, that's right – but only because Jay often lost his temper but he couldn't help it. I wanted Richard, this young man in his suit, to understand. He needed to know that Jay couldn't help it and that made all the difference.

"Did he sometimes do things that frightened you?" he asked next.

I had to agree that Jay did – in wonderment that he could get this so accurately and without my saying anything. He was very young, smartly dressed and good looking. He was much too young to understand all the complexity around Jay's and my relationship.

I tried to explain, "I sometimes remind him of his father – and that would frighten him but make him angry with me... He'd have flashbacks... He couldn't help it..."

He interrupted me again. "Were you ever afraid of him?"

That word – 'ever'. I was, but my word was 'only sometimes'.

I wanted him to understand Jay, "Not all the time. He couldn't help it, you see..."

"Did he ever hit you?"

"No." I was clear about that. "Never – he usually hit things – like the wall or a door or throws something. I usually keep out of reach when I've made him cross. I got it wrong today." My voice was small.

"So he would throw things? Shout at you, swear and threaten you?"

"Yes – but he couldn't help it! He didn't mean it!" I had to make this young man understand that. He had to understand. It sounded terrible the way he put it.

"How long have you been with him?"

I thought for a moment. "Six years."

He looked at me a moment then wrote something down.

"Sounds to me like abuse," he said. "Sounds like you're the victim of long-term emotional or psychological abuse."

It was the first time I'd heard that word or been made to apply it to myself. I opened my mouth to protest but no sound came out. I shook my head. "No," I managed. "No, I'm not – he never meant it – he couldn't help it." My voice faded.

Jay, who could find his way up a sheer wall of granite, fix a car engine, write poetry, leap out of a plane, did not know what he was doing when he was raging.

Richard looked as if he didn't understand at all. It wasn't like that. I was no victim – victims had broken noses and black eyes. I tried to explain again but he interrupted. He said the police had to interview me but they had not 'disclosed' what it was they were charging me with, or the evidence they had, so he didn't know how to advise me. What was it they were going to 'disclose'? He was quite cross with the police – I'd been in the cell for ten hours but they would not tell him what the problem was or what I was going to be charged with. I wished he wasn't cross, it made me nervous.

Well of course they won't tell you, they don't know, I thought. *It's all a hopeless misunderstanding.* As soon as Jay explained about his depression and anger – all would be well.

I had already told them what had happened – in the car, I'd told them it all – what would they want to interview me for?

Richard said I had to be interviewed 'under oath' and 'under caution'. I wondered what difference that made – I'd already told them everything.

He said it made a big difference and they might

charge me later.

My head swam; charged?

The only advice Richard could give me, he said, was to do a 'No Comment' interview because, without the information from the police, he could not advise me what to say or do. I said I would just tell them what had happened again but he shook his head. "That isn't wise," he said. "Things that people say can be twisted or misunderstood."

I knew that. I knew of the Birmingham Six and the Guildford Four and the Bridgewater Four and the McGuire Seven and the Cardiff Three and Winston Silcott – but that didn't apply to me surely because Jay would explain. He would explain about his temper and his flashbacks and his depression which sent him into wild rages where he didn't know what he was doing.

He had explained it to me often enough.

I'd always coped before but now Jay would see that I obviously wasn't coping any more. Now, surely, he'd accept we had to separate.

He'd tell them of his flashbacks and how he hit out sometimes and 'lost it' and how he was scary sometimes when he was in a 'fit'. How he had depression and how this made him totally lose his temper at times and lose all consciousness of what he was doing – even when he hit things or people.

Richard didn't seem to understand all this and just told me I had to say 'no comment' in response to whatever the police asked me.

Two officers came in and a little tape recorder was switched on and they asked me a lot of questions:

about what had happened that morning; why I had hit Jay; what my life with him was like; what he had done that morning?

Several times I looked at Richard as it seemed mad not to take this chance to help the police understand what had happened if they didn't already, but each time he reminded me of his advice so I ploughed ahead, feeling foolish and sensing the police's irritation at my parrot-like repetition of 'no comment'. I knew I was annoying them and it seemed so unnecessary.

I had sat in such interviews before but never in a 'No Comment' scenario which didn't seem to achieve anything.

I felt this was a formality anyway – the police already knew it all as I'd told their colleagues, the police who had arrested me, all about it, only that morning so this was just a formality.

Richard was angry with the police for keeping me in the cells for so long. I asked him not to upset them. He was also angry and let them know it, that they had made his job impossible by not 'disclosing' whatever it was that they needed to disclose. Apparently, they needed to have told him what I was suspected of and what evidence they had.

Later I had another message from Esme that Joe was okay and that she'd put him to bed in Ed's room. I ached to be back with him, and to hold him and know he was okay.

Richard told me that I wasn't being charged – yet – but was on bail to Esme's address. He explained 'bail' didn't mean I had to pay over lots of money and that I'd watched too many American cop shows. Bail meant I could not go back to our house, Hilldene, yet as it was a suspected 'crime scene' and would need to be searched, nor could I go to my parents which I so wanted to do. This felt very over the top and surreal and frightening. But it would be okay once they understood.

Richard gave me his card and left.

As I left the police station, the police told me that the Domestic Abuse Officers would be coming to interview me tomorrow – which was Monday. This could all be sorted out by Tuesday. Obviously the police had understood what I'd told them and wanted to help. My main concern was Jay snatching Joe – at last I'd be able to get some help to keep Joe safe. Maybe it was still counted as 'domestic abuse' – even when the person couldn't help losing their temper, as Jay couldn't. He wasn't an abuser, of course, but they would need to look into it as he often did things which might be dangerous or even mistaken for abuse.

Outside the police station it was dark and I was twenty-five miles away from Joe. I had no money. Luckily, I had my card with me and I drew out some money. The only way back was to get a taxi. It was £70 fare. I wondered what I would have done if I didn't have money in the bank and a card as there were no buses on a Sunday night. When I reached the farm, there was a note on the kitchen table that they had all gone to bed and that a futon mattress was made up for me in one of the spare rooms. I went upstairs and found Joe fast asleep next to Ed, his little friend.

Joe was clutching a small toy, one of Ed's teddies,

and looked as if he'd fallen asleep suddenly, as kids do sometimes when they are overtired, sitting up against the pillows, his hair sticking up all over his head. I gently scooped him up and carried him with me into the little made-up bedroom and lay down with him, smelling him and holding him as I went to sleep.

Everything would be okay. Jay would leave me. I'd get help to stop him taking Joe if he tried – at least until he'd calmed down. He didn't always know what he was doing but, as Richard had said, that didn't make it any safer for me, did it? No, but I had usually managed to keep myself safe, and Joe – hadn't I?

Joe woke up once in the night. He sat up, a little silhouette against the curtains in our little room and said, sleepily, "I thought you weren't here," and went back to sleep snuggled up against me.

I cuddled him as he went back to sleep and told him, "Don't worry darling, you know I have to go away sometimes – but I'll always come back as soon as I can."

Chapter 2

In the morning, I told Esme; told her all about Jay and me and all the stuff I'd kept from her since we'd met. I'd been so lonely and so afraid of driving people away and of people not wanting their kids to play with Joe if they knew our home-life wasn't quite normal.

I'd been so afraid of Jay realising I'd been talking about us, about him – something he really couldn't cope with. I'd told him once, just once, of talking to my colleagues about the work he was doing on the house – I'd stopped talking as I'd seen the change in his face.

He'd changed colour – glaring at me. Then he'd erupted, teeth clenched – holding back the anger. "You've been talking about ME!? I can't stand people talking about me!" Crash, hit, thump. "I can't stand people bloody people – gossiping – as if I'm some object… Why the hell…?" And on and on. Then later, once he'd recovered, he'd told me his family were always talked about by neighbours and other kids at school so it had made him lose his temper as it took him back to that. He was so sorry if he'd frightened me. But I'd learned.

Esme said Joe had been okay during the day: he'd asked for me several times but she'd been able to distract him – except at bedtime when he'd been distraught and wanting to know where I was so she'd done her best with a story and reassurance and cuddles.

She had noticed that he hadn't once asked for 'Daddy' – only 'Mummy'. She was quite clear and very certain about that. It wasn't surprising – I was his main carer, his main 'attachment figure', after all, as the jargon puts it.

Her own children were going off to nursery that morning, Monday morning. Joe didn't usually go on a Monday as I had only started to work on that day a few months previously. Monday had become the day when Jay looked after Joe – from about ten in the morning until five – I used lieu time from the untaken holiday so I didn't have to leave early in the morning, when Jay was usually in a bad mood, and to get home early before he'd get fed up of childcare. They usually spent the day going out in the van or going around the shops in the nearby town. I was expecting Jay to get fed up with this as he had got fed up with other care arrangements in a few more weeks – and by then Joe would be at school and after-school club so this worry would be over.

So Joe didn't usually go to nursery on a Monday but today, as the Domestic Abuse Officers were visiting me, it would probably be best if Joe wasn't around – if I had to talk about stuff he didn't need to hear. Also, he was really enjoying having his friend to play with so I phoned the nursery to see if he could attend as an extra day. No problem. So, the plan was for Joe to go to nursery with Ed and have as normal a day as possible.

I phoned work and left a message on the answering machine that I wouldn't be in.

I also asked the nursery to ring me if his dad turned up and wanted to take Joe out of the nursery – they said they would. They couldn't stop him – as he was a parent – but they could delay until I got there. Joe went off to the nursery with Ed and the other neighbours' children. That left the way clear for me to meet with the Domestic Abuse Officers when they arrived. Esme waited in with me and said she'd come with me to give support when they arrived as she'd noticed a few things which may be helpful to them.

I was keen to meet with the Domestic Abuse officers. It wasn't a usual Domestic Abuse case but I'd explain about Jay and I'd be able to ask them for help.

I phoned my manager to tell her the outline – that I'd been arrested. She said she already knew about it as it had been reported to social services as there had been 'a child present' and that they were going to have a meeting about it and that they'd be in touch later. She didn't ask me how I was. She was very matter-of-fact. Joe had been upstairs but he hadn't been 'present' – had he?

He had been in the house though.

The hours ticked by. The solicitor had advised me not to ring the hospital as I'd wanted to contact Jay, find out how he was, get his phone to him, and talk to him about separating now. He usually said 'sorry' for losing his temper of for frightening me and this time I would be able to say sorry too – for hitting him. He was sometimes okay for days after a 'rage' and, if we spoke on the phone, it would be safer than having to meet; he was more likely to be reasonable. But Richard had said it could be 'misconstrued' if I tried to contact him – so I didn't.

My manager rang again and told me that two social work managers were dealing with the 'case' and would be in touch. Why were they involved?

My heart sank as she named Anastasia Patterson and her sidekick, Dan Pritchard, as the ones who'd be coming to visit. My manager explained that it had to be managers dealing with 'the case' as I was myself, a social worker. That was the rule.

No, not them, anyone but them, I thought, a grey, dull feeling starting in my stomach – I realised it was dread. Surely she knew I was not on good terms with either of them? She'd met with us to try and resolve differences when I'd complained about their attitudes to clients. She knew my concerns about their attitude to people. That was apart from my clashing with them as a shop-steward. But I checked myself for being unreasonable. They were professionals and would help me as anyone else, putting our differences behind them. They were obviously the Domestic Abuse Officers the police had referred to – part of their social work role. I felt sick in my stomach at the thought that they were involved but there seemed no other option.

Later in the afternoon the phone rang and it was Anastasia Patterson. She had been at the meeting they had had and knew about 'the incident'. She asked me where Joe was, I told her he was at nursery and I was waiting for the Domestic Abuse Officers to arrive. It had begun to feel a great relief that more people now knew about what had been going on and what had happened. I would be getting help. Joe would be safer Jay would be getting help. It was going to be better. We were going to be able to separate safely.

She asked me if the people I was staying with were 'supporting me' – I was surprised and touched at her understanding and sympathy. She had obviously been able to put our past differences behind her and was treating me kindly. I reassured her that, yes, Esme and her husband were supporting me. No doubt Anastasia had worked with other women who had been scared out of their wits by their partners and were in need of support and protection.

Joe came back from nursery in high spirits. He asked, "Are we living here now?" and was pleased when I said 'for now' and gave a little 'hooray!' Esme had told me I could stay as long as I needed to – or wanted to. Her husband had asked if Jay was coming after me and had agreed I could stay. They didn't understand the complexities of Jay's problems with life – but they knew I needed their support.

Esme and her husband had a little caravan tucked away inside an outhouse of their farm which Joe and I could live in for the time being. The outhouse was quite ramshackle and grubby but the caravan inside was sound and dry. Their children used it as a play-space on rainy days or for kiddies' parties. Esme and I had spent the Monday, while waiting for the Domestic Abuse officers, cleaning and tidying it up and moving in a table, switching on the heaters and changing the bed. It was quite comfortable. It meant

Joe and I had our own little space to be together – at least until I knew how Jay was feeling and what his plans were. Then I presumed we could move back to our own house, Hilldene, as Jay would leave – he'd probably go back to be with his climbing friends and share with one of them as he had been doing before we'd met.

Joe and I slept that night, the Monday night, in the little caravan; Joe snuggled next to me and I started to see our future. Joe and I could go and live with my parents; I'd quit my job and find something local to them. Joe would be able to go to a nursery near their house and they would love helping me to look after him, he loved being there. He was young enough to easily make new friends, adapt to a new home and routine – and we could visit his old ones. The Domestic Abuse Officers would understand the risk to Joe of Jay snatching him and would take care around arranging visits for him to see his dad so everyone was safe.

The truth about Jay's mental illness and depression would come out and he would probably get more professional help. I had failed in my role as his partner but I had tried my best.

Playing with Joe in this new caravan early the next morning was a treat – we were both so relaxed and enjoying each other's company. Our future could be like this. I had got out the play dough and it was great playing with it without feeling anxious that Jay might appear at any minute and yell at me for using it. Joe seemed very relaxed too and we played hide and seek for a little while as we had done in the old days in our own caravan, giggling. Only two places to hide but always giggles when he found me or me him.

Joe went off to nursery again, with Ed, in Esme's car, after we'd all had breakfast together in Esme's big kitchen. It was a big day for Joe and for Ed as it was the first afternoon at 'proper school' – which was next door to the nursery. I'd already booked off the afternoon from work, weeks ago, so I could be there to meet him after this big First and pick him up at 3pm. I'd now told work I wouldn't be in that morning either. I waited in for the Domestic Abuse Officers again.

My manager had rung me to say that Anastasia and Dan were coming to see me later that morning. I guessed they were in the role of Domestic Abuse Officers or were doing the same job of following up after an incident and being supportive to a family. I had told her that I was afraid of Jay snatching Joe in a temper and that it would be good to get some help around that.

When they arrived, I met them in Esme's kitchen and made them each a cup of tea. Esme went out to give us some privacy. It was odd to be in the room with two people with whom I'd had such acrimonious relationships in my working life. Odd to have them so suddenly arriving in the middle of my personal life and in such a crisis. I felt so vulnerable. They would know the mess my private life was. But I knew I could trust them to be professional and do what they needed to do to protect Joe and make sure his dad wouldn't snatch him.

Anastasia said, "We've spoken to the police."

Well, that was a relief, I'd told the police all about it and it was a relief not to have to go through it all again now when we needed to be talking about Joe.

Anastasia said, "You know why we're here, don't you?"

I agreed that I did. The police had told me to expect two officers. I hadn't realised they had meant social workers when they'd said 'Domestic Abuse Officers' but it made sense that it was part of the social work role to help people in these circumstances and prevent children being snatched.

I explained about Jay's history of mental illness and violence and my fear of him as he often lost control and didn't know what he was doing. They nodded; they seemed to know about that already. The police must have told them after all – I'd said a lot about it in the car.

They went away then as they needed to go and talk to Jay and would come back later. They would liase between us which was helpful. If Jay was in his reasonable mode – as he would be with professionals around – we'd be able to come up with a good plan. Jay was unlikely to lose his temper or threaten anyone in authority. It would work much better than me trying to negotiate with him. He was still in hospital as he'd had to wait for the routine tests.

Esme and her husband came back and I went over to the caravan so as to give them a break from me.

Then Anastasia and her deputy came back and came into the caravan.

Anastasia said, "We think Joe needs to be with his father now."

The world shifted under me.

What?

She got impatient. "You could have killed him, Cathy – he nearly died!"

What?

Her deputy chipped in – "You are a violent person, Cathy, and we need to protect Joe."

"What? But he'd threatened to kill me... He'd lost his temper again... He'd nearly killed someone before... I reminded him of his dad... He was behind me and I heard him starting to rage... I hadn't meant to hit him – just stop him from hitting me..." I was talking too quickly. My heart was racing...

"He's never hit you, Cathy. Never lifted a hand to you. And now he has very serious head injuries!"

Very serious head injuries?

What? My mouth was probably hanging open as I tried to register what they had just said. Serious head injuries?

But the ambulance man had said...?

"I suppose you're going to claim mitigating circumstances?" said Dan, sarcastically.

A mitigating circumstance? What?

"Joe needs to be with his father."

I heard my voice saying, "But Joe's afraid of his dad when Jay loses it. He runs to me when Jay's angry. He's afraid of him when he's raging," I babbled. I had to make them understand. They had to understand.

They looked at each other and snorted as if in

disbelief.

"He's never hit you. Never lifted a finger," she said. "He swears a lot, he admits to it. He can't help it and you've got a problem with him swearing, haven't you Cathy?" The sarcasm again.

"He hits things. He throws things. He threatened to kill me…"

"That's just his anger-management, isn't it? He's had anger-management problems. But he's never hit you, has he?" She was not asking me, she was telling me.

"You're the one in control, aren't you?" Dan said.

What?

"You control the finance. It's role reversal – we've seen it before – you're the main earner so you've taken on the male role," she said.

Male role? What?

"You wouldn't even let him go to his brother-in-law's funeral, would you?"

My mind reeled. Alan's funeral? The entire episode about Jay going, not going, demanding I drop everything last minute and drive Joe 600 miles after not wanting to go months before, demanding hundreds of pounds we didn't have….

"And what happened at Christmas? You hit him then, didn't you? This has happened before hasn't it. You admit you hit him? You hit him – you assaulted him? Before Christmas?" It wasn't really a question. Their tones were of disgust and it showed in their eyes. Why had he told them about that?

Yes I had, he was about to attack me – he'd just smashed the car up, he'd been in a complete blind rage. I'd been terrified then too.

They snorted again. A likely story.

"The damage is still there – in the car – I can show you." I wanted to take them outside and show them where he had kicked the interior of the car until it broke – it was still in pieces –terrifying me in the process. He really didn't know what he was doing when I made him angry.

"We're not interested in the car, Cathy." Now the sarcasm had an edge of long-suffering patience to it. "He's just got anger-management problems, hasn't he? We've seen on his record – he admits it – he's had anger management work – you just don't like him swearing, do you Cathy? You've got a problem with him swearing!"

The sidekick said, "You've obviously been under a lot of stress. Probably that job you do."

That really puzzled me.

"My job doesn't cause me stress – I really like my job." Of all the jobs I'd had in my life it was the least stressful, most rewarding.

But it was her turn again.

"But you're always complaining of it to Jay. Always in tears about your job. He's told us. And if you hit Jay, what's to stop you hitting Joe?"

This was madness. In tears about my job? When? But the other madness was worse – what had they said…?

"I'm never scared of Joe! Why would I ever hit

Joe?" The idea was so mad I couldn't believe they had just said that – but they had. Crying about my job? Occasionally, and never recently Jay had reduced me to tears as I buckled under the hail of abuse as he decimated my character and told me what a vile person I was to live with – but not recently as tears only made him more angry. I had never, ever, not once, ever had to cry about my work to him.

Once, a year ago, I'd cried in supervision – and that had been from sheer frustration at the way these two so-called social workers had been treating a young client who was self-harming and being sexually abused. They had repeatedly dismissed my concerns saying that she was 'old enough to know what she was doing' and was 'obviously lying about her forty-eight-year-old "boyfriend" because she was angry and jealous at him having other "girlfriends"'.

I'd witnessed this before – paedophiles targeting the young and vulnerable in children's homes – offering some kind of attention. No-one took any notice. (It was to be a few years until the media suddenly showed an interest in teenagers being groomed and abused but only because some perpetrators were black or Asian.) This young lass I knew had been emotionally abused for years by her parents but no-one was interested as there were no bruises or anything else that could be measured. The two managers had actually responded with sarcasm when I gave the opinion that she was in need of support.

Panic rose in me as I, too late, remembered just how crass these two could be.

They took it in turns. I tried to speak and to think straight. They interrupted when I tried to speak and even interrupted each other. Sometimes Dan wrote down what I'd said, sometimes he didn't.

"You're the one in control, aren't you Cathy?" Anastasia said again. She was sneering now.

Was I? I was trying to find how that made sense, my mind searching, hunting for a way of seeing where that could be true.

"But he hurts people – he's done GBH on somebody – he's SAS trained – I remind him of his dad…"

"You're the earner," Dan interrupted, "so you control the money."

What? As Jay spent what he liked on what he wanted and turned down work as I ducked and dived between repossession and final demands?

"We've seen it before." It was her turn again. "Role reversal. You've taken on the male role of main earner so you've ended up taking the male role and being aggressive too."

Two hundred years of women's struggle for the right to earn a living curled up and died in this one sentence. My efforts to earn enough to support us all died with it. Also, the myth that a man is naturally aggressive and that being a bully is somehow natural to men was re-established as science and history – and millions of unaggressive men – were silenced and put in a corner by the same sentence.

Also, that I was aggressive. Was I? I tried to speak but my head span – not knowing which point to pick up on.

"He spent the money," was all I could mumble,

confused. Had I been in control? Was that how Jay had seen it? Had that been part of what had upset him?

Then her sidekick leaned towards me and pointed his pen at me. "You nearly killed him. He's got great big cuts all over his head – and on his face – here, here, and here – he nearly died!" He'd pushed his face towards mine and jabbed his finger into his own face to illustrate the dreadful wounds.

My mind spun under the vortex of what this meant.

How could Jay have been so badly injured?

Was Dan lying? He couldn't be lying. Why would he lie? I'd nearly killed him? Jay? How? I'd only fended him off. I'd hit him twice that's all. At most – the first I'd swung out behind me and it had connected. That was all. Wasn't it? I hadn't hit his face. Had I? I hadn't see where the pan had connected as I'd swung it behind me. I'd hit his head, that was true. I hadn't meant to but I had. Must have been his face? A second time, yes, to stop him killing me as he'd roared into total rage after the first contact by the frying pan. But more than that?

Serious head injuries?

The truth came onto me in a flash of realisation and I felt close to fainting, a blackness went across my mind as I realised the dreadful, terrible truth: I must have lost consciousness of what I was doing and hit him more times than I remembered. I must have gone into a kind of 'rage' of my own and hit in a mad frenzy, not knowing what I did. Like Jay did. That was why I could not recall it. That was the only way to square the circle of what they were telling me and what I remembered happening.

I had gone into a similar state of mind that sometimes visited Jay – I must have gone into some kind of rage and caused great damage to Jay – instead of just stopping him from attacking me – but I remembered none of it. I only remembered swinging around to make him back off, the horrible shock as the pan I was holding connected with something, the absolute panic as I realised I'd actually hit him and the hitting out at him in panic to stop him reaching me, then he'd fallen against the door and then onto the bench which he'd hit with his head and lay there – blood spattered onto the toys beneath the bench. I remembered that – like a film in my mind – but not what they were describing – hitting him again and again and again – and deliberately.

"You hit him over and over again," they said. "You nearly killed him!"

They were looking at me, balefully.

All this flashed through my mind but I had said nothing.

What could I say? What had happened to me to make me act in such a way? Had all the years of stress and 'treading on eggs' sent me over the edge?

What had happened to me?

I flatly refused to agree that Joe 'needed to be with his dad'. They then said that this would only be for a few weeks – six or seven – while an assessment was carried out. Dan was very clear about this. Anastasia reassured me I'd be able to see him every day for those few weeks. I knew any assessment would confirm that Joe's main attachment was to me. But why couldn't he be with me while he was assessed?

How would he cope at night? I was always there for him when he woke at night. Anastasia got cross again. I felt the danger of making her annoyed even before she spoke.

Then she said, "If you don't agree to him going to his dad I'll get a Police Protection Order and remove him and put him in foster care – and that could be anywhere in the UK. Is that what you want? Is that what you want for Joe?"

Police Protection Order? Anywhere in the UK? That was true – foster places were in short supply. Kids often got sent miles away. But foster carers were safe. People with violent and unpredictable tempers were not accepted as foster carers. But recently there'd been reports of kids being placed with abusive teenagers and being abused. And Joe would be among strangers. Was that better than with a father who was sometimes frightening? He loved his dad – when he wasn't yelling. This rushed through my mind. I hesitated. Jay was so clever he could get Joe out of the country under these people's noses if he wanted to. He hated any authorities nosing into his life. I didn't know what to do.

Anastasia said, "Right. We'll go and see Jay again," and they left.

When they returned, which was very soon so they must have spoken to him on the phone, Jay had suggested that he go and live with one of his sisters who lived with her husband and mother in a huge house about 100 miles away – and take Joe with him. They put this to me.

"But her sister doesn't know Jay! She doesn't

know what he can be like! She wouldn't be able to cope with Jay when he flips – she hasn't lived with him since he was fifteen – she doesn't know what he's like. And he absolutely hates his mother!" How many times had Jay completely lost his temper over the subject of his mother – whom he blamed more than he did his father for the abuse he had had as a child?

Anastasia said, "Of course she knows him, she's his sister!" She ignored what I'd said about the mother.

This statement summoned up such a vision of happy family radiance and peace – which had about as much to do with the reality of Jay's family life as if she'd asserted that they all lived quite happily on Mars.

"They're estranged! Have been for years! Jay hates his family!" I tried to get this across.

More disbelief. "That's not what Jay told us."

That couldn't be true – Jay was always quite clear about how he felt towards his family – and hate was the word he used the most.

"He hates all of them. His dad sexually abused them all. That's why Jay is the way he is. If Joe goes to live with the family, he'll be able to get to him too!"

Why didn't they understand? They had talked to the police. They'd said they had.

They snorted again. I was talking rubbish. Then she said, "If Jay's dad is a paedophile it'll show on the records."

I thought I'd heard wrong. No, that is what she had said. That any paedophile would be on record. Otherwise I was lying.

"Joe's scared of his dad – he runs to me when he goes into a rage…" I tried again to get this across.

"But Jay looks after him while you were at work for years – ever since he was a baby!"

What?

"No he doesn't – Joe goes to nursery every day that I work – four days a week – only the last few weeks Jay's looked after him just on a Monday – only one day a week – not even the whole day, and never at night – never – and if he's in a bad mood I take the day off. Jay doesn't like looking after him – ask the nursery!"

Why didn't they know this?

"Ask the nursery if you don't believe me – he's been at nursery since he was six months old!"

"You have no reason to be afraid of him, he's never hit you." They returned to this.

"He's done it before – he attacked people – he was convicted – GBH and ABH – he nearly killed somebody in a blind rage! He doesn't know what he's doing when they make him angry! And I make him angry."

She snorted again. "That was when he was a young man – years ago. Hot blooded. Nothing to do with now."

I was desperate for them to talk to someone other than Jay.

"And he's lost his temper with the neighbours – ask them what he's like. He frightened them too! And their kids."

Again, they ignored what I'd said.

"But he told me about it — he gets angry and doesn't know what he's doing — I make him do that sometimes — he can't help it — it's the same…"

Anastasia was shaking her head contemptuously, lips pursed.

She didn't ask how I knew about his violent attacks of the past if it was so long ago and so irrelevant. She didn't ask which neighbours would tell her more. They didn't bother speaking to the nursery. They didn't want to look at the wrecked inside of the car. They didn't want to speak to Joe or to Esme who had been looking after Joe while I'd been in the cell and knew whom he had been asking for — and whom he had not been asking for. Their minds were made up.

I felt they could hardly see me, let alone hear me.

I did not know how to tell her in a way that would make her listen.

They were already getting up to leave.

"And besides," it was his turn again, "this caravan is unfit for any child — there's mould on the walls and it's cold in here. You can't have a child living here."

I was staggered. "We've lived in a caravan for years," I said, "I know how to make it warm — Joe loves being here…"

Now it was her turn. "Oh no, we've seen your caravan — lovely wood burner, nice and snug." Was Jay back at the house then? Had they been in the caravan with him? He obviously hadn't told them about the fumes.

"I'll be back in the house soon," I said desperately.

Jay would leave and Joe and I could live there. If Jay was going to his sister's and mother's and making a reconciliation there – so much the better.

Sidekick Dan shook his head. "The police won't let you back in there," he said.

Wouldn't they? Why wouldn't they? I'd lost the house? Is that what happened? Why couldn't I live there?

"I can live in the house here," I said as they backed me towards the door.

Then he said, "You can't live here with a child – it's up to these people how they want to live but you can't put a child in this place."

This place? These people? How they live? What on earth did he know about Esme's family that I didn't know? What ghastly secret had he unearthed that Esme had never told me?

"The choice is this," Anastasia said, "either you agree to Joe going to live with Jay, at his auntie's, while the assessment is carried out – for about six weeks – you can have contact every day – I'll pay for you to have contact if need be – we'll get the social services there to check on things and make sure everything is going okay – OR – we'll go and get a Police Protection Order and put Joe into foster care – and that could be anywhere."

I was gaping at this point. I couldn't make any sense out of it. I felt sick and dizzy. I couldn't think straight.

"You'll agree to him going with his dad to his auntie's for an assessment? Daily contact with yourself? Social services to monitor? Just for a few weeks? About six weeks – that's all." She looked at her deputy for confirmation and he nodded. It would only be for a few weeks and I could visit every day, the auntie would keep an eye on things, so would social services to keep an eye for any temper problems with Jay, and it would just be for the assessment period. Jay would be bound to have another rage in that time – with his sister or his mother – so they would all realise the problem and Joe would be straight back with me long before the six weeks were up.

If he didn't go to Auntie Agnes' he'd be put with total strangers. But foster carers are not allowed to be bad tempered and unpredictable. But his auntie would monitor. Social services would be there if and when Jay lost it again. Auntie Agnes's house was full of cousins and sane people.

Her husband was a kind, calm man. Joe had visited there once when we'd all gone over when he was about eleven months old. They had a dog, Henry, with which he'd struck up a friendship as kids do with dogs. Fostered children sometimes got hurt and abused by other kids even if not by foster carers. It was only for six weeks. Jay had rarely got angry with Joe. And never badly. If his sister was there – she'd be the one most likely to catch it – not Joe.

And was I really ill? Had I lost consciousness of what I'd done? Had I really hit Jay as badly as they said? Could I be a risk to him?

I found myself nodding, dumbly. There didn't seem to be any alternative.

Chapter 3

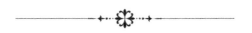

The two managers, Anastasia and her deputy sidekick, Dan, left and returned very soon with a piece of paper for me to sign – which I did. The paper just gave my permission for Joe to go to his auntie's with Jay 'for an assessment period'. There was nothing else on it but that. They were impatient for me to sign. Anastasia repeated the promise of my seeing him every day. I signed. They left, taking the piece of paper. I walked across to the house to see if Esme was there.

I had an odd sensation. I felt like I was moving through invisible treacle which clung to my limbs and to my mind. Everything was distant and unreal. The sounds of the day, spring birdsong, dogs barking, the car driving away, came to me as if down long tunnels. The ground was a long way away. I stopped halfway across the yard and looked at the sky – blue, clear, calm. I stumbled across to the house. I sat with Esme in a daze and looked at the coffee she had made me.

Then Anastasia phoned me again. They had talked to Jay. The plan was this: I was to meet them at the nursery at 3:30. Why 3:30? I wanted to ask. School ends at 3:10. So, I assumed they must be collecting Joe and having a meeting with him and the school or something. Then I was to explain what was happening to Joe – explain to him he was going to visit his auntie with his father. I'd explain to him that I would be visiting soon. I would then leave, as Jay and I must, legally, not meet at any point, and Jay would then arrive to collect Joe from the nursery. That was the plan.

I told Anastasia it wasn't nursery today as it was Joe's first day at school – but she interrupted me impatiently. What was I going to tell Joe? I said I'd thought of telling him my mum was ill so I had to go and look after her – as the reason I wasn't coming with him and his dad. Anastasia said that was okay. I'd also, I thought, emphasise the fact that he would be at his auntie's with other people and I'd be visiting every day as had been agreed. This would soften the fact I was sending him away with his dad. I didn't say that out loud. Anastasia said that Jay's brother was coming over to give a lift to Jay across the country to the auntie's house, with Joe.

I put the phone down. The school day ended at 3:10. That was when I was due, or had been due, to collect Joe after his first afternoon at school. So they must be having a meeting with the school or the teacher – to tell them what was happening. Or something. I mustn't get distracted by details – I had bigger issues to think about.

How was I going to tell my little boy this? How could I tell him I was sending him away? With his shouty, angry daddy who frightened us both on a fairly regular basis? How I could send him to be alone with him? Jay was great with Joe when he was in the mood to be – and for as long as Joe was doing what Jay liked doing – but not otherwise and never for more than a day. How could I send Joe away in a way which would not traumatise him completely? Was there a way? What possible excuse could I give him for doing this which could possibly make it reasonable?

Joe knew very well that I knew about Jay and what he could be like. Joe also knew that I knew that Joe was afraid of his father at least sometimes and wary of him for most. How could I possibly make this okay for him? Should I have gone with the fostering option after all? Could I get away if I just took him? They'd catch us. My job was to make it okay for him – somehow. I remembered Henry the dog. I remembered Joe visiting his auntie and playing on the lawn with me.

And I was obviously ill. I could not remember attacking Jay – I'd hit him, certainly, but to get him away from me. I'd hit him twice – that was all that I could remember – I couldn't remember attacking him in the way the deputy had described to me. There was obviously something very wrong with me. I'd had a flashback in the same way Jay did – doing stuff and then not remembering it. I was scared of what that meant. Maybe all the pressure had affected my mind. I was very scared of what that meant.

Any assessment would find that Joe's main attachment was to me – that was sure. He had been so happy in our new little home for the last two days we had been here. He'd been so relaxed – we both had. He had not once asked or showed any upset at

Jay not being there. After all, he was used to being with me and Jay not being there most of the time.

And now what? I was sending him away to live with Jay, without me to be there – when we both knew I had to be there in case his father had one of his 'moods'.

But the option was even worse – sent off to be among complete strangers. Had I made the right choice? Wouldn't he be safer with strangers? My hope was in Auntie Agnes and her family to do the right thing. When Jay 'blew' they must ring the social workers for Joe's sake. Surely they would do that? They did not know what Jay was like so they were in for a shock. We had visited once – for three days the previous year. Jay had wanted to show off his son to his estranged family.

Jay had not lost his temper with anyone the whole time.

Joe didn't know them as he had been only a year old when we had visited. He might have some idea of their dog, Henry, as he had played with him and we had a photo of them together which we looked at sometimes – keeping the memory alive. Joe really liked dogs – I could use that, to help make this okay.

In a numb daze I accepted Esme's offer of a lift to the nursery/school. I had spent an hour sorting out toys and clothes for Joe – and music tapes for Jay and Joe and Jay's brother to play on the way to the auntie's who lived about 100 miles away. I did everything to make this as okay for my darling as I possibly could. A few weeks wasn't long, I told myself. It would all be over in a few weeks. Everything would be better than normal in a few weeks.

I didn't know why Anastasia had said 3:30 as school finished at 3:10. After the first day he'd need to be in the after-school club until my normal pick-up time after work at 6pm. Jay hadn't been interested in all this. He had waved his hand impatiently to silence me when I'd talked about Jay starting school.

I assumed they must be having a meeting at the school or something before I arrived to explain or something. Presumably they'd let Joe go into the after-school club while the meeting was going on? He'd be okay there as his friends all went to it.

Esme and I got to the nursery about 3:15. There was no sign of the social workers' car. We hung about in the car park. Esme wanted to go and see someone about her own child, Ed. I could see through the window from the car park that Joe was already in the after-school club and I decided to go in and meet him and do what I had to do. My anxiety was climbing, my heart was racing. I had to hold it together in front of Joe – no tears, no distress – that would only frighten him. Pretend everything was fine – that was the only way. If children see their adult carers distressed they get very frightened.

I went into the classroom to find Joe. I heard and saw him at the same moment, in a group around an assistant or teacher. He'd not been in the after-school club before so I hadn't met her. He yelled, "Mummy!" in total delight and hurtled around all the desks and chairs to throw himself into my arms with a great grin on his face. He ran so fast the curl on the front of his forehead blew back and stood upright. He was wearing his favourite Tigger shirt which was blue with Tigger dancing on the front.

Swallowing hard on the awareness of what I had to do, I forced a smile and listened to him chat about his day and I asked him about how his first day had gone, as he sat in my arms, and told him he was a big boy going to school and how pleased I was he'd enjoyed it. He told me happily about some of the things he had done.

Then I said, "I've got a nice surprise today. There's been a change of plan." He looked interested, his face happily expectant. "You'll be going on a little holiday with your daddy to see Auntie Agnes for a little while. You might not remember Auntie Agnes – but do you remember Henry, her dog? You remember Henry?"

His face fell immediately. I babbled on about cousins and 'a little holiday'.

Joe said, his face very still, "Aren't you coming too?"

I went on, "I'll be coming later. I'll be coming to visit. You remember Auntie Agnes? You remember Henry the dog? Remember the lovely garden? And your grown-up cousins will be there. Just for a few weeks. I'll come and visit every day. You remember Uncle Dave?"

I so badly wanted him to remember. I wanted him to know there would be other people about. Nice people, calm people. He wouldn't be alone with that temper.

He wasn't buying it.

"Why aren't you coming?" He wasn't going to be distracted by Henry the dog. His smile had vanished, his face fallen, his mouth down.

I said I had to go and look after my mum who was ill but it would be a nice holiday and I'd come and see them both and Auntie Agnes was looking forward to seeing him again. He'd been there when he was one, I told him, and he'd enjoyed it. There was a big garden. We'd seen rabbits.

His face stayed fallen. He wanted to get down, pushed at my arms and then walked away from me. He was not pleased. "I'll see you every day," I said, to his retreating back, but he went back to playing with his friends and a building toy at one of the little tables. He was angry and upset and I couldn't blame him. I had just betrayed him and I was pretending it was alright. His mother had just sent him away.

I followed him and told him it was just for a short while, he would have a nice holiday with Daddy and Auntie and Henry the dog and I'd see him every day, but his face remained closed. And his back remained turned. He had every right to be angry.

For the whole of his life I'd been there. He had grown up knowing that his dad had a frightening temper sometimes – and that I knew that too. Now here I was – pretending not to know that and sending him off to cope on his own and pretending that was okay.

I had utterly betrayed my child. He trusted me completely to protect him and look after him and now I was sending him into danger. Abandoning him. Pretending I didn't know the risks. Pretending everything was alright. Phoney. False. He was three and a half years old.

I went and fetched the three armfuls of clothes and toys from Esme's car and, on the way back for the third, Anastasia and Dan walked in the door.

So they saw then that I was in the same room as Joe – he was about five yards away at one of the tables. So they saw then that I had got there before them and had been bringing in the clothes and toys.

They saw then that Joe would have already met me, already talked with me and that I had arrived there before them.

There is no way they could not have known all those things.

Anastasia told Dan to wait outside. In return to my greeting she snapped at me, "I said meet us here at 3:30, I think I was quite clear about that!"

She didn't say why 3:30 was so important or why she was cross at my being early. There seemed to be no meeting planned after all.

I mumbled about having had a lift with Esme. I told her that I'd told Joe the plan: for him to go with his father for a few weeks – and I pointed out the pile of clothes and toys I'd brought to go with them to the aunt's house.

She therefore had no doubt, no way of not knowing, that I had been in that classroom for at least a little while and had had a significant conversation with Joe. There was no way she could not have understood that. There was no way that she could not understand that I had met and spoken with Joe and that I had told him what was to happen. I didn't see the significance of this at the time. I told her Joe was not happy with the plan but that I'd done my best to make it okay for him.

The plan was that I would leave in order that Jay could come to the nursery and collect Joe. (The bail conditions stipulated no contact at all between Jay and me.) I had agreed that I would prepare Joe for the trip and say my goodbyes and explain I would be coming to see him every day while he was living at his auntie's with his daddy – then I would leave.

After showing her the pile of clothes etc., and explaining what I'd told Joe, I made to leave but then it hit me that I would not be seeing Joe at the end of the day. For the first time ever, he would not be with me that night. He had never been apart from me for one night in all his life. The ten hours at the police station was the longest I'd ever been apart from him.

When he woke in the night, as he did, as he had every night of his little life, for the first time ever, his mother would not be there. Would his father be there and be cross? "Can't you get him to shut up?" echoed in my head.

Joe was over in the corner at a table playing with the building toys with a couple of his regular pals including Ed and Archie, his oldest friends. I felt I couldn't leave without one more hug and to reinforce my promise. I knew he was cross with me and I didn't blame him.

At times in our lives together, Joe had said to me, "Daddy's not my friend any more," and, "Why is Daddy shouting?" and, "I don't want to go home – it's horrible," when there'd been an 'incident', so he knew that I knew that sometimes he got scared. I'd've taken him and run away several times but I'd been even more scared of what would happen if I did. I'd stuck it out hoping for Jay to decide to leave. Now, if we could stick this out, we'd be back together and safe. No more madness. No more fear.

I went around a couple of tables and squatted down awkwardly behind his chair. He was giving me the cold shoulder. I touched his arm and told him I'd see him the next day, that he'd have a nice time with Daddy and Auntie. I kissed him clumsily – only reaching the side of his turned-away head. He was still focussing on the toys. I told him I loved him and stood up. My eyes had started to cloud and my throat cramped and he mustn't see that. I found my way out of the classroom. I was focussing on the fact I'd be seeing him in a day's time; he would at no point be on his own with his dad; his auntie had two grown-up sons who would also be there and she had worked as a teacher for years so had no 'temper problems'; Henry would be there with his wagging tail and big collie grin; Agnes' husband would be there.

The other social worker, Dan the sidekick, was sitting in the car in the car park. Anastasia was still in the classroom. Esme found me picking over the heap of toys and clothes in the foyer, rearranging it pointlessly, trying to make it look nicer. She got me in the car and took me home. I told her the plan. Today was Tuesday, I'd be going to see Joe on Wednesday or Thursday at the very latest, Anastasia had said, I just had to wait until they'd organised that. All the other kids were in the back of the car so I was whispering. They asked, "Where's Joe?" and Esme spared me from having to tell them by explaining briefly about the 'holiday'.

Esme sat me in her kitchen and made me a cup of tea. I didn't seem to be able to stop talking. The dumb-struck ineptness which had gripped me during the social workers' visit lifted and I explained again and again about Joe and went on to explain why he was now going to live with his dad at his auntie's – and how nice his auntie was even though Jay hated her and on and on.

It was only for a few weeks. The assessment would sort it out. Joe had all his toys with him. His uncle was a nice fellow. The paedophile grandfather lived in another city and did not seem to visit. Jay was less likely to 'kick off' with his sister than with me; they had been close as children, her husband was there too so it would be okay and I'd go and see him tomorrow and take him out. I'd be able to see him every day. So it would be okay. I kept telling myself it would be okay.

Esme listened quietly.

In her house and garden the other kids were milling around and dinner was cooking. I kept looking for Joe. Ed and all his brothers were there. Where was Joe? It was such a lovely house –lovely atmosphere, untidy and fun in a way our house could never be – untidy or fun.

I was alright until the other kids came in the room and Joe was not among them. I was looking among their faces to see if I could spot him. My every instinct told me he was just outside the door, taking off his wellies before coming in. My mind could not accept that he was not there. Every one of my senses was on the alert, looking for him. Except when I was at work, I had not been anywhere without Joe being a few yards from me for the past three and a half years and before that his little body had been growing in me ready to come to life and be him.

Every time the other children hurtled past on some expedition – out to the trampoline, back upstairs – back out into the garden – I habitually looked to spot Joe with them and the shock that he wasn't there would hit me again. Not a cell in my body could accept that he wasn't there. I had to go and look for him. But I knew he was in a car, with his father and uncle driving to another house over 100 miles away. Maybe they were nearly there.

I had sent him away. He didn't know I had no choice. He didn't know I hadn't wanted to. He thought it was my choice. He thought that looking after my mother was more important to me than looking after him. He thought I loved my mother more than I loved him. And, worse, he thought I didn't care that he was on his own, more or less, with the man I was often afraid to be with. I had abandoned him. He couldn't know that I had had no choice.

I couldn't sit down and I couldn't chat with the others. I couldn't stand being alone. I couldn't stand being with other people.

Eventually I had to leave the house and go over to the caravan seeking relief in movement. I got to the caravan but he was not there either. I went back towards the house but through the window I could see the other children. But not mine. I had to keep walking. I had to do something. I went back into the caravan, the empty silence within hit me like a cold wave. But there wasn't any escape. This is what I had done. I had thrown my child to the wolves.

One of Joe's teddies had fallen behind a chair and been left behind in my collecting them all together to go with him. I picked it up and held it. I tried to get a sense of Joe's smell off its fur. The tears came then but brought no relief, only a more physical pain as grief retched and caught in my throat and lungs, leaving me unable to breathe.

Esme came to find me later as it was growing dark and she wondered if I wanted some supper and if I was coping alright. She found me squatted in an arm chair, hugging this teddy to me, my face buried in its fur in a kind of scream. I was rocking to and fro, hugging Joe's teddy to my face. It was all I had of his. I was trying to be with him across 100 miles. Trying to send him my love and protection by thought. Praying for his protection. Praying for his forgiveness. Esme told me the other kids had gone to bed and invited me to have a glass of wine in the house. I crept after her. I tried to put the teddy down but couldn't. I went over to the house with her. I brought the teddy with me.

My body seemed all awkward and distant. I kept tripping on the uneven ground. I had done my child wrong but what else could I have done? Would it have been better for him to go into foster care? Would the magistrate have given a PPO two days after the incident? I hadn't even thought of that option. Why would they have given a PPO? I had fended off my ex who was about to attack me two days ago. I wasn't a risk to anyone. Certainly not my son.

But the social work managers would have asked for a PPO, they were high status so they would probably have got it. No magistrate would know our history or doubt their assessment. Serious head injuries. Serious head injuries? How serious? He'd walked out of the house and down the road to the next farm but one before the ambulance had arrived. The ambulance medic had said, "He'll be alright but we have to take him in for some tests." Had he been wrong? Had I really lost my mind and really hit him over and over again. The social workers had seen the wounds and they were serious.

I drank a glass of wine and wanted more. Seeking oblivion. Unable to stay still or keep company, I went back over to the caravan to sleep.

I got into bed, lay awake and felt a dark pit opening up. I'd been an atheist all my adult life but I prayed for help. The space in the bed where Joe had slept the night before was empty and I kept looking for him. The space next to me, where Joe had slept since the day he was born, three and a half years ago, was empty and its emptiness was loud and filled the whole caravan. In my mind, I could hear his little voice waking and asking for me in the night, not knowing where I was and why I didn't come.

And what if he really was crying for me and what if that annoyed Jay – what then? "Can't you fuckin' shut him up?"

I kept, out of habit, listening for his breathing as I fell asleep and come awake then, not being able to hear him, and then be hit by the fact of his not being there over and over. Or I'd wake from sleep and for a split second I'd be in a state of forgetfulness which would crash away as reality hit again. Where was he now? Was he in bed? Was he asleep? Was he wondering where his mummy was? Was he wondering why I'd sent him away?

Was Jay getting cross with him for asking?

I felt myself spiralling down the pit into madness. I asked God, any god, for help in the dark room of the little caravan. Not sure which god to ask, I asked them all. I thought of the fact that Joe was still alive. He was alive. Elsewhere in the world were women like me, and fathers, who were going through worse than this. I was luckier than them. I would see my child. Car accidents and drones – how many kids had died today? I started counting my blessings. I counted friends who cared about me. My parents, my family. Joe. I was alive. He was alive. I prayed and counted.

The only thing I could do was pray for Joe, for his protection, for help to bring him through and keep him safe, to calm his father's temper and help the auntie look after Joe and be there instead of me when Joe needed her. Was there anyone, or any force there to receive my prayers?

Dawn came. Wednesday. I sat all day at the phone in Esme's kitchen waiting to be told when I could go and visit Joe at his auntie's. I rang the SSD to ask and left messages. They had to arrange the 'contact visit' with Jay and his family so I needed to wait to hear from them. My boss rang and told me she'd be visiting me. I had grabbed the phone thinking this was the plan for me to go and see Joe.

They didn't ring.

My friend from work, Anna, rang to see if I was okay. She had heard the basics. She hadn't known Joe had been taken. I blubbered incoherently down the phone at her. She turned up within the hour with a box of blossoming seedlings – young flowers just coming into bud. She said it was symbolic of hope and that things would turn out alright. She told me that she knew that things would work out alright. The flowers were a sign of that hope. They needed somewhere safe to grow but they'd be alright. She knew Joe and I would be alright too, given time. God would see us right. Having no faith of my own, I clung to hers.

The day closed with no phone call from the social workers. One phone call message to Esme from Aunt Agnes had been left the evening before to tell me that Joe was okay. He and his dad and uncle had arrived and Joe had been playing with the dog and was quite happy. I was overwhelmed with gratitude for the auntie that she had known I needed to know that, and that she had got this message to me. Joe was alright. I hung on to that. I remember a wave of gratitude and relief sweeping me. My little one was okay. The auntie was doing the right thing. And when Jay had one of his uncontrollable rages, she would do the right thing then too and inform whoever it was who was doing the assessment and this nightmare would cease.

I asked Esme what the social worker had said about 'these people' and 'this place' being unfit for a child – asked her to tell me what he might have meant. She looked at me blankly. "You're kidding, right? We have to be squeaky clean – 'cos of Simon's job. He worked with the MOD – they wouldn't tolerate anything dodgy." I had thought Dan had been referring to something they had on record, something terrible, which meant I could not be there with Joe. Then Esme said, "The only thing it might be

– this farm used to be a commune – there were loads of people living here – had a terrible reputation – drugs and all sorts – used to get raided – but that was years ago. We've been here twenty years and it was a farm again before us. But that's the only thing I can think of they might have on record. The address is the same."

So that was it. Out of date records – old news – Dan had thought my friends were part of a drug crazed cult. Deeply ironic given his own reputation for turning up at work off his box at times and rolling around drunk at weekends. But he hadn't thought, he hadn't checked, he had just frightened me with hints and made his mind up on rumours.

The other mystery, the meeting at 3:30 for some odd reason and Joe being in the after-school club I realised was probably something similar: they had obviously asked Jay what time Joe's time at school or nursery ended and he'd guessed. They hadn't checked – if they had, they might have had some clue about what Jay was telling them.

The Wednesday carried on with no news. I'd thought of a lot of information and where Anastasia and Dan could look to get evidence to answer their questions and disbelief. Exhausted with leaving messages that were never answered, I drove the twenty-five miles down to the SSD office to see them but was told they weren't available. A duty officer came down and took my sheets of notepaper. He was coldly disapproving towards me. He asked if Jay was out of hospital yet. He didn't know anything about my seeing Joe. He called it 'contact'. No, he hadn't heard anything. He went back up the stairs.

My boss had come to see me. I was suspended from work 'without prejudice' and was not allowed to see anyone from work or contact them in any way. I could have support from one person – Anna had already volunteered and I accepted that gratefully as she was the person I'd've chosen. There would be an investigation by my employers as well as the criminal investigation to see if I was fit to be a social worker. My manager didn't know anything about my seeing Joe either as 'the team were dealing with that'. I didn't care about anything else she said to me or register the implications.

I now had to ring my parents and let them know what had happened. A few days ago, I had expected to be returning to live with them with Joe – once Jay had agreed we needed to split up after this catastrophe. That seemed a century ago now.

I rang and my dad answered, pleased to hear from me as always. I told them I'd been frightened by Jay and had hit him with a pan and caused him head injuries and he'd had to go to hospital. My dad said, "These things happen."

Surprised at his being so calm, I repeated Jay had had to go to hospital and had head injuries. Serious head injuries. He said he doubted that. I then told him the social workers had said Joe had to go and live with him for a while for an assessment. My dad swore quietly, under his breath. My dad hardly ever swore. My mum came on – when was I coming home? They were more concerned about how I was than anything else.

"It's okay," I said hurriedly. "It's only for a few weeks while they do an assessment."

I heard my mum's voice asking and my dad telling her the outline. My mum came on the phone. "Where are you? Are you coming home? We're worried about you."

I told her I had to stay where I was to sort out things with the solicitor and when I'd see Joe. She said she understood but asked what they could do to help and said that their concern was me and why I had done such a thing, and was I alright? I'd never hit anybody in my life and they knew that.

They had seen Jay being angry once – my dad had offered me a lift and Jay had taken it that my dad was telling us what to do and interfering in our lives – his anger, about 1/10 on the Richter scale of his rages – had reduced my mother to tears and alarmed my dad but they had assumed it was a one-off – and that they must have done something to upset him. Otherwise they knew him as a cheerful, personable man.

They didn't know about how Jay talked about them behind their backs or that the temper they had glimpsed that day was a regular feature of our lives. I had told my mother a little bit about him 'yelling at me' and she had said, "There's a home here for you if you ever want to get away from him," and I'd immediately thought of Jay turning up and pursuing me and Joe, attacking my parents or killing himself or me – as he had threatened, and decided not to do this. I had hoped we could come to a peaceful agreement for all of us. I expected she'd tell my dad and he would talk to me more about it. He never did – and I had no reason then to suspect why this was.

I told them I'd sort out about visiting Joe and come home as soon as I could. Home. I had long since thought of visiting them at weekends, once a month, as 'going home' when my 'home' with Jay had ceased to feel like any such.

Not one word of reproach, not one word of criticism or horror at what I had just told them – only concern and love and support.

The little comments against them which Jay had shared with me as he had spotted, or thought he had spotted, selfishness in their attitude to me or slyness in their intentions, or malice, were laid to nought. He had been wrong. He probably was biased in how he saw other people's parents as his own had treated him so badly. They were all concern and love and wanting to help – I had, for so long, kept from them the truth about my life, thinking they would not understand or thinking they might interfere and be at risk from Jay's anger, not understanding how he couldn't help it – and here they were, only wanting to help however they could.

I explained I needed to arrange to see Joe and sort things out with my solicitor and then I'd be coming home. They sent me love and I put the phone down.

All the times I wanted to tell them but didn't – that there were problems and I was almost not coping – all that secrecy and care – had led us all to this. All the times I'd been at the point of telling them all.

'There's a home here if ever you want it', but that would have meant abandoning Jay – and he would not have coped with that.

Chapter 4

So I rang SSD again and this time I was able to speak to Anastasia. I asked her if there was any news as two days had gone by already. Did she know when I was due to go and visit Joe?

Then Anastasia said, quite casually, "Oh that's all changed. Jay has changed his mind. You can't go and visit him."

She'd said 'can't' not 'can' – but I thought I'd misheard so she repeated it loudly and slowly, with relish it seemed.

"But you said – we agreed – you promised – you said, that's why I agreed to it…" This was not real.

She interrupted, speaking with a sort of bored patience, "It's not up to me, Cathy, *I* can't decide whether you see him or not – it's not *my* decision – it's up to the family and they have said you are not to see him."

What were they thinking of? Why was Jay not sorting this? Couldn't he see that Joe needed to see his mum?

I said, "I told him I'd visit – I said I'd be there – he's expecting me – that's what I told him – he's never been a day…"

Then she said, "He's not missing you, Cathy. I know you want him to, and that's not what you want to hear – but he's not asking for you, he's not missing you at all…" There was amusement in her voice.

I knew that could not be true as Joe consistently asked for me whenever he was upset at nursery – and he'd asked for me when he was at Esme's all day. Plus, I knew in my bones that he was missing me.

I said, "Have you been to see him?" I was incredulous as it was 100 miles to the aunt's house.

She said, "I don't need to see him, Cathy. Jay has told me and his auntie has told me – so you'll have to apply through the courts if you want to see Joe." If I want to see Joe?! "The auntie said you can ring on Wednesdays and speak with him. I have to go now." She sounded very bored as if the whole issue was tiresome, eager to end this tiresome phone call.

What about the written agreement? But there was nothing on that about contact – only my agreeing he could stay with his dad and auntie. Could I drive down and just go and see him? Just call at the house? Would I be arrested?

I was told that, if I went into the area at all without being supervised, Joe would be taken into care.

Jay and his family had said that I was not allowed to see Joe. At least not until I'd had a mental health assessment. It was no longer in her hands. The case was passed into the family private law courts. I would need to apply through the courts if 'I wanted to see

Joe'. The auntie, Agnes, had said I could ring and speak to Joe on the phone – once a week, "If I wanted to."

This was all said with a satisfied sneer. It was nothing to do with her anymore.

She ended the phone call.

The world shifted again. I realised my breath had stopped and I focussed on drawing breath for a while. It was difficult. Blackness swam in front of my eyes as my heart raced.

Joe wasn't missing me? I couldn't go and see him? Maybe he was so excited at being in the big house and with the dog, etc.? I remembered his face falling and him saying, "Are you coming too?" when I'd told him of his sudden 'holiday'. Had he been so annoyed and hurt at my sending him away that he was resolved to forget me? Had I done such a bad job of our parting that he was so hurt? And what about in the night? He still always woke up at least once in the night and called for me, "Mummy!" for a cuddle or for me to fetch him into my own bed. And how was Jay to manage? He got bored and stressed after only hours of being a parent – how was he going to manage whole days? Nights? He'd never looked after him at night, not once.

Esme had made us lunch but I found, hungry as I was, I couldn't actually chew or swallow the food.

I drove down to the SSD offices. I was told I could not come in as I was suspended. I'd forgotten about that. Anastasia would not come out to talk with me but sent one of her minions who was cold and quite rude but matter-of-fact that I was not to be allowed to see Joe and that was the family's decision, not SSD's. I'd written a letter to Anastasia asking her, begging her to see reason and outlining what had happened. Her minion took it reluctantly. I waited outside the office for an hour but no-one came out. There was no reply to my letter.

I walked back to my car. The world seemed to have developed a thin veneer of ice across it. Sounds were muffled and the edges of things were indistinct. I did not seem to be fully present in my surroundings. My hands were shaking slightly except when I gripped them tight. I found my car. I drove back to the farm very slowly as my reflexes seemed to be slower than usual. Again, I tried to eat something but couldn't. I told Esme what had happened. The words seemed far away and a meaningless ramble by somebody else.

At six o'clock the phone rang and Esme told me it was Joe and it was his voice, his little child's voice, when I took the phone from her, his small three-year-old voice speaking into the telephone in the big house to a mummy who had not come to see him after all. But he had no reproach, only, "Where are you? Are you coming in a minute? When are you coming? Where are you?"

I said, "I can't come yet, darling. I'll come as soon as I can. I'll come soon, my love. I love you. Mummy loves you."

"Why can't you?" he said. Why was Mummy lying to him again?

"I have to do some things, my love."

Things to do? What could I possibly have to do, ever had to do, which was more important than being with him, looking after him, seeing to his needs? I blundered on.

"You have a nice time with everyone there and Henry the dog and then you can tell me all about it when I come. Okay?"

"But I want you to come."

It was like talking to him through the bars of a cage, unable to touch him, see him or even to tell the truth which was, 'I can't come and see you darling because someone is telling lies and stopping me.' That was the truth – but it would only frighten him. So I told him again I would come as soon as I could. I asked him about the garden and playing with Henry and seeing his auntie and his grandma too – who lived at the same address in a bungalow in the grounds of the auntie's huge house.

What were they thinking of? And why was Jay not putting them right? He knew who looked after Jay when he wasn't at nursery. And Joe obviously was missing me.

Then I heard the auntie's voice in the background and Joe's little voice said, "I have to go now."

So I told him I loved him, over and over and he told me the same and the phone call ended. But I wasn't coming to see him. Love? Maybe I was ruining the meaning of that word, for him, forever. Maybe I was showing him it was not to be trusted and meant nothing. But if I could tell him I loved him, would that keep him safe?

I'd told him I loved him. What did that mean? I had also just told him that there were things in my life which were more important to me than him – even when he asked me to come to him, I had made excuses and not done so.

Whatever I said – my actions proved otherwise.

I had been told that the family and Jay had said I needed to get a psychological assessment done on myself before they would let me see Joe.

I asked them if they were organising that but it was up to me to do that. How do you organise an assessment of yourself?

I contacted the mental health team and asked for an appointment urgently and they booked me in. It was for the following week. A week.

I went to see Richard.

Jay had made a statement regarding the incident which Richard read to me. I had hoped that Jay would explain about his temper and problems and everything would be sorted out as he was always sorry about his temper-rages when he had calmed down.

But the statement wasn't quite what I'd expected.

The statement spoke of my suddenly attacking him with the frying pan for no reason as he had been getting dressed that morning and of blows 'raining down' repeatedly upon his head. It spoke of my uneven temper and fragile disposition – frequently crying on return from work. It spoke of his being beholden to me for money and unable to work himself for an illness he had which caused him to swear – and that I didn't like him swearing; of the fact he'd gone out the night before and that I was always jealous when he did this.

I was unable to speak.

The statement spoke of the incident at Christmas: apparently I'd thrown him to the ground, using karate skills, pressed my knee into the small of his back and kept it there while I hit him again and again over the head, full force, with a large stone I had carried about with me for some time. He had had to go to the GP with his injuries after this incident. The statement accused me of trying to kill him.

I read it through myself. I checked the name at the bottom of the page – it was Jay's. My mind whirled around in this new strange place. Richard watched me as I scrambled about.

"His dad used to hit him around the head a lot – maybe it was a flashback? Maybe he mixed it up? He had no injuries in the Christmas incident – none at all – he didn't even flinch. I hit at the side of his head to stop him hitting me and it just caught the side of his hat – then he grabbed me and threw me on the ground. He didn't 'fall over' or anything of the kind..." My voice trailed off.

"Did he go to his GP?"

"No. Not that I know of. He was fine. He was fine after he'd calmed down and we had Christmas at my parents' so he couldn't have gone to his doctor's for that week. He had no injury – it was nothing like he said! I barely hit him – he was in a rage and coming at me. And this last incident – I hit him twice at most – I was scared he was going to lose it completely and hurt me or even kill me not knowing what he was doing... it must be a flashback – if it isn't a flashback he would be telling lies – and being malicious."

Then I blurted out what I was really scared of.

"Or I lost sense of what I was doing? I must have done if I hurt him that much because I don't remember it like that at all. Did I go into a rage same as he used to do?"

Richard looked at me quietly. "No, I don't think so," he said. "Has that ever happened to you before? Lost consciousness of what you were doing?"

"No – but I've never been so scared before."

Then he said, "I think Jay's telling lies. And I think he is being malicious."

I looked at him. "But why would he do that?" I floundered. It didn't make any sense.

The room was very quiet. Someone was typing in the next room.

I looked at the statement again. I'd twice hit out at him in fear to fend him off or to stop him from venting the rage on me – both times were after I'd told him I felt we needed to separate and when his anger towards me had escalated generally: once before Christmas after he'd lost his temper and smashed the inside of the car up and seemed about to start on me, and then again on the Sunday morning when I'd annoyed him somehow, probably by leaving the telly on too loud, and then failed to get out of his way once he'd got in a rage. Before Christmas I'd grabbed a paperweight which had been on the side and hit at him – if I'd been bigger and stronger I might have punched him to keep him away. But I'd grabbed the stone. He'd flinched out of its way; it had just connected with the side of his hat, that was all.

On the Sunday morning, I'd hit him the first time accidentally as I swung out behind me to keep him away and again to stop him attacking me when I realised I'd hit him the first time – he had stumbled but was straightening up and would certainly 'lose it' with me worse than ever before. What he had told the police and social workers was rather different.

He had told them that, in the incident before Christmas, I'd crept up behind him and got him onto the ground with a martial arts move then proceeded to hold him down with my knee in his back while I repeatedly struck him very hard on his head with a large rock.

On the Sunday, he had written in the statement, that I'd crept into his room while he was dressing quite peacefully and suddenly, and without warning, I had started to lay about him with the pan and the 'blows had rained down upon his head' while he tried to restrain me. He was frightened for Joe's safety. If I could do that to him, Jay, how was Joe safe, he asked? Nothing about his own temper or rages. Nothing. Not one word. Just 'an illness which causes him to swear'.

My mind ran around on the end of its leash trying to find a point of view from which this made sense. It found one. I had had a lot of practise trying to understand strange stuff in the past few years. I was well trained. I saw the answer.

"He must have had a flashback," I said. "His dad was always hitting him around the head. So when I hit him it must have set off a flashback."

Richard looked at me.

"That isn't what happened before Christmas," I continued. "Unless I remember it wrongly – I only hit the side of his head – only connected – to stop him hitting me – he was out of his mind and coming for me. He'd just smashed the car up. He didn't fall over…"

Richard interrupted me.

"If you had hit him like he said you did," he said calmly, "he would have been dead – or at least very badly injured indeed. Did he go to hospital?"

"No – he wasn't injured at all It wasn't that kind of a hit. He must be mixing it up with something that happened to him before."

Pause.

"Otherwise," I said, floundering, "he'd just be being malicious and why would he do that?"

Richard said, "Does he like to be in control?'

In control? Jay struggled to control his temper – especially when I did something that triggered him. He would grit his teeth and clench his fists and keep the roar of anger tight in his throat as he struggled to stay in control of his temper. He'd change colour with the effort.

I explained this to Richard. He folded his arms.

"No, I didn't mean controlling himself," Richard said. "I meant controlling you."

Controlling me? No, that was silly. I supported Jay as best I could – I also knew something about psychology so that helped me look after him. I explained this to Richard. It was very subtle stuff so he might not have grasped it as he was used to dealing with actual abuse cases – not situations like mine and Jay's where he couldn't help it and didn't mean to frighten me or hurt me.

Richard listened quietly.

I read and re-read what Jay had written.

"But this isn't true! None of it is!" There were so many points in the statement which were so far from what had actually happened that its connection to real events was tenuous. In every point, Jay depicted me as deliberately malicious and intent on hurting him. Outside of the incidents I was portrayed as bullying, heartless and controlling and himself as trying to cope with a domineering, unpredictable partner – me.

He had given, as an example of this, was my not letting him go to his brother-in-law's funeral and my being obsessed with money at all times! I had insisted on putting Joe into crèche and nursery, he had written, which was totally against Jay's own principles but he had been afraid to object as I always had my own way on everything, he'd said. No mention of finding it too dull and boring looking after his son. No mention of not being able to stand living in the same caravan as us. None at all.

I was aware I was gaping in disbelief and closed my mouth.

Richard nodded. "I also think he is being malicious because he has asked the police to charge you with attempted murder."

He suddenly seemed to be speaking to me from a long way away although he was only on the other side of the desk. Jay? Jay who had the uncontrollable fits of rage when he would hurt those he was close to because he was unable to stop himself and then be unable to remember what he had said or done? Jay? Who had smashed crockery and phones and spades by breaking them against walls when the 'red mist', he had described, descended and struggled so hard against the terrible depression which held him in its grip?

Who nearly always would say 'sorry' and want to stay with me – despite the fact I irritated him so much and so often because I reminded him of the people he hated most? Who would weep in agony when telling me of the pain he suffered and how the thought of us separating made it all worse? Now accusing me of attacking him and of bullying him? Jay who would weep real tears when I had told him we needed to separate as I couldn't cope with the fear anymore? Jay, whom I had been looking after and supporting as best I could for the past six years?

The room was quiet again except, perhaps, for the sound of pennies beginning to drop.

I had long been convinced that Jay couldn't help what he did. His terrible childhood had left him with deep scars. Being close to anyone was painful as both his parents had betrayed him, rejected him and abused him. I'd come across many teenagers who would throw your proffered friendship or kindness or your Christmas presents in your face precisely because anytime people had been kind before had always been the prelude to more abuse, more hurt or a further rejection. Why take the risk again?

I told Richard about the explosive uncontrollable rages within which Jay had no idea what he was doing and the history of him having hospitalised someone who had triggered these and the way I, too, was constantly reminding him of his father – hatred of whom was the root cause of the rage and the violence.

But Jay had not told the police about his rages, his mental health problems, his inability to cope with stress, his history of depression, the fact his previous two partners had run away from him, or the fact that he had two convictions for violent attacks on people because he had lost all sense of what he was doing because they had 'triggered' him – the same way I 'triggered' him on a regular basis. Instead, he told them I had tried to kill him, out of the blue, unprovoked and for no good reason.

Jay hadn't told them that he was prone to angry, out-of-control episodes or that he sometimes hit or threatened people without knowing what he was doing. He didn't tell them that he had almost killed someone once in a blind rage, using a hunk of wood, because that person had reminded him of his dad – and that I was forever reminding him of his dad. He had told them, and they had believed him, that the two convictions he had had as a younger man for ABH and GBH were just 'hot-blooded youthful fights'. 'High spirits'.

He hadn't told them about smashing the car up before Christmas and screaming at me then raising his arms and my hitting him away. He hadn't mentioned smashing plates and glasses against the wall if I ever spoke out of turn or threatening to break my neck if I talked of us splitting up. He hadn't told them he'd threatened to snatch Joe from me.

He also told them that he wanted me charged with attempted murder.

Besides, what evidence did I have that he wasn't telling the truth? He had serious injuries all over his head.

I wrote a statement of my own in response to Jay's and Richard put it in to be typed. I went back to the farm. Two days had already gone by and I still didn't know how I was going to see Joe.

Richard had given me the name of a colleague who did 'child and family law' as he didn't. I'd gone to see them and they had said they had to follow what the social workers had said and apply through the courts. Then colleagues, via Anna, sent me the name of another family law solicitor and I decided to go and see her, hoping she'd say something different.

This was the next expert to enter my life – Ms Pane. She was recommended to me by several friends and colleagues who knew of her fearsome reputation in custody and divorce cases. A colleague had gone to her during her divorce from a vicious thug of a bully who had beaten and terrorised her for years and Ms Pane had done the right thing and got her through the divorce. I was amazed to hear her story as this small woman, who had worked across the corridor from me as a clerk, told me of her experience with her husband.

This was something else which had started happening to me: as I told people of what had happened – stammering and shame-faced, telling them of Jay's behaviour and my mistake of hitting him – they would open up to me: totally respectable people with apparently uncomplicated pasts would tell me of their own nightmares. One had been beaten and humiliated by her very well-to-do husband for years and she had only escaped by being rescued by friends; another had had a dagger held against her throat by her drunk partner of years –which had been the final straw and which prompted her to run away. Another had assumed a new identity to keep safe; another had hit her partner over the head with a bottle during an episode – he had left and not pressed charges.

Ms Pane had worked in the area of domestic abuse for years.

So she would know a lot about abuse – even more than Richard. And she was a woman – so she'd know.

Her office was in the town. At first the receptionist told me that Ms Pane was not taking on any more clients. She advised me, over her shoulder, to find someone else to go to who took on Legal Aid clients. I explained I was not a Legal Aid client – I would be paying privately. Immediately her manner changed from cold, dismissive drizzle to warm, welcoming sunshine and I was given an appointment and ushered into the waiting room and fetched tea.

I went into Ms Pane and made a statement for about an hour which she wrote down and then posted to me along with the bill. It arrived about a week later. She hadn't seemed a 'warm' person – very matter-of-fact and apparently quite bored by my account and uncomfortable in her tweed suit. She hadn't asked me to elaborate on anything I said and I considered how often she must have sat and listened to accounts such as mine and how she'd have to protect herself from the hurt of others' lives just to function.

She could not get emotional about every sad tale she heard of fear and violence or she'd go mad.

The report she had written and had typed out arrived the following week on yellow paper with a note asking me to read and sign. Strangely, the account I had given her was all sort of tangled up, in the report she had written, with events in the wrong order and causal connections drawn where none existed in reality and details which I had not included as they had not happened.

Two of the sentences incriminated me as she had reversed the order of events and she said that Joe had been present in the room and pulling me away and me acting in a temper rather than in fear. Where had she got that from? Had she assumed it? Hadn't I explained it clearly enough? I had told her of Joe grabbing my hand sometimes during Jay's rants and pulling me 'this way Mummy' to get me further away from Jay. But he hadn't been anywhere near me when I had fended Jay off that last day. He had been upstairs and I had told her that quite clearly.

She must have misheard. Friends told me it was easy to get things mixed up in accounts. This was why I had to read it first and sign it. I sent it back almost covered in corrections and amendments.

The response I got was another appointment – this time with another partner in the firm and a secretary who would make the notes and we went through it all again, this time in more detail about the relationship and very detailed accounts of what had happened during the incidents when I had hit Jay. I even had to act out what had happened that morning in a sort of mad choreography. I realised that his telling the exaggerated story of what had happened before Christmas had condemned me in many eyes. However, what he had said were lies and so could be proved to be so, I was sure – he had said I'd hit him many times and he had had to go to his doctor previously.

The meeting then produced another report – this time on blue paper and another, even bigger, bill. This report was more accurate. It still held a few surprising inaccuracies but I was so anxious to get things moving – it was already a week since Joe had been 'placed' with Jay after all, I signed it anyway – enclosing a note pointing out the discrepancies – did they think it worth rewriting to get this accurate? They didn't reply. I didn't want to appear tiresome. They were the experts. They set about writing to SSD and Jay to try and sort out more 'contact'. They identified someone who could give a psychological assessment of me and of Jay and see if the need to supervise me on contact could be lifted. They would write to Jay's solicitors on my behalf etc. £200 per hour? I assented. The estimated cost would be £10,000 to get the case sorted out and concluded.

They sent me attached files of copies of the letters over the following weeks but I didn't know how to access these as they would open into what appeared to be hieroglyphics and very tiny. My brother came round to show me how to open them properly. I wrote and asked if they would please post copies to me as my computer skills were poor – but they did not respond to this.

Ms Pane told me she was pessimistic about my not going to prison, given the severity of the serious head injuries which I had caused on two occasions. I knew Joe could not be left with Jay – when the truth about his mental health and anger issues was realised – so would Joe be taken for adoption then?

Would he be placed in the family or would they all be considered as unsuitable? My mum reassured me that if it came to that, she and my dad would look after Joe. My dad pointed out that social services would not accept them as 'we are too old'. My brother and sister-in-law told me they would look after him if I was 'sent away' – but would Jay allow that? Would he have the right to refuse for Joe to be placed with my family even if the truth about his own temper problems eventually came out? My mind was running ahead in a panic trying to find a safe place for Joe if the worst happened. Ms Pane listened and said we couldn't make plans yet.

My appointments with the family solicitor were to become part of my routine. She had seemed distant, slightly bored with my account of what had happened but friends reassured me that this would be her professional mask – her way of protecting herself from the pain of others. She had half-moon spectacles and looked at me over them like something out of Dickens. She was about six feet tall and of large build. I imagined Jay or anyone trying to intimidate her. I wondered if she'd ever been scared.

Papers had arrived from the social workers detailing the injuries I had caused to Jay in the second 'incident'.

"This sounds very nasty," she'd said. "You hit him more than once. You must have been very angry."

I explained about how I must have had a blackout as I could not recall causing such harm. Or hitting him so often with the pan. There wasn't time to tell her all about the years of living with Jay and what he was like in a temper so I write a long letter detailing all the incidents I could remember and describing his threats and loss of consciousness as an explanation of why I might have gone into 'flashback' of my own, as well as being scared out of my wits that morning. I thought that maybe I'd wanted subconsciously wanted to hurt Jay? It seemed the only explanation of why the injuries were so bad.

The idea of the blackout was the only way I could square the difference between what everyone seemed to be saying about his injuries and what I remembered happening.

Chapter 5

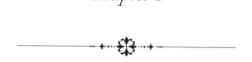

The conditions of my bail had changed to allow me to live elsewhere and the only condition now was that I did not go anywhere near Jay. And this suited me very well as I was afraid to go anywhere near him. I would have risked it if it meant seeing Joe but this was not on offer.

It was a long drive – from Esme's to my mum and dad's home.

I went past our house, Hilldene, still strange behind the surreal black and yellow 'crime scene tapes'. I had had to meet police officers there one day to hand over the keys. I would be allowed back a week or so later, Richard had said, so Dan, the sidekick, had been wrong there too as he had implied I'd not be allowed to live there for the foreseeable future, or ever.

So, I went home. The journey was difficult as there was no little face in the rear-view mirror, no Joe in the back seat smiling at me, happy to be going on these jaunts to see his grandparents – as there always had been on this journey, this, our little escape for a weekend of freedom. We'd drive along, chatting; I'd point out sights along the way. Or, if Jay were with us I'd keep quiet as he preferred it that way. Today, I drove past the familiar sights and there was no-one, to point them out to.

When I arrived home my mum and dad were at the door to welcome me. My dad was solemn as he hugged me and offered reassurance that things would work out and my mum was delighted – but then confused. Where was Joe? My dad reminded her and she looked stricken.

For some time, she had been forgetting things. Where's my handbag? Where are we going? Who was that? And, 'why don't you take me home?' And my dad patiently explaining that this is our home for the umpteenth time. That was on bad days. On other days she was my mum as usual.

My mum said, "Where's Joe?" again as we arrived in the living room and was shushed by my dad. I hugged them both and they took me in and sat me down. Dad brought a drink and told me it would all be sorted out soon. Any idiot, he said, could see that Joe should be with me, a three-year-old with his mum. I realised my mum never had passed on that conversation I'd had with her about Jay's temper, never raised the subject with my dad. I realised now that this was because she had probably forgotten about our conversations minutes later.

But that wasn't all that had been forgotten: in the time it took between my phone call telling of the disaster and my arrival home they had made up an album of photographs; they were all of my life. Photos of my childhood, teenage days, walking in the hills, holidays with my parents and brother, young adulthood, friends, first teaching job, boyfriends, friends, first car, paintings now long sold, early middle age, travels abroad – then Joe – and blank pages afterwards. Pictures of Jay were not included. I recognised the smiling stranger looking back at me from these photos of my life. Me. I hadn't always been what I had become.

"Because your life goes on," said my mum, drawing my attention to the blank pages, as yet unfilled with photographs. "This is a crisis – but your life goes on – you get over it – find a way of coping – and your life will go on."

And then I let myself cry. I'll never know how my mum, struggling with dementia slowly extending its grip on her mind, knew exactly what I needed to cope with what was happening to me, but she did: there it was – evidence for me that I hadn't always been this mess I was now. I had been a child, a teenager, a student, a daughter, a teacher, a social worker, a painter, and a mother – kind, capable, loving, loved.

My dad let me cry on his shoulder on days when, sat in a daze in front of the television a film would come on, a war film, and I would be overwhelmed with knowing how scared those soldiers were and I'd cry and shake and blubber. Or each day would pass with no news of seeing Joe and his face would be before me in my mind's eye.

At this time there was an advert being put on the television for something or other which featured a baby apparently lying on the edge of a cliff. I had to leave the room when it came on. That is what I had done to my baby.

Sometimes my mum would say, "What's she crying about?" because she'd forget. Many times, when I'd been upstairs, making a phone call or whatever I'd come downstairs and she'd say to me with a conspiratorial smile, "Is he asleep?" referring to the Joe she imagined I'd just left sleeping upstairs. This would hit me like a wrecking ball and I'd have to leave the room, my mum bewildered as my dad explained once more that Joe was with his dad.

My mum's dementia had progressed to the point where she couldn't retain this and "Where's Joe?" was a recurring question in the house, as if my senses, searching for him in every shadow and every other child's face, were being voiced by another.

I waited to hear of the mental health assessment which would let me see Joe. I was allowed to ring him every Wednesday evening and we talked for ten minutes.

If an advert came on which featured a child I had to walk out of the room and escape upstairs. But there was no escape. I watched whatever was on television to fill my waking hours and stop me thinking or feeling anything as all I could think or feel was that Joe was not with me and I did not know if he was safe.

If even a domestic comedy included any rows or raised voices I would tense in every limb and find it unbearable. My mum and dad took me to the supermarket when they went to get the weekly shop. I collapsed in choking tears in the back of the car at the sight of the supermarket – I had always had Joe with me when we shopped; he'd go for a ride in the trolley and sample the goods on the way to the till, giggling and learning the names of things.

I stayed in the car as my mum and dad did the shop.

I told my mum and dad that I would go to prison if I was found guilty and how would they cope with that? My dad said he didn't think that would happen. I said, "They might find me guilty."

He said, evenly, "They might not." My dad believed in the system.

My mother told me she believed in me, that I was a good person and that I had to start believing in myself. But it wasn't my belief that was the problem — it was everybody else's.

Nights were painful, dark, lonely times when I could hear in my mind's ear my child crying for me, but I was unable to go to him. I could see in my mind's eye Jay getting angry, yelling at Joe — maybe worse — but I was not there to pick him up and get him to a safe place. I'd lie awake, praying fervently, just in case there was a God or Angels — anybody. Friends reassured me that there was and that things would come out alright and I clung to this idea. If I drifted into sleep I'd wake again to the horror of the gap beside me.

Walking down the road or going in the kitchen, all my senses would still be telling me that Joe was just around the edge of the curtain or the door and I'd look to see him. Everywhere was full of memory-images of when we had been there together, playing, laughing. He was behind me, I'd look. He was just in the room next door. He was asleep upstairs and would wake up any minute. I was haunted every waking minute and in sleep it was worse.

If I saw other children anywhere I'd stare at them like a mad woman to spot my own among them. I'd see likenesses in their smiles or ways of running. All my senses screamed at me to find him. My brain knew he was 100 miles away with his dad and aunt but it was as if my body did not believe this or had not been told and was searching, searching. Sleeping pills from the doctor helped knock me out at night so I got some relief. She'd asked me if I had ever contemplated suicide before she prescribed them.

It beckoned. Smiling. Sweet oblivion. End to pain. But there was another vision. Joe. Maybe years later. A teenager, wanting to know. "Why did my mother leave me? Why didn't she wait for me? Why did she abandon me – twice?"

So there was no escape. If I took that way out I'd be abandoning Joe.

The physical side of this was strange. My whole body from just below my ribs to down below my waist seemed to go a dull kind of achy numb. The space which Joe had lived in safely for nine months. I was hungry but I couldn't eat. I'd put out a bowl of cereal and milk and want to eat it but I couldn't. My whole stomach would rebel at the idea of food even though the hunger was clawing at me.

A strange numbness started to form. It wasn't on any part of my body. It was sort of between me and the outside world. It wasn't quite like deafness but everything everyone said was echoey and distant. When I answered them, my own voice sounded mechanised and far away as if someone else was talking.

A van had arrived one morning and the driver handed me a big brown envelope telling me he was serving me papers. The letter told me of the hearing at the court near to the auntie's house and that Jay had applied for a residency order.

I didn't sleep and left at 1am on the morning of the hearing, as being still was unbearable, and at least driving lent me the illusion of doing something useful. I arrived in the strange town at 4am and located the family court: a square, utilitarian building. I drove around looking for somewhere to park and stopped in a side street near the court. Here I was able to sleep, setting my alarm to be in time for the hearing at 10am. I knew the light would wake me way before then. I wondered at my chances of being arrested for vagrancy and I wondered if that would impress the judge, or maybe not?

My dad had wished me good luck and I had imaginings of the judge seeing the obvious mistakes that had been made and ordering Joe's immediate return to the mother he missed so much and arrangements made to ensure his safety during visits with the father who had such a difficult mental health problem.

I went into the court when it opened and was told where to wait. I was the only person in the room, having arrived early. The usher asked me suddenly if I was a social worker and I said yes thinking it must be on some notes somewhere.

Then she asked me to follow her and showed me into a small 'consulting' room and asked me to wait. Then she came back with another woman who was carrying a large file of papers and who told me in crisp tones that the adoption would take a while. I gaped at them as she continued, my world spinning – my worst fears – they had realised Jay's mental health problems and found me guilty of not protecting my son. Then the second woman said, "So I've just spoken to the mother and she says …"

I found my voice, "But I'm the mother!"

They both looked at me blankly as if I was mad.

"I'm the mother!" I repeated. "I'm Joe's mother!"

The usher asked me my name and wasn't I a social worker? I told them, yes I was but I was the mother. They looked at each other and then left the room. I was obviously the wrong name, the wrong social worker and the wrong mother in the wrong case – and they hadn't been talking about Joe. I realised I was very close to a total panic attack and went to the window. I felt sick and weak and had to sit down again quickly.

One of Ms Pane's juniors then found me and we talked about 'the case' and any concerns I might have about Joe living with his father. She seemed a bit overwhelmed when I told her. I mentioned my concern about Jay's paedophile dad being allowed to visit and have access to Joe. And Jay having a history of out-of-control rages – and the fact I was being charged with assault as I had caused him serious head injuries as I'd been so scared – and that Jay could not tolerate any misbehaviour or noise. This all seemed to be a big surprise to her. I wondered afterwards if she'd been told anything at all about the 'case' – the 'case' being Joe's life.

I hadn't seen Jay since he had left the house

wrapped in a duvet and the towel. Then I had been all concern and shock. Since then I had seen his statement accusing me of attempted murder and he had taken away my child and seen to it that I was unable to see him, or he me.

I had begun to realise that he had never been 'out of control' or in need of my help or support. He had been in control. Not ill, not in pain, not in a flashback – but in control.

The idea of walking into the court and seeing him was clawing at me. Ms Pane's junior assistant would be with me – she seemed about seventeen years old and naïve. What would happen?

There is a Native American way to gain strength from others when we lack our own. I was in need of it. I closed my eyes and imagined myself, as the method describes, descending a rope into the middle of the earth and sitting in the dark, asking for my power animal to show itself and come to my aid: several creatures scampered by my mind's eye, scuttering away as I asked each one, desperately, for help. Then, from somewhere in my mind's eye, from somewhere inside the scared hollow of me, a huge elephant, yellow with dust, massive with power, strolled forward and picked me up and I felt the strength of its weight and of the earth itself rolling beneath my feet. Together with the strength of that mighty, female yellow elephant, I stood up and walked into the court in a daze. Ms Pane's junior padding beside me never knew I had other company, giving me strength.

I have long supported the cause of indigenous people's fight for their rights and language and cultures and 'Bury My Heart At Wounded Knee' was the book which opened the door on the real world to my teenage self – and on that day in court, it was as if I was receiving a thank you.

I was aware of Jay being there in the court but I didn't have to speak or look at him.

At the hearing, I'd imagined the judge understanding and seeing that a child should be with his or her main carer and to know that I'd hit the father out of fear, and to allow Joe to return to me but he just said, "We can't do much today," and to agree Joe to live with Jay until 'things were resolved'. Ms Pane's assistant didn't say anything. Jay's legal team told the judge of the serious head injuries I had caused and that was that.

Ms Pane's assistant offered to walk with me to my car, which was kind and she also asked me if I'd read the social workers' report which had arrived. I said I hadn't. I thanked her for her help.

I went home. I still hadn't been able to see Joe.

Yet another week went by. I was allowed to talk to Joe again briefly on the phone on the Wednesday. He'd been to see some ships with his dad and for a walk with Henry. He wanted to know when I'd be coming. Anna had advised me what to say, "I don't know darling but I will come there as soon as I can, I will come, I can't say yet. You have to do nice things and tell me about them and enjoy them until I can get there."

I had to give him some certainty but this was all I could give him without making the situation any worse for him with more false promises.

I'd agreed that I would have a 'psychological assessment'. I was desperately trying to find someone who could do it – and it had to be someone acceptable to Jay. All my colleagues had heard of this and offered to do it but it had to be someone 'neutral'. I had visited the local mental health team when the solicitor said the manager could do a mental health assessment which would be acceptable. I made an appointment – nothing available for a week – then two. They went by. The world did not think any of this was important or urgent – my hell was all just routine.

I went for a mental health assessment. The mental health social work team manager was congenial, thorough, and asked me a lot of questions. I answered them in between blubbing as I recalled incidents in my home life and was overwhelmed with shame at how this must sound to a normal person as I described my pathetic life. I didn't mention anything about yellow elephants or power animals. Mental health has a proud history of slapping mental illness labels on folk who don't have a mainstream culture.

I emphasised that Jay had always, or nearly always, said he was sorry.

"And what does sorry mean?" the assessor asked, quietly.

I thought about it and suggested that it means an expression of regret about having done something.

He disagreed. "I think it means more than that – it means regret, certainly, but it also means a commitment to not doing the same thing or similar ever again. Or trying very hard not to do so. It does not mean – 'you must forget all about this and I will do it again just as soon as I feel like it.' That seems to me to be what Jay seemed to mean by it."

That took a while to sink in.

Over and over again, I had accepted Jay's apology as meaning it would not happen again – and over and over and over again, it had.

The assessor concluded I was not a risk to anyone but then in his report suggested I be 'supported' in seeing Joe – that ambiguous word again – until I was emotionally stronger. He did not clarify why he thought I needed 'support' during contact – this was left open to interpretation. Weeks went by again.

Once a week, which was a spot which I crawled towards throughout the rest of the week, I was allowed to talk to Joe on the phone for ten minutes. Whatever I said, that I'd been in the garden or to town his little voice would say, "Can I do that with you? Can I come there with you?" And, "When are you coming? Where are you?" Then voices in the background would murmur and Joe would recite what he'd been doing: he'd been to the stream or the café or the shops or a cousin had taken him out or he'd been playing with Henry. I thanked God for Henry. So the voices in the background knew every time he asked for me and how much he was missing me. Who was it who had told the social worker, Anastasia, that he wasn't?

I was grateful to know he was being looked after but was it only in the phone call that he wanted to see me? It would be such a relief to believe that – but I knew it wasn't true as he told me: he missed me.

Where was I? We had always been together, outside of nursery.

I learned very quickly not to tell him of my day but would tell him stories which I thought might help – about children who lost a toy and had to look for a long time before they found it again, or children who went on a big adventure which felt strange sometimes and scary but it all worked out in the end. He'd listen. He'd always liked stories. Then the phone call had to end, a voice would murmur and Joe would say, "I've got to go now," and I'd tell him I loved him as big as all the sky, as big as all the solar system and blue whales and the call would end, the handset would click and burr in my hand – and the week would stretch ahead in pain and grey.

One Sunday, another one of Jay's sisters rang me, the one I'd met at the funeral. She asked me why I'd hit her brother. I told her I'd been afraid. I was amazed at this phone call out of the blue, especially as she lived hundreds of miles away from the auntie where Joe and Jay were staying. Maybe she had visited. She was the eldest child of the family – the one they all looked to, the one who sorted things. She asked me why I wasn't seeing Joe and that he needed to see me. I explained I was not being allowed to – but I hesitated and didn't say that it was Jay who was stopping me. I didn't want to say negative things to her about her brother – that wouldn't help. Surely she would know that? She said that was ridiculous and that Joe needed to see me. The phone call ended.

The next morning, a Monday, I'd driven to see the family solicitor and someone in social services called on my mobile as I was pulling into the car park. I was asked if I 'was available to go and see Joe this Thursday'. The suddenness, the unexpectedness of the call and the sheer madness of the question left me breathless. As if I'd have something more important to do! I said yes as tears again overwhelmed me. I thanked the caller again and again in hysteria through tears. I later tried to find out what had happened to bring about this change, I asked the social worker who had been assigned 'the case' what had happened to bring about the change but I was just told, "Don't worry about that." I never did find out why it had suddenly changed but remain convinced it was this elder sister stepping in for Joe's sake.

The details of my 'contact' with Joe were: I was not allowed to be in the same room as Jay at all, I had to be supervised with Joe – the mental health report was ambiguous, saying that I should be 'supported' in contact – and the contact was for two hours on the Thursday at the auntie's house.

As I drove back my mobile rang: it was Debbie – our neighbour. My friend whom Jay had disliked. She said, "I'll make a statement about his temper so the police will understand."

I'd forgotten the incident, Jay yelling at Debbie and Ron, their children frightened – it might only have been 5/10 on his personal Richter scale but Jay had had temper rages and had frightened others apart from me. Maybe I wasn't on my own after all?

A small hope opened in the dark.

Chapter 6

When I told them about the contact happening in a few days my parents were ecstatic for me. They too missed Joe and were afraid of what was happening to me.

My mother, as the dementia gnawed away at her memory, constantly forgot that Joe was not with me. She'd be aghast again as my father shushed at her and again told her that Joe was living with his dad 'for now' and my mum would ask why this was.

But she caught the delight that I was going to see him that week although she had no idea that I hadn't seen him – for a whole month.

A month ago I had told him I'd be coming the next day. A month ago I had agreed with the social workers that he could live with is dad, at his auntie's for six or seven weeks for an assessment, and I had not seen him since. I had trusted them. A month is a long time – especially when you are three. I couldn't help wonder if he'd recognise me. Anna assured me he would not have forgotten me.

I drove the hundred miles. The car was packed

with a picnic big enough for a street party and I'd bought a new ball and a toy to give him. I thought these would be useful to distract him from my leaving again at the end of the two hours. He had had plenty of experience of my leaving him at the start of crèche and later of nursery – I had been leaving him since he was six months old. We had had practice.

I arrived in the village and parked in a lay-by to await permission to go to the house. I remembered the house from our visit two years previously. Then the supervisor phoned and I drove to the house and up the drive. Joe's social worker was there, he left when the supervisor had arrived.

The auntie and uncle lived in a huge house with a massive garden with a long sweeping drive. One of the cousins came to the door and I was let into the kitchen. The supervisor was there. We waited. I heard a car come into the drive and car doors close. Then the kitchen door opened and I heard the auntie saying, "Who's here then? Who's this? Who can this be?" and Joe was there.

He didn't see me at first as there were kitchen stools between us but then he did and he ran to me, calling, "Mummy, Mummy, Mummy!" and ran into my arms at last and I lifted him up to sit in my arms once more. I just wanted to hold him forever. He sat smiling down at me as I greeted him and chatted. Everyone else in the room was irrelevant. The world spun back into place. I stopped hurting.

Joe chatted very fast, telling me all about all sorts of things and wanting to show me toys and the dog. I'd brought some flowers for the auntie and she seemed to accept them and put them in a vase. I'd brought my dressing gown and put it on to read Joe a story – to revisit what he was used to in our being together. He cuddled into the dressing gown like it was an old friend and wrapped it around him like he had always used to and followed the story in the book as always. He used the word 'Mummy' a lot as if enjoying being able to use it again. He showed me where he slept and where he kept his toys. He showed me trees in the garden and books. I couldn't take my eyes off him. We played 'catch' in the kitchen and hide and seek and included the supervisor, I wanted it all to be as normal as possible for Joe.

We'd always played hide and seek in the caravan. I'd make much of not being able to find him – as he hid in one of only two places in the caravan where it was possible to hide. I'd go around saying, "Where is he?" Where's my little boy?" as he giggled in delight at my confusion.

And I did this now, "Where is my little boy? I will find him. It might take me a long time but I will find him. I love my little boy even though I can't see him, I'll never stop loving him, where is my little boy?"

I didn't know if this would help at all but it was all I could think of. Joe crouched under a chair giggling in delight as his mum wandered past saying these things.

The next two hours went very quickly. They were like five minutes in most people's lives – people who are not separated from their child. I'd asked the kind supervisor to let me know when I had fifteen minutes left. I needed this so I could prepare Joe for my leaving so he would not be shocked or distressed. I told him I'd have to go 'in a minute' but that I'd be coming back 'very soon'. He asked, "How many sleeps?" I had to say I didn't know but that it wouldn't be so long this time. And I quickly showed him the toy I'd brought and talked of him playing with it with his auntie. I asked after the family dog and we went to find him and started a game.

I asked the supervisor to carry on the game as I left. The auntie was ready to come and pick up the game. I gave Joe a big hug and repeated that I'd be back soon. The last time I'd parted from him, I'd lied to him. Did he remember? He kept asking me to come and look at this and that in an effort to keep me. Did he really think I wanted to go because I was bored? I told him again that I had to go. Told him to go to his auntie.

We cuddled and chatted and it was just like it always had been between us – he showed no resentment. He asked why I had to go and I used the agreed lie that I had to look after my mum who was ill. His face had fallen but I told him we could look forward to next time and gave him his new toys and told him he could now play with these new things with his auntie and the dog – I was building him a bridge away from me to make it easier for him. He looked solemn as he listened to my burblings but he seemed to accept it. He climbed onto my lap and pressed his face into mine, his eyes right up to mine, as if looking right into me. He had never done that before. Had he sensed I was lying? I only knew to smile at him and treat it as a game.

After a final 'big cuddle' and carrying him, spinning him around and a last 'big kiss' and talk of 'next time' and throwing the new ball to the dog, I left.

I held it together until I reached a lay-by where I

could pull in and cry until I had stopped shaking and was fit to drive home. Home that could never be home without Joe. Very often tears bring relief – others you just cry because you are trying to get the pain to move, but the tears do nothing and the racking, jerking, empty spasms only cause physical pain. This is some relief from emotional pain. And praying. Praying, I discovered, is what you do when the tears no longer help. Physical pain is tangible and finite – unlike emotional pain which stretches to all our horizons. It also helps. Pinching myself hard until I bruised helped to focus what I was feeling and make it finite, manageable. I had to drive home.

All the way home I held the moments which we had had in my mind. Playing hide and seek, reading some books, pig-a back around the kitchen, throwing his teddy, him telling me all his news, just the joy of being with him again and seeing he was alright.

There was a god after all and he would see us alright. He would look after my baby and see that right was done.

That became my routine. Days and nights of a strange, zombie-like existence trailing around after my parents or staring at the television, unseeing, and nights spent praying and trying to find sleep to have a few hours of oblivion. I'd telephone Joe for the few precious minutes – "Are you coming tomorrow? Where are you?" in his little three-year-old voice. "When are you coming?" How many sleeps?" and, "Too many sleeps."

And then the two-and-a-half-hour drive and the two hours with each other into which we tried to pack our all. And the two-and-a-half-hour drive back.

But the criminal trial had moved ever further away. Dates would be set but then kept getting postponed. I hadn't even been charged yet. I thought it would be sorted out in a few weeks but there was no sign nor of the 'assessment' which was supposed to have taken 'a few weeks'.

I now knew that with every passing day, my chances of Joe being returned to me were slipping away. I now knew that the agreement with the social workers hadn't been an agreement at all but just a ploy to get Joe away from me so they could close the case and leave it to the courts.

They had lied. Like Jay, they had lied.

I never knew from one week to the next when contact would be. I was only allowed two hours per week – usually at the end of the week. I could not see him without being supervised. The people who were sent to supervise us were wonderful. They joined in and played and were kind.

They told me they were not used to supervising where they were so obviously not needed. They were used to having to prompt the parent to play or talk to the child. They were used to supervising where the adult wanted to spend the time talking to them about herself/himself or who was preoccupied with their own needs. We charged about playing 'owls' or chase or Joe would sit on the picnic rug and I'd drag it around the garden with Joe riding it as if on a sledge. We were still meeting in the garden of Jay's sister Agnes's huge house.

Sometime during the week I'd get a phone call from the social work office saying contact was arranged for such and such a date and I'd claw my way towards that day.

Ms Pane forwarded to me the report written by Anastasia and Dan which had been filed with the family court. I had not seen it before nor signed it. My understanding of such reports is that they need to be signed and agreed and any differences recorded – but somehow not this time.

The report said that, when I'd arrived at the nursery, Joe had been reluctant, as if afraid, to go to me. Anastasia had written that she had witnessed my arrival at the after-school club – and that Joe had kept away from me. There it was, in black and white.

Immediately I phoned the school and asked to speak to the teacher who had run the after-school club – there was just a chance she would remember Joe's hurtling across the classroom to greet me. I gave my name and was put through to the headteacher who said I could not speak to the teacher – but that she remembered that day well and what she remembered was that, at 3:10, when the day ended, there had been no-one there to collect Joe – so they had put him in the after-school club. Her voice was rich with disapproval. From her point of view, I had failed to collect my child after school – on his first day.

There was a heap of detail I could give her about how I was told to go there at 3:30, not before, and how I needed the teacher to speak up for me – to say how Joe had been delighted to see me – to prove that Anastasia was lying – but she was quite clear – I could not speak with her and the conversation was over. She agreed to ask the teacher herself. She rang back later: she had asked the after-school teacher and she remembered nothing of that day. It had been a long shot, I knew. Why would anyone remember a child delighted to see his mummy at the end of the day?

I told Ms Pane the report was misleading and it needed to be challenged – she said it was 'historical' and the judge would not be interested in a social worker's behaviour. Again, everything which provided context was disregarded. That report sat on the file for everyone to see. Esme wrote a statement about how Joe had been with me during his time at her house and when she was looking after me – asking for me. She was very clear he had been asking for me and missing me. I hoped it would help – but who would believe Esme against a 'professional'.

The spiral downwards got faster now I knew how bad things were against me. Nights were painful, dark, lonely times. I could see in my mind's eye Jay getting angry, yelling at Joe, fear of worst – the hitting out – but I was not there to pick him up and get him to a safe place. I'd lie awake. Praying helped as it gave me the sense of being able to do something; an illusion or false hope, maybe – but anyone who sneers at false hope can only do so because they do not know what it is to have none of the real kind. When there is no other, you clutch at false hope and hug it close, as it helps you to keep breathing, even while your rational mind watches in scorn.

Friends like Anna and Esme and my parents and wonderful brother and sister-in-law all reassured me that things would come out alright and I clung to this idea and their friendship, clutching at their hands held out to me from the shore as I floundered, choking – without them I would have undoubtedly gone under.

Sleep, pill-driven, was oblivion of sorts. I'd get to sleep as the pills took hold but I'd wake in the night hearing Joe's voice in my mind calling for me as he did in the night.

Was his father tending to him – or was he being angry at being woken? Was he applying his own philosophy of leaving him to cry abandoned?

Friends advised me to pray – to a God I didn't believe in and a universal force for good I'd never found. But there was some relief in it. Some sense of asking for help from some greater power, to take care of my child and comfort him when I could not. I learned during this time, that tears don't always bring relief. Some tears there are which really do tear. Racking, tearing tears which just left emptiness all through mind and body with no relief, only a rawer, more present pain.

"Religion," said Marx, "is the opium of the people, the sigh of the oppressed – a heart in a heartless world." In his time opium was the new miracle painkiller and I drank deep, finding it put something between me and the pain.

Keeping moving helped – it gave the illusion that I was going somewhere, getting away from the pain, doing something – so I'd blunder about the house and garden, never sitting or staying anywhere for long. It was a relief to have to drive to attend for bail or to go and see the solicitor – either Richard or Ms Pane – just to have something to do which felt positive.

Nobody seemed in any hurry to resolve the situation. I'd assumed it would be sorted very quickly

– Jay would tell them of his temper problems or he would 'lose it' with his sister and all would become clear, the social services would do their assessment of where Joe was most attached and he would be back with me. But neither of those things had happened.

The weeks turned into months.

One day, aimless and trying to find somewhere to get to where I wouldn't feel like this, I drove over the common, thinking to go to the highest point to walk awhile. The wind was strong and a storm was coming in. It was difficult to find anywhere which did not have some remembrance of being there with Joe – and this was worse in the house so getting out and walking in different places was some relief. There were places where I'd go and pray. There was a spot in the woods where I'd sit, at the foot of a large tree, away from the track, and ask for help, beg for help. As I drove up the hill and onto the plateau of the common, the wind was roaring in from the sea, leaves, rain and litter sped horizontally past the windscreen. There was no shelter anywhere. The trees on the common writhed in the wind.

Then I saw, on the side of the road, a small group of wild ponies, all colours, grey, beige, and white, brown, black. They were in the full force of the wind and rain. The storm lashed around them. They weren't going anywhere. They weren't panic-stricken or restless. They stood heads down, facing into the wind, eyes half-closed, patiently waiting. One in particular, the smallest, grey and white, watched me as I looked over at the group as the rain lashed. Why were they not afraid of the storm? What were they waiting for? Then it struck me – these horses *knew* that the storm would end. They knew, by instinct, that if they stood long enough, that the howling wind and rain would cease. All they had to do was survive and keep breathing until it was over. How did they know that? How did they know that, when I didn't? I got back in my car and drove home. I kept the grey and white pony in my mind when the storm returned. I focussed on facing it patiently, and waiting.

If this had been a film it would have been easy. No sitting around pretending to be ponies –I would have been heroic and active. But in real life this is not allowed: paperwork must come first, procedures must be awaited.

If heroes and gods came back now they too would have to fill in a form and wait in the queue. Poor God. Once we had whole pantheons of gods who had fun – frolicking, failing and fornicating like we do – but now he has to be perfect and sit listening to our wails and justifying this mess of a world we blame him for.

I prayed because I didn't know what else to do. I was in maximum stress and minimum power. There was nothing I could do to help Joe without making things worse. I thought of driving to the auntie's house and finding Joe in the garden. He would see me and run over. Maybe we could get to the airport? *And then what?* said Rational Mind. I had no connections abroad, nowhere to go. It would be kidnapping as Jay had the right to have Joe in residence with him. I'd be caught and arrested and Joe taken from me by force and we'd both be in a worse state than now.

My friends had helped me. They'd told me of things they had learned of how to keep going. Anna told me of prayer: she had a huge faith in a god which seemed to inform her actions in the world – she was always kind and compassionate and she urged me to find help there.

And Ruth, a friend and colleague, gave me a card where she had written: "Some days you will only be able to do three things – do them – and all will be well... Some days, you will only be able to do two things – do those two things and all will be well. On some days, you will only be able to breathe – so breathe, and all will be well." The effect of these was to help me, in a situation where I could do nothing but where every instinct screamed at me to do something, to become a little calmer and to focus on keeping going – and on not going mad. Many days all I could do was breathe, so I did. Sometimes staying alive and staying sane is challenge enough and takes all your energy.

There were many things which supported me during this time. Without any one of them I would have gone under, sank into soft folds of madness and given up the effort.

I focussed on them – my mind spinning at the thought of how many must arrive at this point and not have such support.

We have evolved, after all, to make sense of our world; as deer have evolved to run, humans have evolved to think – to analyse our environment, what our senses tell us – to make sense of it and know how to act. But what if the world no longer makes sense? What then? Does the mind fold back on itself in defeat? I felt my grip on sanity slipping by the day. Nothing made sense. I clung onto things which seemed real: without the persistent kindness of others, my father especially, I would have gone under.

I carried an image of Joe in my mind wherever I went. The smile of delight when we met. Times we had had together in the past. The two hours per week we had now. The next time I would see him. The pictures he did and gave to me I had stuck on the walls. I'd plan and prepare games he'd like and fetch books from the library. I went to car boot sales and bought toys – far too many – but it was some way of being with him.

My dad was a beacon from the beach as I ducked and swallowed sea water and disappeared under dark waves. Every morning, every single morning, when he awoke he would go downstairs and make tea for himself and my mum. They had developed this routine over the years. He'd then bring in a mug of tea and set it down by my bed. I hardly drank it. I was amazed that among the hell of Joe not being with me and solicitors' letters which I couldn't comprehend and not being able to eat or sleep that he would think a mundane nonsense like a mug of tea could be important. But it was. Every day, each morning, I got that message of my own importance and that I mattered to someone, and that someone cared. It was a routine of love while the world bucked and swirled around me.

Other people who sustained me were folk whose names I do not even know. I had one image in my heart. It is a woman standing among a ruined house in Palestine, holding up the body of a dead child, her face utterly contorted with grief. And disbelief as well as pain and horror. When the unspeakable happens to you the overriding sensation, I'd realised, is one of disbelief.

Another picture, a man laying down the body of a small child – about Joe's age. The child is well dressed, wrapped against the cold and looks as if he is sleeping. The man is laying him, very gently down alongside three others of the same age, similarly wrapped and also as if asleep.

They are not asleep. They are all dead. A bombing attack on Palestine. The faces of the adults. Somehow, they were coping with a pain worse than mine. They would not play with their children on Friday for two hours. They would give all they had to be in my place and be able to see their child again for a moment, never mind two whole hours. If they could cope with what they were going through – then I had to be able to cope with this. I crawled on.

My mother had long been showing signs of short-term memory problems but we all looked the other way. We couldn't cope with it, that's why. Always the hub of the family, the only extrovert among us. The chatty one. The one who made things happen. Creative. Glamorous. Keen on art and science and maths. Twelve times in one day she'd now lose her handbag and get distressed and we'd trawl the house to find it. She'd put it in 'a safe place' and, ten minutes later, off we'd all go again, hunting.

So when I arrived back in their lives on a full-time basis – without partner and without child – it took a little while to adjust. She'd ask me, "Where's Joe?" whenever we encountered each other around the house or when we were watching television.

When social services finally decided they were not going to provide supervisors for my time with Joe anymore as it 'did not meet their criteria' Jay was still insistent that I was not allowed to see Joe on my own. All my friends immediately volunteered their time to come with me so I could see Joe. Jay turned every single one of them down where he could find any chance of doing so. He lied.

He said, for example, he did not know Esme and nor did Joe. Esme sent photographs of Joe at her house with her own son, playing and even one of Jay himself on one of the rare occasions he had come with us on a visit. These were all ignored by the solicitor and none of my friends were allowed to be supervisors – even though they were school governors, parents themselves, and mothers of Joe's friends – which would have meant he could at last see his friends again after all these months.

The only people Jay accepted as supervisors were my family members – he even turned down an adult nephew – well into his twenties, in work, not a blemish on his character – saying he was too young. He used any excuse. He said Marianne was unacceptable 'because she smoked'. The court accepted this without a murmur. As if she chain-smoked all the time she was with children – rather than the odd cigarette she'd go outside to have a couple of times a day. The only people I could turn to, to accompany me on the 200-mile, eight-hour round trip to see my son were my dad, my brother – who worked full-time, and his wife, my sister-in-law who had her own household and life – and Anna, who lived forty miles further away from Joe than I did. The court went along with this. It was nothing about Joe's needs – to see me or his friends – it was all about Jay's right to control. And he wanted to make it as difficult for me to see Joe as possible.

If there was one sure way of breaking the bond between Joe and me it would be for me to become unreliable. To repeatedly not show up. Eventually Joe would learn not to trust. Not to care. He'd already been let down for a month of his mother not coming to see him – when she had said she would be there every day.

The court had my psychological assessment; they had umpteen character references from colleagues and friends. They even had the photographs which proved Jay to be a liar when he said Joe didn't know Esme or that that he didn't – as the pictures showed him and Joe at Esme's house – but they all counted for nothing. I was told the outcome by a slightly distracted barrister who had not so much as raised one objection to Jay's assertions – of the many I'd put before her.

So my octogenarian dad came with me on the 200-mile round trip to supervise me seeing Joe. We could now go outside the grounds of the auntie's house. We went to play places together, my dad strolling along with us, chatting at times but usually quiet, enjoying the time together. We left my mum with my sister-in-law but this could not go on happening. My sister-in-law was exhausted after each day. My mother, who had now been diagnosed with Alzheimer's, had been frantic without my dad – putting on her coat and running up the road to find him in a panic of feeling herself deserted. Anyone who has seen how dementia progresses, knows that the main carer becomes someone on whom the person with dementia absolutely relies and cannot be without. My dad was my mum's main carer. She could not cope with being separated from him.

So my mum came with us. The wise court officials, who had accepted that my friends were too smoky or too young or too unknown to Joe to supervise my time with my son, accepted instead that my Alzheimic mother accompanying my father was a better alternative. This madness involved us once a week persuading her into the car and charging up the motorway answering her repeated questions of, "Where are we going? Where are you taking me? Why are we going here?" And relentless insistence of, "Take me home," or worse, "drop me off here, I'll walk home from here. Drop me off. Let me out, let me out."

*

The court had agreed I could now see Joe twice a week and my sister-in-law could attend once, my brother when his work allowed. She would come with me on the Tuesday and we would take Joe out. When the SSD dropped their provision of supervision they also agreed I could take Joe out of the aunt's garden which was a relief. My sister-in-law would chat with Joe and fit in with whatever I wanted to do. My mother on the other hand could not do this.

I'll always remember one time when we arrived at the soft play place we had found and adopted as a regular place to bring Joe for our time together – my mother getting do so distressed my dad had to say we had to leave and go home. Joe had to be more grown up than my mother and accept he had to go back early.

My mother would ask why I left Joe at the aunt's and why I didn't want to take him home. All of this was agony as each time it happened it was like a scab had been pulled off the wound.

Each week my dad would tell me he really didn't think he could ask my mum to go through it again. And every week I'd explain why we had to and insist that we did. The alternative was my not turning up to see Joe, letting him down. So, my mum and dad went through this hell. The 200-mile round trip. The total distress of someone with dementia not knowing where they are – because Jay insisted I needed supervising when with my son. To do otherwise, Jay would have had to admit that I had had some cause to hit him as I did. That, yes, I might have been frightened by his anger and his mindless rages and threats. He could not admit that so the pretence went on and the court went along with the wishes of this, obviously very ill, man.

Jay could not find a reason to refuse my family the 'right' to 'supervise' me. I knew he had tried as he had refused all the others on unreasonable grounds – but he had probably been advised not to appear unreasonable in front of the judge. But the judge needed to see that unreasonableness if he or she was to understand the situation.

The other person whom Jay could not find a reason to refuse was Anna.

Anna had already volunteered and been accepted as a 'supervisor' because, as my fellow social worker, she was qualified in childcare, didn't smoke and had already known Joe. Jay probably could find no reasonable-sounding reason to refuse her offer – so she would come with me once a week to visit Joe. To do this she had to get to her local train station at some ungodly hour and travel to where I was living. I'd pick her up and we'd head off down the motorway. She knew Joe as we'd visited her house together and we'd played in her garden. She'd brought her grandson to his third birthday party a million years before. She had asked me then why Jay had not come to his son's party and been bemused at my mumbled, "He's very busy."

I leaned on her like a fallen tree.

Anna had a strong faith in God and believed that all would turn out to be well, that God would not let my son suffer and Right would be established. She also thought that through suffering God was teaching me something. I asked her if God would mind awfully if I ducked out of class and stayed ignorant as I wasn't sure I wanted to know anything more about pain than I did already – and could Joe skip the class too?

Anna. Without Anna, how many times would I have failed to make the journey up that motorway? How many times would I have had to let Joe down? How much worse a mother would I have been to him? Jay could not find a reason to refuse this woman the 'right' to accompany and supervise me. And she had taken this on. When the social services workers had been withdrawn – 'case closed – wait for the private courts' – and before Jay had graciously given permission for some of my family to supervise – Anna had stepped in and enabled me to see my little

111

boy. I could imagine what this had cost her. She had her own family, people who needed her support at home, and yet she quit them and came to help Joe and me.

On the set days – and often they were only set as a day's notice as Jay would cancel and rearrange or messages would not get through – she would get up two hours earlier to catch the train to where I lived now from the little station in the village a few miles from her house. I would meet her at my local station in the early morning and we'd drive the 100+ miles to where we met Joe. Then she would come with us to the park, the museum, the lake, the river and join in with our play. She'd talk to my little boy, play with him, help me help him cope with the parting, and she would sit with me while I cried my pain out enough to manage the drive home. Not one word of complaint. No criticism. No exasperation at the mess I had made of these lives.

I had confided something of my life to her when we had been working together but not the full extent. I was now mortified by the thought I had thought this amazing woman was capable of rejecting me or of ridiculing me. Jay's hatred of me had done good work in convincing me that no-one could possibly like the real me if they knew me well enough. I'd kept everyone distant.

Weeks went by and then my family were able to supervise. But even then, they could not cover all the days. Often, they were having to work or were ill or my father was exhausted at trying to persuade my mother to get in the car for another mad sojourn and Anna would stand in.

There are many wonderful people in the world. But I don't think there are many like Anna.

She was with me when I sat in the park and told Joe something of why he could not live with me 'for now'. I told him I had hit his daddy because I'd been scared. The story that I was looking after my mum had got a bit thin: he was asking me who looked after her when I was visiting him. Bright lad, spotting the hole in the lie. Joe listened and said, "Don't bash my daddy again!" And, "But I miss you!" So we fed bread to the ducks and left the sad conversation under the tree.

For months Anna accompanied me and comforted me on those journeys back when I was fresh again in the pain of bereavement. When Joe asked me why he couldn't be with me, why I had to go, why was it so many 'sleeps' until I came again, she had the answer to comfort him. She made us both look forward to 'the next time' and to treasure whatever activity we had had this time. She had the idea of giving him a little gift – a shell or button to 'look after' for me until next time – as a tangible way of telling him I'd be back.

He and his dad had been living in Jay's sister's house – a huge place with many rooms. We played in the garden and sometimes inside if it rained. I had long hoped for some signs that the family did know about Jay's temper but that hope evaporated. I had long left my phone on overnight, waiting for their call to tell me what had happened, Jay had 'had a fit of rage' and that they had called the police and could I come and get Joe. That call had never come.

Once freed from the aunt's garden we explored the locality. We found parks and 'family farms' where we could see the goats and feed the guinea pigs. We played ball in the park and played our many games of old – the 'shop game' with me pretending to be an array of strange animal customers asking Joe-shopkeeper for an array of unlikely commodities in a suitable animal voice, Joe giggling at my fierce snake and doleful elephant asking for jelly and bacon sandwiches. We found a museum which didn't charge entrance fee – like a miracle – just for us. We used its room shamelessly on rainy days to play and sit and chat and read and the museum workers smiled indulgently and never asked us to leave – even when we played hide and seek in and out of the many rooms, giggling.

I began to realise angels are of this earth and very real. But they're not supernatural beings with halos and long gowns. They are humans – but special ones – and it's kindness which makes them special.

Ms Pane had recommended I find work of some kind to help pay for the petrol and other costs of the journeys and the court costs, her fees for example. She also thought it would help if I started making preparations for a new line of work as my chances of working as a social worker again, even if I didn't go to prison, which seemed unlikely, were negligible. All my salary (I was still suspended on full pay) effectively went straight to her office.

I hunted around and eventually got taken on as 'hot-wash' in a local kitchen, putting dirty dishes from the restaurant in the steaming hot-washer and pushing in the new basket full and pulling out the one full of freshly steamed clean dishes, and emptying these into the various cupboards. I was glad of the work. My first job as a teenager had been as a kitchen hand. I had my own dingy cubby hole at the back of the kitchen and it was noisy so I didn't have to chat with the other kitchen hands much which was necessary as I felt too raw all over to socialise like normal people. There was no 'safe' subject of conversation I could hide in. I focussed on what the money was for – trips to see Joe.

Alienated workers the world over find common ground to chat about – as part of the art of making horrible jobs bearable, or even fun. What we have in common is that we have friends, previous jobs, parents, kids – and an antagonistic relationship with the boss who wants us to work more for less – while we want to work less for more.

I'd been a shop steward all my working life so it was natural to think in these terms especially when we were working for a pittance in awful conditions in a hotel which was making a mint each week. I couldn't risk losing my job by trying to build a union, even if I'd been in a mentally stable state to do so. I would have to spend time sussing out who was safe to talk to and who not. I was in no position or state of mental health – I realised – to call a meeting or to take the risks. I was in the job by my fingernails. Any change would be traceable to me so that subject was closed.

So another part of my identity had to hide awhile. It is possible to unionise any workplace but you have to be surreptitious about it until most people are 'in' and careful in the meanwhile you don't inform any 'scab'. I remember organising a meeting to support the strike in a school and seeing after the meeting, the other steward going to see the boss and, judging by the boss's comments to me later on, telling him all about it. Dependant on his references, I hadn't subsequently been able to find work in that industry again. Some of us do want to change the world but there are those in power who, strangely, want to keep it exactly as it is. So here I was in an un-unionised workplace with all its dangerous working conditions, hours and low pay. At least the part of my life spent improving working conditions was vindicated, I felt – without unions, we'd all still be in sweatshops. Maybe my life hadn't been such a waste after all?

As for chatting about my family – I could chat about my mum and dad but I kept the fact of my having a child a secret. I did not mention Joe to anyone. Luckily the place was full of young folk from all over the world who were not that interested in this odd, middle-aged woman in their midst. Two of the chefs would banter with me, telling jokes which were incredibly rude and funny and I found myself laughing. They kept up this banter in the dark, windowless kitchen where they worked for sometimes thirteen hours on the stretch, and they would never know how grateful I was.

I hadn't laughed for a very long time.

So that became my routine. Trips to see the solicitors, working in the kitchen, trips in the other direction to see Joe – my darling Joe. What did he make of the mother who had loved him so much for the first three years of his life and then abandoned him? What had that taught him about the world? Would he trust it again? Would he love again? Was there anything I could ever do to dress that wound I had inflicted? What did he make of the fact I never came to see him alone but always had my brother, or my sister-in-law with me, or Anna, or my mum and dad?

During the months, when all this had been dragging through hearings which seemed to achieve nothing, my mother's condition had deteriorated. She was totally dependent on my dad and followed him about the house. If he went into the garden she'd follow after him and ask him to 'come in for dinner' – at ten in the morning. If he went out without her she became agitated –sometimes leaving the house to go and look for him, heading off down the road. She'd forget things – everything – and tell you false memories or repeatedly go around the same conversation. She told me the same anecdotes over and over. She'd sit and watch the same film over and over with no recall that we'd watched the same one the night before – and the night before that.

Anyone who has watched a loved one sliding into the oblivion which is Alzheimer's will know this story. We kept thinking she'd get better. I'll never know if the stress around what was happening with me helped to speed the illness along.

But in amongst her illness' savage advance across our lives, my mother left me with some gems which I will carry with me all my life.

I was sitting in the garden. My mum and dad had retired to this new house in a new part of the country fifteen years previously to be near my brother's children who were then infants – now grown-ups. The big potential garden had been the main attraction of the house and they had turned what had been a field into a place of beauty with mature trees and flowering shrubs all year round. I would go there at times. Sitting in the garden one day, I was crying – as I often was at that time, I couldn't help it. My mother came across the garden and sat next to me.

"What are you crying about?" she asked, noticing my red eyes.

I mentioned Joe not being here and worries about the court case. I didn't go into details. She would forget in a short while so there was no point in distressing her.

"Now then," she said. "Listen to me now. The bomb has gone off. In everybody's life, a bomb goes off. And Life is now teaching you how to cope with it. I'm going to tell you how to cope with it as someone once told me."

She took my arm – we are not a 'touchy-feely' family so we don't hold hands and all that usually.

"You have to put all this pain in a box." She went on, "Then you have to close the lid. Then you have to get on with what you have to do. You put the box away. You get on with your life. You go and see Joe. He's okay. Kids cope with things like this. Then once a day you open the box. But after a while you must close it again and put it away. You can't be in pain all the time."

An hour or so later we were again going through every cupboard and nook in the house trying to find her handbag while she fretted about wanting to 'go home' as she stood in her own kitchen of the house where she'd lived for sixteen years.

My dad told me that, when they had visited Jay

and me at our house, my mum would always want to 'go home' – as she did wherever they went because of the Alzheimer's – and he had not wanted to tell me about that so he made up the excuses, 'not wanting to drive in the dark' being the main one, to protect me from the fact my mother was becoming ill. I had thought they had just wanted to go home and had felt sad they did not want to stay longer. Thus we make strangers of each other by keeping our secrets. I hadn't told them about Jay, and they hadn't told me their little secret either.

But my mother's wise words stayed with me and I started to practice it. Consciously, when the chasm beckoned, I'd wrap a large box around it in my mind and close up the pain. It didn't always work but it meant I could sometimes go whole hours focussing on what I could do, on preparing a meal, even if I couldn't eat it, on planning my next visit, on gardening, on surviving.

I had told my brother what had happened a few days after I'd arrived home. Always someone I'd looked up to, I had dreaded telling him of what had happened. I told him, I had caused Jay serious head injuries.

He had sounded worried and asked, "Which hospital is he in then?"

I had said, "No, he's at his sister's. He was in hospital for tests for two days."

And my brother, a medic, said, "Well he hasn't got serious head injuries then has he?" And he explained what 'serious' meant. Serious head injuries are a fractured skull, brain damage, concussion.

Another friend and colleague responded the same way, she snorted in derision when I'd described what the social workers had told me and said, "He'll have a couple of little scars which he'll cover with his hair." They explained that the head, when cut even slightly, bleeds a lot – it's an important part of the body and rich with blood vessels to repair quickly any harm done. They were not impressed with the 'serious' adjective.

As my brother said, "Serious head injuries mean you're in hospital for weeks, even months – not two days!"

So why had I been told otherwise? Maybe I hadn't 'lost it' as I'd feared.

Maybe, just maybe, the way I remembered that awful morning, and the day before Christmas was, in fact, the way they had happened.

Maybe I wasn't mad after all.

Chapter 7

The family court solicitor said the case about Joe and where he was going to live couldn't even start until the trial, for the charges against me of two counts of assault, was finished, as I might go to prison, so we had to wait.

The criminal trial date had been set months ago but each time it approached it would be put back to make room for a more important case than mine. Than Joe's. Jay was still asking that I be charged with attempted murder but I was eventually charged with two charges – one of GBH Section 20 – which sounded, to me, a lot less damning than attempted murder, and one count of ABH – for the incident at Christmas. ABH means Actual Bodily Harm – although there hadn't been any. I was amazed they didn't just go along with Jay's wishes. I was worried he'd be angry at their decision not to go along with his wishes to charge me with attempted murder – and that Joe would reap the reward of his rage.

When not at work, or seeing Joe or seeing one of the solicitors or trying to sleep, I'd cook or garden or when I could not do those things any more I'd sit in the house staring at the television.

There was still no sign of the SSD assessment.

They had no idea when it would happen. I phoned SSD and asked when the assessment – of where Joe should be – was due to start. They had not appointed anyone yet.

Anastasia and Dan, the two social work managers, had said 'a few weeks' but they hadn't even had anyone to start the assessment – and must have known that at the time. Another lie which I'd gullibly believed.

Someone had recommended that I went to Women's Aid to get some support around what had happened to me. I found the office in a dingy part of town with a very hard-to-spot sign on the door. I was told this was for safety's sake and to avoid the office becoming a target.

I told them something of my history and was invited onto a course called 'The Freedom Course'. It sounded a bit flighty but I thought I'd go along. Of course it wouldn't teach me much. I'd worked with clients who had gone to Women's Aid and on courses like the 'Freedom Course'.

They had been very vulnerable women. Often addicted to something. Often badly beaten by a succession of partners. I was a professional, trained social worker in my forties. What on earth would I learn from it? But it might help to be able to talk to people about what had happened.

I knew they wouldn't understand about Jay – about his childhood and how my behaviour made him lose his temper and how he had blackouts so, when he became violent, he didn't know what he was doing. They would be used to dealing with physical abuse and battered women. Would they really be interested in what I had experienced?

The family solicitor, Ms Pane, told me, dismissively, when I had told her what Jay was like, "A lot of women put up with a lot worse than that."

At the first meeting, there were about six other women who had been, or who were still, in abusive relationships, me, and the two facilitators. What I hadn't known was that this particular course wasn't about physical abuse at all. It was about psychological/emotional abuse. It was about the kind of abuse Richard had talked about. Again, I didn't think I'd learn much from it as 'Jay was different'.

After introductions, the facilitator gave us a list to read. It was a list of the 'typical' behaviours of someone who carries out psychological abuse on his (or her) partner.

I read it, re-read it – and then had to leave the room. I was convulsed in wave after wave of shock, grief, and disbelief, all of which expressed themselves in tears and instant denial. One of the facilitators came with me into the little kitchen and put the kettle on as I tried to come to terms with what I had just realised.

On this list, this piece of typed paper in this dingy office, was every kind of behaviour Jay had carried out with me: it was like someone had been hidden in the house, watching and then had jotted down events of our lives together and then put them in list form.

Jay wasn't 'exceptional' or different. I hadn't been

helping him or 'different' in any way from other victims of abuse. He was an abuser like any other and I was a victim like any other. Everything I had believed in or had come to believe in for the past six years came crashing down around me as I stood shaking and gibbering in the tiny kitchen. The facilitator stood nodding understandingly as I gibbered about the list and that was what he'd done and that was all true... She kindly made me a hot drink and eventually we rejoined the group. My face was tearstained and I listened to the rest of the talk quietly, the other women telling their story. One told of having precious things taken and hidden. I told them about the cooking pot hidden under the caravan and of the videos and the cups and glasses; others nodded and told their own stories of precious belongings being hidden, broken, damaged, and lost. I was not alone. The empty prairie I was wandering in alone was now populated with others like me, others just like me.

The list I remember included:

You feel responsible for his behaviour — he tells you that you are the cause of it.

Uses past violence s/he has committed — or tells you s/he has committed — to frighten you and let you know what s/he is capable of.

Makes your friends unwelcome — for example, he'll be sitting in his underwear when they arrive or he'll be rude to them or even aggressive. Or he may flirt with your friends.

He'll hint that he knows or has noticed

something about your friends or family that means they are not to be trusted by you.

He may compare you unfavourably with other women.

He makes it difficult for you to see your relatives or friends, any people who care about you. Will insinuate that these people are not your real friends, or don't really care about you. As there are gaps in any friendship/relationship he will focus on these to exaggerate/exacerbate them to encourage you to end these friendships or not see your family anymore. He will find fault in their behaviour and encourage you to break off with them He will lie to you about them – what they said to him/didn't say.

Will frequently change the goal posts so you do not know what is expected of you. The reasons for the abuse will keep changing.

Will want to know where you are at any time. Might buy you a mobile or tell you to leave it on. Will say it makes him feel insecure if he doesn't know where you are at any time.

Will be totally charming to outsiders so you think it is only you who 'has a problem'.

Will try and separate you from your children. Tell you that you are a bad mother.

Criticise your appearance – maybe in a subtle way at first. 'Why do you always wear blue?' Or buy you clothes you would not have chosen for yourself and then be upset unless you wear them.

When he 'accidentally' breaks things it will be

things that belong to you, especially things which were gifts from those important to you.

He will follow through a period of temper and abuse with charm and apologies and being very loving – to you and the children.

He will threaten to kill himself – or you – or the children if you talk of leaving.

He will have told you of his unfortunate experiences of other women – how they hurt and controlled him. His own record will be blameless.

He will insist that 'only you' understand him and can help him. Nobody else has ever understood or made him feel loved.

If you ever assert yourself, he will escalate the abuse – emotional abuse may begin to include physical abuse, physical abuse may escalate to be more severe. This will also be 'your fault' as you 'provoked him'.

Plays mind games with you – telling you he told you such and such – 'Don't you remember?' – when he hasn't at all so you begin to doubt your own memory/mind. He'll do this also to cover up lies. He'll make you doubt your own sanity by saying you said so and so, or that he'd told you something when he hasn't, or that your responses are abnormal.

Hiding things which are important to you. Or throwing them away. Or breaking them. Then saying, 'Oh you didn't want that old thing, did you?'

He may become financially dependent on you

by losing his job or moving in with you very early in the relationship. Again, you are responsible for him.

The abuse would get progressively worse as the abuser's control and sense of 'entitlement' increases and the victim's ability to cope or assert herself/himself diminishes.

This list was like someone had been watching our relationship and making notes. But it wasn't. It was just a list of how typical abusive people behave. They use these methods to tie their victim to themselves with complicated emotional bonds – use our very ability to love to control us. In a million subtle ways, they cut us off from others who may help us.

I realised Jay had nearly given himself away there as he had always 'had a fit' before I went to see my folks – telling me it provoked him – but then had said to me, one day, in a cool mood, "Haven't you noticed I always lose my temper when you're going to see your f—in' family? Haven't you noticed that?" It had crossed my mind, at the time, if he wasn't aware of his 'rages' how come he remembered this pattern? But, as usual, I'd pushed this question away, turning away from its implications.

He'd often ranted his anger at my close relationship with my parents – when he'd met me I'd told him of big rows with my parents so how come I was close to them now? I had told him of my teenage years. I was not fifteen anymore and had long accepted my parents for the flawed beings they are, as they had accepted me. He had not understood this.

So he had tried to stop me visiting my parents – certainly he'd stopped the plan to move nearer to them – but he hadn't managed to break that relationship. Had he also been worried that if he'd got too violent, I'd go to them? Loving them and being loved by them had protected me from worse.

And the times when I'd been puzzled by things he said which contradicted other things he'd said had been no mystery – he had been lying, that was all. Or when he'd say, "Don't you remember me telling you that?" and I'd feared I was losing my memory. He'd been lying and covering up, that was all.

The other shock was the 'cycle of abuse' analysis – where an abuser goes from being threatening and frightening to loving, caring and apologetic, and then back again. I had long thought that these were 'mood swings' and to do with his depression. He had told me so often enough. He said doctors had told him that he was prone to depression and had to avoid all sources of stress. So the 'mood swings' were, of course, always my fault as I had said or done, or not said or not done, something which 'caused' his 'stress'. Similarly, he'd told me 'the doctors' had told him he needed to avoid things which made him angry – so it was my fault if I said or did something which 'made him' angry.

Anger was never his choice then – it was always something I forced him into.

But the cycle of abuse, as I read in the booklet Women's Aid provided, is where an abuser entraps his victim by being alternately abusive and controlling, then loving and caring as a way of continuing the abuse. If he – or she – was consistently aggressive, the victim would be more likely to understand what was happening and get away.

So none of it – none of it – had been behaviour he 'couldn't help'. I hadn't been helping him or special. We hadn't been 'in love'. He wasn't a tortured soul wrestling with shadows from his past and unable to do anything to stop the rages which engulfed him, forcing him to scream abuse and smash things against the wall. It was an act. It had all just been his abuse and control of just another victim – me. And Joe.

None of this was a huge surprise to Richard who just nodded and said yes. He already knew this, I realised. Had known it the minute he'd met me in the police station and asked me what had happened. His job involved a lot to do with domestic abuse, which always included emotional abuse either alone or as part of the other kinds of abuse – so he had learned a lot about it – and had training, etc., in the patterns. He already knew what I was just beginning to learn.

My social work training course had spent a lot of time on behavioural psychology and statistics but nothing about this.

Training courses had all been about the physical abuse – the broken bones, the bruised faces. For years I had looked at leaflets depicting this with the heading, 'Is your partner abusive?' and had dismissed the possibility, which had occurred to me from time to time, because Jay had threatened but had never actually hit me.

He had often seemed about to do so but had just managed to restrain himself – or so I thought. So it couldn't count as 'abuse'. And anyway, 'it was different', Jay didn't mean to do what he did, I had told myself, so that made it different. Yes, I was often afraid of him – but he wasn't doing that deliberately and that made all the difference.

So I was now entering a world of experts who knew more about my life than I did. This was a terrible shock – to my ego, to my sense of self, to my status as a professional, trained expert in the dynamics of people's problems, looking after children from abusive homes, etc., etc. My sense of self, or that aspect of myself, lay in tatters. I wasn't someone who had been 'helping' Joe – I was just a stupid mug who had been taken in by him – and now Joe was paying the price of my stupidity.

The darkness closed in around me.

I was in a pit.

Sanity left me.

Angels came to me then in my darkness. But they did not have halos – or bright robes. They were memories. They were of the kids I'd known over the years – none of them perfect, all of them flawed with life's scars in an imperfect world – and they reminded me of who I was. I was kind, I was sympathetic and that was not a crime. I had helped them – at least sometimes. Kindness had helped them recover from their abuse. Now, they kindly brought me memories of who I am – and am not.

We are mostly defined by what we are not – our senses keeping out most of the information provided by the universe – otherwise we'd be overwhelmed and dissolve – and part of what I was not and never would be, was someone who hurt others deliberately; I would never be someone who took advantage of someone more vulnerable, lied for money or deliberately twisted truth for my own ends. Whatever else he did to me, Jay could never make me be like him.

I climbed out of the pit. I would fall back in frequently but these memory angels returned when I needed them.

At least my worst fears had receded with the new information from Women's Aid. I understood that Jay was not at all 'out of control' when he lashed out or ranted or vented his apparent anger by hitting repeatedly at whatever was nearest. On the contrary – he was well in control. This explained why my mobile phone, left on in the night since the first day of my separation from Joe, had never rung. I'd always expected it to ring – with news of people realising Jay was not safe to look after a child, and would I come and collect Joe please? It had never rung and never would ring – Jay knew, and always had known, exactly what he was doing. Jay had found ways to control me – using my tendency to empathise with those in pain and using fear to back this up.

He had controlled me without having to use actual physical violence as assuredly as if he had held a gun to my head. Like a chameleon he had changed his colours to match the territory – that was why he'd taken trouble to find out my values when we first met, asking me about my life, watching to find how I thought, how I felt.

He had got it exactly right: he had used my ability to care, to empathise, my wanting to help – to control me. Whenever I had wanted to leave all he had had to do was cry about his wounds and I'd come back to him – while he laughed behind his crocodile tears. All the time, I'd thought I was 'coping' and helping him towards some wonderful recovery.

So Joe was safe. Ish. As long as he toed the line. He was safe from being inadvertently killed in a blind rage anyway – which was the fear which had clawed at me every night and day in between phone calls. Now I knew. Jay was not likely to lose his temper in that way. He would control Joe in other ways – certainly – Joe had told me of 'Daddy shouting and I go and hide under the bed' – but at least he would not be thrown against a wall in a fit of Jay 'not knowing what he was doing'.

I wasn't 100% assured – was Women's Aid wrong after all? Jay really had been very convincing if he had been 'putting it on' – but I began to be able to sleep at nights at times.

I realised that 'Jays' had been written about for years but I'd not noticed them before: In Austen's 'Northanger Abbey', a psychological abuser, Colonel Tierney, is featured – who 'had sucked the joy and life out of her' by his cruel treatment and Joss, in 'Jamaica Inn' – the most famous domestic abuser – Du Maurier had made it perfectly clear that he had destroyed his wife and terrorised his niece – but had never actually hit either of them. These too had used the emotional weapons and the victims' personalities to control and degrade them. In the centuries where the nuclear family and marriage were exonerated as the ultimate joys – some, Austen and Du Maurier among them, had spotted a flaw.

But I found then that Jay's abuse hadn't 'just' been emotional after all.

I was still trying to sell the house. It seemed the only way to pay the fees for the court case which, Ms Pane said, would be about ten thousand pounds.

Jay had eventually agreed to let the house go onto the market some months before I was arrested. What we were going to do after it had sold, I didn't know – I had clung onto his having once said he would agree to our splitting up once the house had sold. I had felt so relieved when he had agreed to this as I believed it was a sign he was accepting that we needed to split up and that he was going to let me go.

Jay had been insistent on not involving estate agent or building inspectors all the time he was working on the house. They were parasites and knew little of building, he said. I had bowed to his experience as well as fear of annoying him and gone along with it. He was a master builder, after all, and did not need their interference.

Before agreeing to put it on the market he had had another plan: a year previously, he had insisted that the farm next door would want to buy it privately, add five acres to it from their farmland and then re-sell it as a smallholding and make a fortune. I'd agreed to this as a plan. It seemed a reasonable idea which the farmers next door may well find interesting. Jay would not go and ask them straightaway, but at least he was agreeing to selling up and splitting up. He wouldn't let me visit to ask if they were interested. He insisted that he would do this and I was not to do it. A whole year went by while I waited. If I mentioned it, it was to my cost. When he eventually went to ask them, they said they were not interested. Farmers don't sell off their land easily.

After another month Jay agreed to involving the estate agents, they visited, assessed its market value and put up a for sale sign. This was a few weeks before the 'Christmas incident'. In the spring, a couple had come to see the house and were taken with it.

They returned, months later and after I'd gone to live at my parents', with an architect to look at the renovation work. I then got a letter from the agent listing the problems and irregularities with the house, and could they see the certificates or speak to the building inspector who had been involved, as 'the renovations didn't seem to come up to standard'?

There was no building inspector, there was no planning permission. The estate agent contacted Jay but got no helpful response. The architect advised the couple to withdraw and advised the estate agent what he had found. He had found major shortcomings in the work Jay had done to the house: the wrong materials had been used; procedures which were illegal and which actually made the house dangerous had been carried out – by Jay –the 'master builder'.

My life savings had gone into the house and Jay's work on it. It was illegal and unsellable and worth less, much less, than when I'd bought it. No mortgage company would approve it. No-one could buy it. The mortgage company still needed my payments. I was working as a hot wash. My period of being on full-pay suspension was coming to an end.

I went up to the loft where Jay had stored all the receipts of all the materials he had used on the house. Since the Women's Aid revelations and the architect's discoveries I had my suspicions. I emptied the bag which was stuffed full of all the pink receipts and white receipts. I looked closer – only the white papers were receipts – the others were all just delivery notices or order forms, only proof that the items or materials had been delivered. The actual receipts added up to less than half the money I'd paid over to Jay in utter trust to pay for items he said he'd bought and used.

I sat in the dusty loft surrounded by pink and white papers. I listened again to the sound of pennies beginning to drop.

I saw myself as I had been so few years ago – middle-aged and lonely – after attempts at relationships through dating agencies and personal ads having spent too many years in the caring professions, working nights and weekends, and surrounded by women and married folk.

Then I'd met Jay, as if out of the blue – so intense, so keen on me, so like me in values and interests – books and poetry and art, changing the world, love of the outdoors – but what had he met?

A fairly attractive woman, caring, fairly well off – or at least with a good income – and gullible. Most of all, gullible. Useful. Caring, sympathetic – and idiotic.

All the time I'd thought I was looking after him, supporting him, helping him to recover from his difficult past – he was using me, laughing up his sleeve as he told me another one. I'd believed everything he'd told me – every story of his childhood, every 'uncontrollable rage', all the stuff about his violent past, his depression, his wonderful building skills and how the law worked around houses. All of it.

But what was his motivation? To lie and deceive – for years? For a fairly comfortable living and occasional access to a vagina? To have something pretty to hang on his arm and show off to his mates? Was 'being in control', just an end in itself, sufficient motivation for this?

Now I remembered a couple of times he had told me of 'having a flutter' and winning 'a few quid'. He'd had a tip from someone he'd met, he'd told me, and placed a bet and won some money. That was what he had told me – but what had been the reality? How many of the hundreds or thousands of pounds, represented by the 'pink slips' now before me, had gone on 'flutters' of which I had not heard? All those trips into town when I was at work. He had done some work on the house – just enough to cover his tracks and keep me fooled into thinking we were a partnership, working together.

Also, I could not sell it now to raise money to pay for the court case. The criminal trial qualified for Legal Aid – but the family court hearings did not. A year had gone by and payments to Ms Pane took all my salary – I was still suspended on full pay. If I kept my job, after the investigation, this could continue – but what if I didn't keep it? What if I was struck off, which was much more likely? As well as prison, the house would be repossessed. I wouldn't even have that to leave to Joe.

I told Ms Pane of these developments and she advised me to apply for Legal Aid and sent me a bundle of forms which I filled in and sent off.

She seemed sympathetic. I explained I could not raise any more money by mortgaging the house, nor could I sell it.

I told Marianne and Esme what had happened. Marianne, familiar with the world of housing and finance, and also with how horrible people can be and not at all surprised that Jay had turned out to be a charlatan and a cheat as well as a bully, rang me with a rescue package.

Marianne explained: for some reason, houses which could not be mortgaged by people wanting to buy them could still be mortgaged by owners wanting to rent them out: so a house which was sub-standard could be mortgaged as long as it was going to be rented out, not sold. This didn't seem to make any sense but it was true.

Esme and Marianne rallied around and helped me get the house looking clean. They both turned up with cloths and bottles of bleach and worked all day for days. More angels. Marianne helped me arrange to remortgage it to let out. I borrowed a huge amount on the mortgage so I could pay the solicitor and a family moved in. Marianne agreed to act as liaison with the tenants given I was living a long way away now at my parents.

A family moved in – two adults, three kids. A family – like we should have been. They liked the house and were paying rent which covered the mortgage.

Within weeks Marianne phoned up. The family were having problems with the plumbing and she had gone round to investigate. Human faeces were rising up out of the plumbing into the garden. The pipes which Jay had put in were inadequate and the 'new cesspit' he had said he had put in – was non-existent. The toilet was effectively draining into the garden, into the ditch outside and thence into the headwaters of the local river and water-table. This from the man who would rant and rave about other people's neglect of the environment!

He'd have happily sold this house to a family. Terrified, I phoned the Environment Agency who came out with a building inspector. I saw this being added to the charges against. me. It was my house so I was responsible for poisoning the water table and the main river in the area with human faeces. I knew massive fines of tens of thousands of pounds were charged against people caught polluting the environment like this. Worse, I envisaged someone becoming seriously ill or even dying – a swimmer maybe or a child – as a result of the poisoned waters. I was in such a fragile state I found everything catastrophic.

But far from being incompetent busy-bodies they just sorted it out. A local builder came to put in a cesspit. He dug the earth with an electric digger to check drainage. The earth was too clay and held the water – which meant a cesspit could not be put in. All seemed lost. The EA guy said, helpfully, dig deeper. He did so – down to the next layer of soil – and the water drained away. In went the cesspit – sorted. I couldn't pay all the bill but the builder was looking for a home for his brother and took the caravan, mine and Joe's haven, in part-payment. I watched it being towed away. I had to go and sit in another part of the garden as memories of being there with my child crashed in on me.

But also, another memory – of Jay charging across the garden yelling at Joe and me as we played with water in that part of the garden. That took on a whole new meaning. He had known full well what he had done and knew the danger of Joe getting faeces in his eyes or mouth and had yelled at us that we were annoying him. We had never played in our own garden after that –I'd long since stopped trying to garden in it – and we always went to parks or other people's gardens to play. After then I had stopped trying to use the garden at all – for me doing gardening which always annoyed Jay or for Joe to play in – I saw now it was because he, Jay, knew that the drains were not working so did not want his own son to be affected. I remember him saying later – "I've got work on around there so keep away." But he had been happy for someone else's child to be put at risk.

But so it went on, Jay had done work on the house to make it look good. He'd done surface work; he'd covered over damp and put in fancy-looking features and details. But the basics like the drainage and the wiring were actually dangerous. Some of the ceiling was at risk of falling in as he'd taken out structural supports. All of it needed redoing. Money went to the solicitors and to plumbers and electricians to gradually mend the house. Jay was nothing but a con-man. Had I ever known him at all?

In between going to see Joe, playing with him, making out all was okay and that what was happening was perfectly fine, organising the house to be fit for human habitation so the tenants wouldn't leave, persuading my father to bully my mother into one more trip each week and trying to decipher the tiny letters sent to me in email by the solicitor who still didn't seem to be able to hear what I was telling her, the day of the criminal trial kept getting postponed.

Joe kept asking me when he was coming home.

I kept on lying to him.

All the walls of my world had fallen down. I had seen myself as the patient, helping partner. I wasn't. I was instead, a doormat, a mug, a victim. An idiot who had failed even to protect her child.

This was my new identity.

Chapter 8

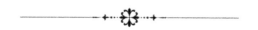

The long awaited 'core'-assessment – which the social workers had said would take 'six or seven' weeks began. It was now five months after I'd allowed Joe to go and stay 'for a little holiday' with his father and aunt.

The woman to do the assessment was a semi-retired social worker, Beryl. I had moved into a biosphere where suddenly everybody wore suits. She looked at me over her glasses in a way I hadn't seen for some years. I didn't know this at the time but she'd been appointed and given an outline of the case by the two managers, Dan and Anastasia. They had appointed her out of semi-retirement on a temporary contract just to do this assessment.

"So why didn't you leave?" Beryl asked in a bored voice when I'd described what life with Jay was like. I no longer justified his behaviour with the refrain of 'he couldn't help it'. I'd learned something at least.

Why didn't I leave? Such a simple little question. So many simple little answers:

Because he had threatened to kill me if I did?

Because he'd threatened to snatch Joe? Because sometimes it seemed to be getting better? Because I didn't want Joe to lose his dad? Because he'd threatened suicide if ever he had to cope again with someone leaving him as his wife had done? Because I hoped he'd get better? Because I felt guilty for punishing him for something he couldn't help? Because he'd already had too much pain in his life? Because I'd loved him and hoped he'd recover? Because he was always going to seek out another therapy, another cure? Because he was always so sorry and contrite and totally convinced and convincing he'd never, no never, do it again? Because I was scared of what he would do if I tried.

She made notes as she listened as I stumbled through the answer, trying to make it sound coherent, rational. As Graham Norton once said, 'The heart is such an idiot.' Her eyebrows remained arched. She didn't look at me. She didn't question anything I said. She didn't ask me to clarify or illustrate. She just wrote it down. Quickly. Eyebrows arched. Then the next bored question.

I told myself this was just something she had to do every day. She was probably an expert on cases like mine and had heard all about domestic abuse so many times it was tedious. I had entered a world of processes – assessments, meetings and hearings. Before seeing my son, I had had to have a mental health assessment – as Jay insisted I had had no reason to hit him and that I was a bad-tempered, unpredictable person who might be a danger to my son and the social workers seemed to have believed this.

That assessment had found that I wasn't a violent person after all. So he had been lying.

Surely the experts would spot this?

That first assessment had been enough to allow me to see Joe only for a few hours and only when I was supervised – at Jay's insistence. I then had this assessment by a social worker – a 'core assessment' by a retired social worker who looked at me with disdain and asked why I hadn't 'just left'. She didn't seem to understand me when I explained that I was afraid to do so because of Jay's violent and erratic behaviour. Nor could she comprehend why I hadn't gone to the police. With what? The other times I had gone to the police in the past drifted into my mind. I told her I didn't think they'd believe me or do anything. She asked me about my previous relationships presumably because she wondered if I made a habit of hitting folk with pans.

Then there was a long wait for her assessment to come out. It was full of misinterpretations of what I'd said and mix-ups as to what and where – but that is what happens when you don't check with the person you are interviewing that you've understood them right: did what you think you heard correspond with what they meant to say? Worlds fall through the gap between those two entities.

There are chasms along the way – between what the person is trying to express and what they actually say, between that and what you hear, between that and what you understand – and between that and what you write down.

As the meaning changes subtly within all these

gaps – what eventually gets written down can bear little or no resemblance to what the person was trying to describe. She wrote quickly as I spoke and then moved on to the next question. Her report was full of her own assumptions to bridge the gaps between what I had told her – and what Dan and Anastasia had already told her.

I'd been trained in how to interview people about complex issues – to ensure that people's meanings don't get lost in the long voyage from their mind to their mouth, then through the ears and mind and down through the pen of the interviewer. It is impossible not to lose at least some of the reality on that voyage but, when you don't check, when you ignore your own prejudices, your own assumptions and value judgements, you can lose all of it.

I realised from her report that the two social workers had given her an 'outline' of 'the case' before she had come to meet me or Jay: their interpretation of it. The rest of her report kept referring back to their instruction and she seemed to have expected to find me to be an aggressive, violent person. She seemed to be unnerved at not having been able to find that. Everything I said had to fit into that outline.

In science this is called an a priori assumption – that which is not questioned. It lies outside the area which is being scrutinised. They that lay it down have power indeed. Everything outside it cannot be questioned, voted on or changed.

Beryl came to see my parents. I spent days frantically trying to make the house look perfect in every way. I got obsessive about the place-mats for some reason. My mother looked dishevelled and I tried to get her to change her skirt as she'd spilled some water on it and there was a small mark, as if that would make any difference.

Beryl spoke to them alone as I waited in the other room.

My dad told me afterwards that she had asked them what they knew of what had happened. My dad told her what he remembered of what I'd told him. My mum didn't remember what I'd told her but had helpfully made up her own account to fill in the gap – which is what people with dementia do with gaps in the memory. If they can't remember what they had for dinner, when asked, they will make up something as a way of covering up the gap in their memory as a way of feeling normal. I did not know about this until I read the assessor's report. I was horrified. Again, the assessor hadn't queried why my mum's account was so at variance with my own or with my dad's – but had just written it down verbatim.

She had not even picked up on my mother being affected by dementia, just wrote down her account and commented that I seemed to have lied to my mother. She also reported my brother, saying he had been surprised at the police having been involved as evidence that I had lied to him too – pretending the police were not involved – but I hadn't told him any such lie.

Beryl also went to see Jay and wrote down everything he said. This was at some variance from what I had said. She did establish that Jay had been lying about our childcare arrangements and that Joe had been at nursery four days a week – which showed he had lied about that to the social workers. Another lie had surfaced. Was anyone watching?

She concluded she could not assess who was telling the truth so recommended another assessment. Then she went away. The waiting went on. Months rolled by. My criminal trial kept getting postponed.

We waited for a psychologist to be appointed to make a new assessment.

As I began to realise the extent of Jay's deception of me and of others about this time, I began to wonder if I was the only one to have been taken in by Jay. My friend, Marianne, asked if I knew any of his previous partners.

My little fantasy world where I was looking after, protecting and helping a very fragile man cope with the stresses of his life and start to recover from the horrors of his past and head towards leading a loving 'normal' life in a stable relationship – now had more than a few cracks in it.

I'd been duped, like any other mug.

I wondered at things he'd told me – about his past – about his previous relationships. Were they true?

"It's a pity you can't talk to some of his ex-partners. You can bet you're not the first he's done this to," said Marianne.

He'd told me of his previous relationships: the wife, Sue, he'd married at nineteen and who'd heartlessly run off with his best friend when he'd thought all was well – I'd never met Sue although he had told me he knew where she lived. He had traced her and meant to go and find her but had then met Sophie. Sophie, whom he'd been with for six years, was the mother of his daughter, Chloe. Sophie, he'd told me, had gone off with another man and had left him with their child – then returned to take Chloe away and left Jay broken hearted. Then there was the girl friend just before me, Wendy. They'd only been together a few weeks, he'd said, and only slept together once – but she had come at him with a knife and once threw a can of beer at him and caused his teeth to come out.

He had, when we had first met, told me it was a fall whilst rock climbing which had so damaged his teeth – he was still recovering from the operations when we had met. He said he had told me this as he'd been embarrassed by the truth but later on he had told me that Wendy had done this, by hitting him with a full drinks can – which is why he had ended the relationship. He had had to have extensive bridge work to get rid of the B-Movie horror look. He had had great difficulty extricating himself from that relationship, he'd said.

He had, during our time together, told me of various events which had happened 'while I was with Wendy' – it seemed to have been a very crowded week now I thought about it, with an awful lot crammed into their short relationship – parties and trips away as well as fights involving a knife and a cola can.

Was any of it at all true? Going by what he'd told the social workers and police about me – maybe it wasn't. I'd prided myself on being able to succeed – on loving and understanding this man where others had failed, on being able to cope because I 'understood' the causes of his rages and other weird behaviour – hiding things, not being able to cope with friendships or with my having friendships. That pride was in tatters as I'd realised the truth.

I had no idea where the other 'exes' were but he had taken me once to visit Sophie, the mother of his child. They lived in the north-west and I remembered Jay and I, before Joe was born, turning off the motorway and driving into the area and arriving at the house – but not much in between. Jay had been driving and had known the way. But how many roads can there be in this area – among the lakes and hills? I got out the map. There were dozens. But only dozens. I saw the house in my mind's eye. I could picture it clearly – set back from the road – at the end of double tracks with a shed to the right. I knew if I could just drive past it I'd recognise it. Would she still be living there?

I had a whole week before I could see my boy again. I only had one shift at the hotel hot wash that week. Having something to do acted like a narcotic on the pain. I told my parents of my plan, packed some sandwiches, filled up the car with petrol and left.

I headed off before dawn to give myself time to get there and still have daylight to start the search. Heading into the rural district's woods and fields I tried to resurrect the memory of that trip from years ago. But I hadn't made any notes or memories of the direction or the road so the only option was to drive as systematically as I could and hope something would trigger a memory.

I started in the North-East corner of the region and started combing my way down by driving up and down all the main roads and through the villages looking at the houses. I had an idea the house was on the main road through a small village – but even that was hazy. By the time dusk fell and it was too dark to go on I was exhausted with driving. I pulled over into a parking space where there were a few other cars parked and stopped. In case someone in the adjoining houses had seen me arrive I got out and walked away as if I was visiting someone. It was good to stretch my legs. Then, when it was quite dark, I went back to the car and lowered the front seat, pulled the car rug over me, pulled my hat over my face in case anyone was glancing into cars and spotted my face, pale in the dark interior, and, exhausted, slept.

I had started to become dispirited by the number of roads there were – which simply weren't on the large-scale map I had – and the sheer number of houses in each apparently tiny village.

I remembered his daughter – a teenager then. Not a happy girl. She'd told me something of the temper and aggression of her childhood. When her father had raged at her during her brief one stay with us she'd said to me, "I'm used to it." I'd liked her: her father was unable to accept she was no longer his little docile princess and wanted to do her own thing – see her own friends and not tail along behind him like a well-trained obedient servant – as I'd learned to do.

I hadn't seen her since she'd left after the one day of her visit. She had then applied to go into care on the grounds of estrangement from both parents and Jay hadn't opposed it. I'd encouraged Jay to write to her and, once, he'd gone to see her and take her out and that had seemed to go well. She'd been about eighteen by then and now she'd be in her twenties. It wasn't her I needed to see. She could hardly be expected to speak against her own father. It was his ex-partner, Sophie, Chloe's mother. Did she have something to tell the court to prove what Jay was like?

When dawn broke I began again. I stopped at a local shop and bought bread rolls and a tin of spread. Seven hours later, I knew I was beaten. I'd covered the entire area and not found the house. I headed home feeling utterly wretched. I'd let my son down again. How else was I going to help the courts see the danger my son was in if I couldn't find other witnesses to Jay's temper?

My mum and dad greeted me and I sat and looked at the television, unseeing.

Talking to Marianne on the phone she asked me why I didn't look up Sophie's address by her surname. I explained that I didn't know it.

"Isn't it the same as her daughter's? Do you know his daughter's surname?" she asked.

I explained what Jay had told me: his daughter, Chloe, he'd said, did not have the same name as himself or as her mother. His daughter, he'd said all those years ago, had taken the surname of 'one or other' of the men Sophie had lived with for a while after leaving him. I remembered feeling sorry for the daughter when he'd told me this as she'd obviously lost two fathers – her birth dad – Jay – and the one to whom she'd felt close enough to want to have his surname. Poor kid!

Marianne said, "You don't think that's a lie?"

I said, "He told me that ages ago when things were alright between us so it can't be a lie."

I heard her being patient. I had a rethink.

"Maybe it was."

She said, "He was covering his tracks – that's what they do! I'll bet that was a lie."

There was one place there might be a clue. I got back in the car and drove back to our house, Hilldene, and went up to the attic. There was a box of old letters, cards, and other papers and I started to go through them.

I found it. A letter regarding his daughter – the one confirming she was going into care 'estranged from both parents' the first name – and there, unknown to me before then, a surname – Endsleigh. I rang Marianne again.

"Okay, I'll look that up. Give me a minute."

She came back on. "There's a Mrs Endsleigh living at..." and she gave me an address in the north-west. It was in a village I'd driven through.

The site she was using didn't give the phone number but gave the phone numbers of houses nearby. I rang one and a woman answered. I asked to speak to Mrs Endsleigh.

"Oh, you want next door," she replied – I apologised and rang off.

I wrote down the 'next door' address and got back in my car and headed back. Several hours later I pulled up outside the house which I recognised from all those years ago. The memory paints its own pictures and fills in all the blanks if you want it to but it was basically the same. It was on the main road through the village – but this particular village had two main roads in it, one leading off the other – and I had missed this one.

I'd driven past less than 500 yards away from this house on my mad journeyings.

I got out of the car and headed up the drive. A woman came out. I didn't really recognise her but I remembered the hair colour. She looked at me and knew who I was immediately. Maybe she'd been expecting me. She gave me a warm welcome and relief flooded me. She knew what had really happened and she would help me. She would take this chance to tell the truth about Jay and save my son.

The daughter, Chloe, was also in the house – I hadn't expected that as she now lived independently. The mother insisted on her being part of our meeting. I was very uncomfortable knowing even adult children remain loyal and attached to their parents.

They told me one of Jay's sisters had rung them the evening of his having gone into hospital after I'd hit him with the frying pan – and had told them Jay was 'dying in hospital'. They'd rung the hospital in a panic – and been put straight through to chat with Jay who was far from dying or anything of the sort.

I said, "I'm sorry you got told that," because I was. It must have been terrible – especially for the daughter. It was also a long way from the truth.

The daughter was very cold towards me and I felt she had believed what the sister had said and what Jay had probably told her since.

I explained why I was there – that Joe was now living with his dad and could she – the ex-partner – tell the courts her own story so the court would know who Jay really was and the risks to Joe?

I asked her if Jay had ever threatened or frightened her. The two women looked at each other.

She said, "We both know what it's like to be at the sharp end of Jay's temper."

The daughter concurred with this. Her mother told her, "I've not told you all of this but I'll tell it now." So she did. She told me the real story behind Jay's colourful version which I had heard from him.

When their daughter had been tiny they'd gone to live in Portugal where Jay had had work with a local property developer renovating sites. I remembered him waxing nostalgic about Portugal and how there was no 'red tape' decreeing what you can build and how – now I knew why he hated those laws.

Things had become very difficult between them, with Jay demanding her obedience and not liking her to leave the house at any time when he was not with her. He was erratic in his moods and got nasty very quickly if crossed. All this was familiar to me. One time, when the little girl had been about three years old, Sophie had been so scared by Jay's behaviour she had run away and taken a flight back to Britain, leaving her daughter with Jay.

Sophie had gone to find a place to live so she could bring her daughter to live with her. She had then received a letter via her parents' address from Jay, from Portugal. The letter had told her that he had arranged passports for himself and for Chloe and 'you will never see your daughter again. If you don't come back I'll leave with her for good.' I felt my heart go cold as I remembered him threatening to take Joe away from me and disappear. He was capable of it. He could live outside the law. He had connections all over the world and wasn't encumbered with the niceties of legal living like most people were. Sophie had taken the next plane out and travelled back to the village where they had all been living a week previously. She had passed the house where a local Gypsy family were living. They'd called out to her, "You've come to get the child?" She'd asked them for help.

Some had come with her to the house and they had stood with her while she confronted Jay. Up against numbers and an organised family, he'd turned on the charm and agreed to the little girl going with her mother. They had gone into the house and passed the little girl out of the downstairs window to her mother – keeping Sophie safe from having to go into the house. Jay had agreed to this – he had not had much choice.

She'd set up house with her daughter. There was later some trouble from time to time with Jay turning up on the doorstep drunk at all hours demanding to see his daughter at all times and not sticking to arrangements. This had got so bad she'd moved house a few times. She then had met the man she whom she was still living with now – sixteen years later – far from the story Jay had given me. Jay had told me Sophie had gone through many short relationships and was so hung up on drugs and drink no-one could stay with her. Chloe had taken this man's name and regarded him as her father. Jay had often failed to turn up to see his daughter at arranged, agreed times. It was all very erratic. She had often been afraid of him. She had actually run away because she'd been scared it was getting worse. Like me, she'd felt the anger was aimed at her more than the child. The little girl was right in the middle. Sophie said she often 'gave as good as she got' but this had not been the case later in the relationship as he'd get worse if she argued back or tried to stand up to him.

I explained that was why I was afraid for my little boy and they both nodded in agreement and understood why I'd be scared. They agreed they'd better do something to stop Jay getting control of Joe. I was so glad they understood. I explained it wasn't for me but for Joe. He was already scared and wary of his dad's temper and being on his own with him would compound that fear until it became normal. I remembered why I was there and that my little boy was now living on his own with this man who frightened adults, never mind kids, and I felt I'd better leave.

I drove back home, having left my address and with their reassurance they would write and tell all in a statement to court. They would bear witness to Jay's terrible temper, threats to hurt and to snatch.

So he'd even lied to me about his daughter's name. For no other reason than to sling mud at her mother – making out she had had so many relationships and was high on drugs most of the time.

And maybe to cover his tracks? Even years ago, he'd been lying.

Was there anything I knew about this man after all, or had it absolutely all been lies?

I told Marianne the outcome and thanked her for her detective work. I wondered if there were others I could contact.

If the court could hear from several women the truth about this man – Joe would be saved.

I knew Jay'd been married – to someone called Sue – when he'd been a soldier in Aldershot during his training. A young marriage. She had run away to Australia with his best friend eight years later. Jay'd returned home to a letter on the table and an empty house and had had a nervous breakdown, teetering on the edge of suicide. He'd said. I knew that story. It had played its part in preventing me from running away in the same way – the thought of Jay taking his own life because he'd been abandoned again was a horrible enough thought to make me pause.

I wrote to the records department to get a copy of the marriage certificate. When it arrived, on it was the address-town of Sue's parents. On the telephone number finding site which Marianne had told me about, there were two addresses of that name in the town and I wrote to both of them saying I was trying to contact 'Sue'. I did not get a reply. I wrote again, recorded delivery putting 'please forward' on the envelopes. No reply. I had included my phone number.

After sending the second letters I tried something else. I looked up all the secondary schools in that town and went looking on the 'reunion' sites. People had listed their previous names and put a little sketch of their autobiography by them. There were three Sues across the three schools in the town who were in approximately the right school years. One little sketch spoke of a marriage in her late teens, a divorce and 'living in South Africa' for some years. And living in a certain area of Britain now. And there shimmered onto the screen a word which I realised must be the current surname.

Back to the telephone number site – and ten minutes later a woman answered the phone. It was Sue.

Yes, she'd had the letters. Yes, she agreed Jay was a frightening prospect. Yes, she was sorry he had custody of my child. Yes, she agreed that Jay should not be bringing up a child as he had a fearsome temper. No, she would not help me. I begged. For the sake of my child, I begged. No.

She would not help me because if she did Jay may disrupt the life she had now – comfortable, new relationship, two houses, nice car, etc. And if I'd found her, Jay could too. I didn't want to tell her he already did know which town she lived in (he had told me he'd traced his ex-wife and he'd told me the area – and he'd been right) as that seemed unhelpful and likely to panic her. That was all she would say and I was not to call her again.

She wished me luck. The phone bleeped and went silent in my hand.

Knowing that a three-year-old child was at risk, this adult woman turned away. Back to her comfy life.

The following morning a letter arrived from Sophie. It wasn't quite the letter she had promised. She apologised and said she did not want to cause upset in the family by telling the court her story as this would upset Jay and they had been on okay terms for years so why disrupt this? She enclosed a statement which was very bland compared to what she had told me. It mentioned she'd been to

Women's Aid to get help but not much else. It was almost useless. After my conversation with Sue this was another blow and a sense of hopelessness threatened. These women were not at risk, they had homes and other adults in the home to take their part. They were not three years old and alone. I kept the bland statement and the letter apologising for it – surely the judge would see the story that was there? Surely he would understand her apologising to me and not giving me the statement would let him see she was afraid too?

The only other ex-partner I knew about was the one with whom Jay had had a short relationship – of the overcrowded week, just before I came along; Wendy. I remembered she had offered to give me her phone number when we had met in the town one time and I'd wondered why. She'd said, "In case something happens – you never know with Jay." And I'd thought she was being nasty or trying to poison our new relationship. Now something had 'happened'. I only had her first name and the nickname with which she was known by her friends.

I phoned the papers local to her area and asked to take out a personal ad. 'Desperately Seeking' in one of them. I used her nickname and put in my mobile number. The guy in the office at one paper, when I explained I was trying to find someone, said, "Oh we don't do that," and refused to help – but the other I contacted shoe-horned it into the personal section with a coloured headline to make it stand out. I hoped she, or a friend would see it.

A week later, heading back from the common after a walk one evening and feeling very low I asked the angels for some help and the phone rang. I knew her voice immediately.

"Hello there," she said. "What's he done now?"

A friend of hers had seen my ad in the paper and called her, saying, "Somebody's looking for you." I'd put my first name in the ad with my phone number and she'd had a good guess which 'Cathy' it was and why I was searching for her.

We talked for an hour. I agreed to meet her at the train station in her town so we could talk properly. She agreed I'd need a statement and that she'd write one. She hadn't been with him for a 'few weeks' as he had told me. She'd lived with him for six years. With her, his aggression had escalated to holding her head under water so she thought she would drown and hitting her with a little rubber length which left no bruising. He had held a knife to her throat and threatened to kill her if she left. Yes, she had hit him in the face with a can of drink on one occasion to get him away from her. The blow had knocked out all his front teeth and he had bled a lot but he had backed off . With a shock, as she told me this, I remembered him telling me he had had to have dental work after a bad fall onto rock while out climbing. I remembered my being amazed his jaw and nose had escaped damage and his saying he didn't want to talk further about it. Of course he hadn't – it had just been another lie. It was no fall that had broken his teeth but a previous girlfriend defending herself with a well-placed can of beer. She'd got her family of friends involved in helping her to get away and they had threatened Jay into leaving her alone. She was horrified at what the social workers had done and said she would do anything she could to help me and my son.

This time it was a train journey. I arrived at the small town's station at the time agreed. There was no-one there. I waited an hour. There was no reply when I dialled her phone. I stood in the darkening road for an hour.

A friend arrived, looking for me – she was at home ill.

We spent the afternoon talking over our experiences with Jay. Wendy promised a statement detailing his temper and brutality and how he had treated her. She knew of others who had witnessed some of it who may also help. I drafted out the kind of statement I was needing and she said it was too vague, but she signed it anyway and said she'd send a real one and give proper details about his behaviour during the years she'd lived with him.

I caught my train home.

Her letter never arrived. The solicitor wrote to her asking for a statement. She never replied. I filed what she had given me with the solicitors. I sent her a card asking her to reconsider. Begged. I never had a reply.

"There is no unity among the oppressed," Tony Cliff would say. "Oppression does not unite people – it divides them." This seemed to be have been proved true once more.

One oppressed person will find relief in the oppression of another. An oppressed person from one oppressed group can turn the anger onto someone of the same group – or of a different oppressed group. Women can turn against each other, gay people can find relief in attacking black people and vice versa, recent immigrants will join forces versus more recent arrivals, one 'type' of traveller will scapegoat another – oppression does not unite – it divides. All the other women I could contact who had been attacked, emotionally or physically by this man, all ran for cover when I begged for help. Begged for my child. They were safe, they had houses and partners and family around them. They would not swap their comfort to help my child.

The view of human nature which I held dear – the view of people as wanting to help, empathic, eager to stand up for justice and to defend the helpless – took a nose dive at last and depression wrapped me in its soft dark fur.

My times with Joe were the times when I lived. The times in between I concentrated on breathing. I crawled about the wreckage of my life with a millstone on my neck of dread and a body numb with pain from shock. Seeing Joe once a week was like a window of light where I could be myself again.

Long ago I'd read the biography of Douglas Bader – a young man who had had both his legs amputated following an airplane accident. The loss of his legs was ultimately to save his life as he was able to get out of his stricken Spitfire when, without artificial legs, he would have gone down with his plane. But that was later.

The part I remembered now was when he was dying in hospital after the operation. He had been in agony. The pain had wracked him day and night. And then it had started to recede. A warm painlessness had begun to arrive and he had sunk towards sleep.

Through this nice comfortable release, he had suddenly heard the voice of a nurse outside the ward. She was telling people to 'shush' as 'there's a boy dying in there'. He had realised that the 'boy' was himself and that the reason for the retreat of pain was his death approaching. Death was coming – driving pain away. He had fought back to the pain and welcomed its return.

Pain had meant he was alive.

As the months went by, not thinking of Joe became a way of having respite from pain. I became adept at pushing away thoughts or emotions. The love of my child was the root of pain. Was it better to be in pain or to let this die – if only a little? Being alive was painful – but if that was the cost of continuing to be his mother and a responsive parent then so be it – I would not be without that pain. My new prayers included one that he was not having similar pain and that, if so, it would be put onto me, not him. Friends tried to assure me that children live in a 'now bubble' and adapt to whatever happens to them, and I hoped this applied to Joe. He continued to be overjoyed to see me every time I visited and to want to chat on the phone and he still asked at times. "When am I coming home?" – but I hoped and prayed that he no longer called for me in the night and was finding a way to like the life he had and that the only life wrecked would be mine.

Chapter 9

Then the criminal trial court date finally arrived: it was a whole year since I'd been arrested. I had been assessed and reassessed. No-one had actually spent any time with Joe. Jay had moved out of his sister's house and was living alone with Joe in a small rented house in the village a mile away from the sister's house. The date for the criminal trial had been set several times and then postponed as other, 'more pressing matters' had had to be fitted into the schedule. The little matter of domestic assault kept being pushed down the queue. We had celebrated Joe's fourth birthday in a park with my father on a visit. Jay's millionaire sister had put on a party inviting his whole class at her mansion of a house.

Joe's time away from me kept on extending. He was getting more and more used to my being only a visitor in his life. More used to living with his father. More used to temper and lack of empathy and being controlled rather than nurtured. More used to having to please his father and suppress his own needs and personality for fear of triggering his father's rage. He'd already learned how to play the 'delightful' child at all times as the safest way of keeping on his father's good side. I was always glad that he felt safer with me and to have the odd bad mood or to protest or express his own views. I treasured these as signs that he knew, with me, he could be himself and relax.

I had waited for months to hear from the police what my charge was going to be. I thought of the police, putty in Jay's hands as he wove his story, as I had been. The charge was going to be attempted murder, I believed, as that was what Jay wanted it to be. Richard, my solicitor, had told me it wouldn't be but I felt he was being nice. Richard didn't think that Jay would be able to charge me with attempted murder and I asked what would stop him. It was very difficult to stop Jay doing whatever he wanted. He'd get angry if anybody tried.

Richard said, "He's not in control now, you have to stop letting him control you. He doesn't control everybody."

The future looked as if I'd be in prison, Jay would eventually get tired or be found out and Joe would be put up for adoption. My brother and sister-in-law would step forward but Jay would insist on his being 'placed' in his own, much larger family. I might never see him again.

Even the day before the criminal trial, I expected it to be postponed yet again. Every time it was postponed it became less likely that Joe would come back to me. He was fast developing a whole new life. Jay had started him at the local school in 'reception'. For a second time, he had started school. He still asked me about his old friends – he hadn't seen them for all these months after spending four days a week in their company at nursery and playing at their houses at weekends. I would tell him, "I don't know when you will see them again but you will see them."

The criminal trial was in the Crown Court as Jay had been hit with 'a weapon' and the charges against me were very serious – the upside of this, if there was an upside, was that I therefore qualified for Legal Aid to pay Richard and the barrister he appointed to represent me, Dafydd.

I had met with Dafydd and he had questioned me closely about exactly what had happened during the two incidents with which I was charged.

Now, over a year later, we were going to trial.

Three days beforehand, the neighbour, Debbie, and her husband, Ron, who had made a statement after having been scared by Jay yelling at her and frightening their children, suddenly withdrew their statements. I begged them – for Joe's sake but they were concerned at what Jay might do if they spoke against him. I begged them again. They refused.

Similarly, the neighbour whom Jay had frightened one day, when she had been walking her horse, had made a statement about his raging anger that day – but she would not attend court so the statement could not be admitted.

The three ex-partners – all of whom had their own tale to tell – would not stand witness. The letters from two of them were of no use unless they attended court to confirm what they had written.

Jay's ex-partners had all refused or failed to deliver statements about what he had done to them. The most useful were the ambiguous letters from Sophie –

which at least mentioned going to a refuge and being afraid sometimes – and the semi-statement signed by Wendy – but these were useless for the criminal trial as neither would attend court to confirm and answer questions so neither piece of evidence could be submitted.

How is it expected that people attend court to testify against someone they are afraid of?

Neither of the people to whom I'd told a little of what was happening at the time could act as witnesses as their experiences were second-hand – only heard by them from me. They had not directly witnessed Jay's behaviour so their statements could not be allowed in a criminal court. I had confided to Anna most of an incident of Jay losing his temper in the van and I'd told a colleague and friend Ruby something of problems at home: I'd bumped into her when I'd run with Joe to the local supermarket to escape an episode. I'd also told Anna of some episodes when we worked together and she'd asked questions, gently, and prised some of the truth out of me – Ruby and Anna were both prepared to come to court but their evidence was second-hand so not allowed in a criminal court.

I was alone.

We had statements from the GP – showing that Jay had been lying when he had claimed to have gone to her after the 'first incident'. He had said in his statement I had held him down and repeatedly struck him with a large rock and that he'd gone to his GP afterwards. He had told the social workers this and they had believed him. They hadn't checked. He had had no injuries at all as I'd hardly hit him at all. I also had photographs of the car's dashboard which he had just destroyed before I'd hit him with the stone I'd grabbed up. The photographs from the hospital showing the horrible cuts to his head I had made with the pan were to be shown to the jury. Some of the character references from my colleagues could be used. They'd worked with me for years and not seen any aggression or violence or unreasonable behaviour at all.

They were also qualified, middle-class people. I wondered how people like me fared when their only associates who could vouch for them were not so high status.

Also, I had broken down in tears one time when I'd attended for acupuncture treatment and told the practitioner how scared I was of him – she had agreed to let the court see her treatment notes as evidence and Ms Pane, the solicitor, had told me this was 'very powerful evidence' as the acupuncturist was a professional and I had told her how afraid I was long before the incidents for which I was arrested – but no, even she wouldn't attend court. Again, I'd begged her. But no, she 'just couldn't'. Jay did not know her or her address or even where her treatment clinic was. But no.

But I was not alone. My dad attended court for two of the three days. He sat and watched his daughter go through the trial. He heard about my life – what I had been keeping from him for years – protecting him – deceiving him.

And Esme, Marianne and Anna came too. They deliberately dressed to impress – Esme left her farming gear at home and came dressed to the nines and Marianne turned out in one of her immaculate suits. And Anna too dressed more formally than I'd ever seen her.

On the days of the trial Joe was to be at nursery and looked after by another aunt. Jay attended my trial with two of his sisters and his brother. Jay was chief witness for the prosecution. The police who had arrested me were also being called for the prosecution. I was chief witness for the defence. And only witness for the defence. My mad driving around and hunting through websites and calling on neighbours – all had led to nothing but false hope of help which never arrived.

The first event in court was the swearing in of the jury. About twenty people were in the room and names were called out by a sort of raffle. I watched anxiously. I looked at their faces. Did any of them know what it is like to be afraid? To be in almost constant fear? I watched the ones who were not chosen leave. Were they the ones who might have understood?

I had been led to a little stand at the back of the court. It was surrounded by a little wooden fence. A police officer stood next to it. I was high up and could see the court.

There were two barristers – the prosecutor and my defending counsel, Dafydd, in wigs and gowns. The jurors in their box and the clerk at the front. There were my friends and my dad sitting in the public gallery to the left, there was Jay and his family and someone from the papers. We all stood up as the judge came in wearing a red cape and a wig.

Jay gave evidence. He cried briefly and accepted the offer of a glass of water. He told the court I had attacked him for no reason on two occasions, causing him injuries. When asked about some entries in his diary which referred to his own temper he said he was a bit of a poet and liked to make up stories. The photographs of the injuries were shown to the jury. They looked at them and then at me and then at Jay.

It was confirmed that Jay had previous history of convictions for violence when in a temper. The defence read out statements he had made – about having to go to the GP with injuries –contrasting with the GP's own statement that he hadn't. When Jay wasn't in the dock he sat with two of his sisters, in between them. I noticed they were holding him by the arms – to a casual observer maybe just resting their arms over his. But they were calming him. I realised, they knew their brother. They might have left him as a teenager and been estranged from them since but they knew he was likely to 'blow' at any minute. I prayed for that to happen. Then they'd see. But they were helping him, covering up.

The two social work managers, Anastasia and Dan, had been called to give evidence. When we went out for lunch they were sitting in the café – with another ex-colleague plus someone from HR for their 'support'. No-one there for my support. My employers had already found me guilty.

My friends sat with me and got me a chair sitting with my back to them so I did not have to look at them. They were the people who had taken Joe from me. I could remember the lies they had told to get me to agree. "Just a few weeks. Social services will monitor. Just until the assessment is over." It was nightly torture to me that maybe if I had refused they would have failed to get the PPO and would not have been able to take Joe. It was nightly torture to me that they had spent no time whatsoever with me and Joe together so had had no idea of our relationship or Joe's feelings on the matter. It was just a day's work to them. It was torture to me that I had allowed Joe to go to Jay: If I had insisted he go to foster carers, at least the foster – carers, wherever they had been, would not have lied about who it was Joe was asking for and cried for in the night – and he would have been back with me.

I had been a social worker for twenty years. I had worked with children in homes and in foster care. I had always believed that I did so as part of an honourable web of child protection. But how many had been taken away from loving mothers like me – by lying social workers like them? Sure, I had seen deliberate cigarette burns on some children and healed scars on others – but there were others who had told me 'the social workers took me away but my mummy loved, me and she hadn't done anything wrong' I'd always assumed that they were telling a fantasy, as children do, to fill in the blanks – but in how many cases had that been actually the case?

My whole life seemed a lie.

I'd crossed those two managers as a shop steward and as a professional – disagreeing with their bullying manager tactics and with their appalling practice. I had made enemies but never suspected they would stoop as low as they did in revenge, how blind it had made them. But how many other families had made similar powerful enemies and been torn apart? What did my life, given as I'd thought, to the care of children, really then add up to? Was I just another part of a huge failed con which took children away – like Joe had been taken from me? Was this the pain I was in suffered by my 'victims' whose children I had helped to keep from them?

When we went back, the defence barrister, Dafydd, pointed out to the court that their evidence, of Anastasia and Dan, could not be allowed as they had not been investigating a crime but looking at child protection issues so their evidence was hearsay – as much as the witness statements not present had not been allowed. They had questioned me but as social workers, not as investigators of a crime. Any evidence they offered could not be relied upon. I had had no legal advice. I had had no caution. This was true. I had been told by the social workers, for example, that I had 'assaulted' Jay and I had believed them – not realising the legal weight of that word and thinking they must understand the law so must be right.

But 'assault' is not, legally, synonymous with 'hit'. If you hit someone in self-defence – it is not assault and that word should not be used.

You live and learn.

They had told me I would not be allowed back into my own house – and again I had believed them and they then said the caravan I was in was unfit for a child. They had told me that Jay's injuries were serious and I had gone into shock – believing him to be badly injured and thinking I must have lost consciousness and hit him more than I remembered. But he hadn't been injured seriously. I was to be allowed back into my house in a few days.

Also, a PPO was unlikely to have been granted as I had only hit my partner, and that two days previously. I had been living with Esme ever since, with Joe, quite happily. I had no record of violence. This was also a source of torture – if I had not agreed with them for the 'short stay' at his father and auntie's – would they have been able to get the PPO which they had threatened to go and get? If Joe had been with me that day, in the caravan, and they had seen how we were with each other, heard his protestations about leaving, the outcome of that dreadful interview would have been quite different. Joe, maybe, would not have been taken from his mother. Maybe?

There was some argument in the court among the barristers about the two social workers but it was found that their evidence was 'unsafe' and an usher was sent to tell them they were not needed. It was a tiny victory.

The defence counsel showed the photographs of the smashed dashboard and glove compartment to the jury. Jay had kicked and kicked at it until it broke into pieces while he smashed his hand on the dashboards screaming the whole time – with Joe sitting in the back seat and me driving back to the house shaking – unable to go on driving back to my parents' house for the Christmas break. Jay had then got out of the car and strode to the front of the house still ranting and hitting out at plants or air as he passed.

I'd given Joe a book to look at, whispered I'd be back and gone to see if Jay had gone into the house or up the garden. If up the garden I would take Joe in the house until all was calm. If into the house I'd take him into the cold, unused caravan to play for a while. Coming to the corner of the house I realised my mistake – Jay had done neither and was heading back to the car and I'd nearly collided with him; his arms were raised, I spun round away from him, a white object on the top of the water butt was just in front of me as I ducked instinctively away from his raised hands. He was still shouting in anger, he was just behind me, I grabbed the stone up and span round to face him again – the stone in my raised hand, and it connected with the hat he was wearing, bumping the side of his head. He sprang back, he'd stopped yelling in shock. I still held the rock. I was aware my heart was beating fast. He grabbed my arm and pulled me into a head lock. I thought I was going to die and saw my glasses on the floor, I thought they were the last thing I was ever going to see.

But then he pushed me and I fell forward onto the floor and he swore at me and went off around the house, past the car and onto the front lawn. I ran to the car, got Joe out and took him into the house and upstairs. I had no keys to lock the door. Jay stayed outside for a while; I could see him shouting at the road. Joe asked, "Why is Daddy shouting?" and I said I didn't know and took him into the bathroom to play with water and the taps.

I then heard him come in downstairs and he seemed to have calmed down from what I could hear. He called up that there was tea being made. He said he was stressed as 'Christmas always' made him stressed. I suggested he not bother with Christmas – I'd just take Joe to my parents' house and Jay didn't have to bother. I had an idea we could get to my parents safely and not come back. But Jay said he'd feel sad not to have a Christmas so came with us and we left again – with the damaged car – as if nothing had happened. Another episode in my bizarre life. Joe had then been three years old. Four months later, I had hit out again, thinking I was about to be attacked by an enraged Jay when I'd got in the way and that time Jay had been injured and I'd been arrested.

The photographs of the damage to the car's interior were shown to the jury. Jay was asked about the damage to the car. It was then that I was very surprised. I had expected him to come out with a very elaborate, carefully thought out lie to explain the state of the car. I had by now, started to become aware of how good a liar he was. But when he was asked about the state of the car and whether he'd kicked it until it broke that morning – he said no, he hadn't and that it had just fallen off all by itself.

This was so obvious a lie it was almost as if he was making a joke.

When I was called to the dock I looked at my friends and my dad as I walked past them. I needed to look in their eyes as people I loved and who knew me. From them I drew strength.

The defence counsel asked me to describe what had happened on the morning of the first incident and I did. He would ask me to tell then to pause there if he needed to ask me again to clarify something. It seemed to go on forever. I realised I was thinking everybody in the court must be sick of my voice and desperate for me to shut up. I realised that was probably the effect of living with Jay for too long and him not being able to stand my speaking more than a few words.

Then the barrister asked me about what had happened on the morning of the second incident. Again, he would stop and ask for clarification as we went along the sad tale. I described the day before, how Jay had been very angry and so I'd been on edge the following morning as he seemed to still be in a bad mood and likely to 'blow', my sad attempts to keep things normal, make the breakfast; my fateful, pathetic decision to try and turn the television down to prevent him losing his temper about the adverts, as he often did, and his sudden outburst of anger behind me, the sudden roaring in the throat which always preceded an explosion and my panic-stricken reaction attempting to ward him off – then the complete panic when I realised I had actually hit him and I would probably die if I didn't get out of that room. The second blow to keep him away, his fall onto the edge of the bench, the door slamming as he fell past it, Joe coming in, my ringing the ambulance, Jay leaving to go to get a lift from the neighbour.

The transcript of my call to the ambulance was read out to see if it was consistent.

The prosecution called the arresting police officers to give evidence. I waited to hear the damning account, not expecting anything good from police: but instead she told what had happened that morning, what I had told them, what they had found, how I had been with them – and with my child. I remember thinking that I was wrong about police – they weren't all out to get a 'nick' at any price. She told the truth – and it did not help the prosecution at all.

Extracts from Jay's diary were referred to and

showed he had been lying about his mood swings and feelings of anger. His dissatisfaction with his life.

The jury withdrew.

While we were waiting my friends kept me company. If I was found guilty it would be very unlikely for Joe to be returned to me. Why would they place a child with someone who lost her temper and went about hitting people for no reason?

The jury were out all over lunchtime.

*

Carol said later than when the jury came out she knew what the verdict was because they were looking at me and at my friends with some smiles. I didn't see any of this as I was standing up and staring at my hands folded on the wooden fence.

There were two charges. Two counts – both Not Guilty.

My dad and sister-in-law, Carol, were taking it in turns to look after my mum. On this the last day, my mum came into court with Carol, not able to cope at being separated from my dad. She saw me in the dock and came over, not knowing what I was doing there or what was happening. I gave her a hug over the wooden fence of the dock. No-one tried to stop us. The dementia was obvious from her attire and hair and manner.

My sister-in-law had brought my mum into court to be with my dad and, her in her long overcoat and trainers, we hugged over the little wooden fence of the dock and she smiled around at all the court. That dazzling smile. She had some idea of what had just happened.

"You can go now," said the police officer, and opened the little wooden gate.

I said thank you. I tried to say thank you to the jury but I had no voice.

I didn't know where to go and my legs wouldn't work, my sister-in-law, Carol, came over to hold me up and help me out of the door. Tears came. They had understood.

I would not be going to prison.

I had to then go and see and thank my barrister and his team and sort out details and sign stuff. When I got back to the café, Carol was in tears. Jay's sister, Agnes, had asked to speak to her and, once Carol had left the café and the company of my friends, had shouted at her in anger and disapproval of the verdict and that I was no longer allowed to collect Joe from her house. This was the woman whom I had trusted would protect Joe.

Jay hadn't been there for the last day. I wondered if he'd been advised to stay away as his agitated 'edgy' demeanour in court in front of the jury was giving the game away.

I sent texts to friends and colleagues. My dad was not surprised. He had had no doubt, having faith in the legal system which I did not have, that all would be well. He said that Joe would be home soon and the nightmare over.

I went home.

Chapter 10

It had taken a whole year. From my arrest, the social workers deciding I must be guilty, threatening to put Joe in care if I didn't agree to the 'few weeks' with his aunt and father – a whole year had gone by.

His fourth birthday with me was spent in a park where we played all his favourite games and had a cake I had made and brought over in the car with my dad. I had bought him a model of his favourite dinosaur. We acted out the story Joe loved best – the three Billy Goats Gruff – where we took it in turns to be the Big Billy Goat and the big bullying Troll. A park bench stood in for the bridge in the story and we took it in turns to lurk behind the wooden trellis and leap out and roar.

Next time I saw him he told me his dad had taken the dinosaur off him and 'put it away' somewhere.

The barrister at the next Family Court Hearing told me it wouldn't make 'much difference' – the fact I'd been found not guilty. It didn't seem to matter to any of them – that fact that Jay had been lying for a year about my mental health, about what had happened and why I 'could not be trusted' with Joe.

He had prevented Joe from seeing me, his mum, for an entire month, allowed Joe to be crying and distressed at my absence, kept him from seeing his old friends, insisted on my being supervised – all for no good reason, just for malice or the need to control.

None of this was, to them, of any significance.

Life went on. I was still not allowed to see Joe without a supervisor. My family and Anna still had to travel up with me. My solicitor told me arrangements around contact would only be looked at the 'Fact-Finding Hearing' which was in a few months. So, seeing Joe was as before. Except now we were not able to collect Joe from his auntie's house, after Jay had dropped him there, but now we had to wait down the lane at a lay-by where his auntie or his grandma would bring him. We'd pick him up, put him in the car, delighted to see me and chatting away the minute we connected. Then we'd return him to this lay-by three hours later after visiting a park or a museum and playing and chatting as much as we could cram into the few hours we had.

I was allowed to see him twice a week now. He still asked, "How many sleeps?" When it was more than two until our next time he would always say, "Too many sleeps."

He rarely cried now on our parting. Even when I had used to drop him off, as a six-month-old baby at the crèche or nursery, he had learned that crying did not bring me back so became hardened to this mini, daily desertion and had learned it was not for long. He had also enjoyed his time with the other kids and carers at the crèche or nursery. We had become experts, even then, at managing being separated. By now we both had PhDs in leaving each other and burying our feelings. I knew exactly how not to upset him with my own grief. That was saved for when I was safely out of sight or in the dark hours when I'd wake.

So now we picked up and dropped off at the lay-by.

The first time we did this it was on a glorious sunny day and we had been in the park. As we drew in to the lay-by, a single grey cloud arrived overhead and opened up, raining on the auntie and on Joe as they walked back towards the big house as we watched, sat in the car. Anna had said she thought God had a sense of humour.

"Shall we offer them a lift?" said my dad.

The next part of the procedure was a Fact-Finding Hearing. At this I'd need to go again through the whole history of what had happened during the two incidents for which I'd been arrested – but this time in the family court rather than the criminal court which was all rather mystifying.

I was told it was at a 'different level of proof'.

There would be no jury.

The family courts do not have juries. It is said that this is in order to protect the identity of the child. At least that was what I was told. I would be cross-questioned again, this time by Jay's family court barrister, so I'd just have to tell again what had happened and about my life with Jay.

At least it would make things clear to the judge.

The evidence that had come out at the criminal court could be included. I paid three thousand pounds to my solicitor for a transcript of the criminal court case to be made and sent into the family court so none of the evidence would be missed. The transcript included everything I'd said in the witness box and what Jay had said.

Parts of Jay's diary had shown his strange state of mind and outlook and had been read out in the criminal court. That diary had also been forwarded to the family court solicitor.

I also put forward for filing the letters which I had had from Sophie and from Wendy – the two exes. Separately they did not add up to much but together they painted a clear enough picture: this man was a bully and a liar and had either a terrible temper which he could not control – or the appearance of such which he used to control others. I still didn't know which it was.

Ruby and Anna agreed to travel the long miles to the court and speak in support of their statements. To both of them I had confided some small part of what was happening to me – and the court could now hear this for Joe's sake. My solicitor told me I'd be cross-questioned again and I nodded as I had understood this. I asked if the evidence from the hospital would be available: the social workers had declared Jay's injuries to be 'serious' and 'life-threatening' – and Jay had told his family this – but the doctor at the hospital had found them to be 'superficial and not serious' and had written a report stating this.

I suspected that Jay had also been the one to give the social workers the 'analysis' of 'serious head wounds' and that they hadn't even bothered to check it – being only to keen to believe the worst of me.

How could I blame them for believing Jay? I, who had believed him for so long and so completely?

I drove the 100 miles and arrived early as always. I waited in one of the little rooms and prayed for help, for protection of Joe and for help for the judge to understand at last.

The barristers and solicitors arrived in a swarm of designer suits and wheelie bags. They met and discussed and went from room to room between Jay and me. Jay's team were anxious to discuss things before the Finding of Fact hearing got under way.

Anna and Ruby were waiting 150 miles away to drive up to the court. The hearing was to take place over three days – they would probably be called for the second afternoon. I would probably be cross-questioned first. It felt quite like déjà vu. All I had to do was tell it all again and all would become clear. This time I'd have the backing of other witnesses. The truth about Jay would be in the open for the judge to see. The evidence from the criminal trial was already on file.

The criminal court team had sent the evidence – the diary belonging to Jay, the letters from the exes, the character references which they couldn't use in a criminal court, to the family solicitor, knowing it would help inform the family law case. When the judge had read them, he would have a much better understanding of the context of the case, of Jay's temper and the need to not leave Joe in his custody a moment longer.

As the family court needed a 'different level of proof' we were going to go through all the evidence again in the family court for the family court judge to decide for himself what had happened – regardless of the findings of the criminal court.

The advantage of this was that, in the family court, the statements by witnesses whom I'd told of events at the time, even though they had not seen anything themselves, was admissible evidence – unlike in the criminal court. This meant that the three people to whom I had told something of Jay's behaviour would be able to come to court and tell what they had been told, Even if they didn't, their written statements would still be counted as some kind of evidence. The statements written out by my neighbours would be counted – the two women whom Jay had frightened in his rages – they had refused to come to the criminal court but their statements could be included in the family court trial. Also, I had told Anna, at the time, of one incident of Jay's temper; she had spotted me looking stressed at work one day after he had lost his temper driving the van, yelling abuse at me, swerving all over the road – all because I'd suggested we stop awhile and have a break – and she had asked me and I had blurted out some of it. Also, I had bumped into Ruby at the supermarket one evening when I'd taken Joe and ran out of the house and driven to the supermarket just to have a safe place to be for a while away from Jay when he was in a rage. Seeing I was in something of a state, Ruby had asked and I had told her something of what was happening at home.

Even more crucially, I had gone for some acupuncture treatment and, under treatment, under the gentle questions of the diagnosis I'd burst into tears and blurted out my fear. The acupuncturist had written it all in her notes and had submitted these as evidence when my solicitor had asked me 'had I ever told anyone anything?' My solicitor, Ms Pane, had been impressed with the acupuncture aspect as this was a professional person who would not lie or put their livelihood on the line.

Anna and Ruby's evidence was also 'powerful' as they too were professionals and would have credibility, she said.

I had copies of Sophie's letters – the letter she had written plus the one where she apologised for not wanting to upset things between her and Jay and acknowledging the letter she had given me was not the one I had been expecting. Surely the judge would see the significance of this – a witness acknowledging she dare not disclose all for fear of upsetting Jay. She was obviously, moreover, not afraid of upsetting me by thus letting me down.

The diary containing the passages where Jay wrote of his own mood swings and resentment towards me had also been forwarded. He'd also written an account of the first incident which contradicted completely what he had later told the police and social worker.

The letter from the hospital showed he had also lied when describing his injuries to the social workers – he had told them, and they had told me, that he was 'almost killed' and the injuries were very serious – but they were not.

He had not had serious head injuries at all.

I was originally told by 'my team' that the

arrangements around contact could be looked at and maybe change during the Finding of Facts hearing. Now I was told that no decision about custody or contact could be made at today's hearing – that couldn't happen until the Final Hearing which was many months away. Also, the Finding of Fact hearing was such a long procedure that there would be not time after it-whatever the outcome – to discuss any changes to contact arrangement. This was a shock to me as I'd been told that contact arrangements would be discussed today or tomorrow as part of the hearing. But now I was told that, whatever the outcome, I'd still need to be supervised, and still only see Joe twice a week.

When I arrived at the court for the Fact Finding hearing the barristers were in consultation. Jay's barristers and my own were in a meeting behind closed doors.

Jay's barristers had read the court transcript – the evidence from the criminal court.

They had a proposal to make.

My barrister was in favour of this and told me it would be to my advantage. So was the CAFCASS officer.

The proposal was that, instead of going through it all again, we would reach an agreement today, called a 'Compromise Agreement' which Jay and I would both sign – and then we could go ahead with looking at custody and be sure that the events for which I had been arrested would not be referred to again.

I said no. There were two witnesses ready to attend. There was no way the judge would ever understand what Jay was about unless he heard the whole truth about what had happened. The only way he could hear this evidence was if we went ahead with the hearing.

My barrister reassured me. "It will all be on the file," she said.

The court judges, she and the CAFCASS officer assured me, already knew 'all about' domestic abuse and what happened so nothing would be lost. It would be also be to my advantage – because if we reached this agreement today – 'we would then be able to go on and look at the contact arrangements and get them changed'. They had years of experience in the family court – and what did I know?

There'd be no need for supervision anymore, they said.

But if we went ahead with the Fact Finding – whatever the outcome, we would have 'no time to look at contact arrangements'.

I saw in front of me my mother, confused and stressed, sitting in the car as we drove the hundred miles. My father, trying his best to look after her as we lurched around the park or soft play place with Joe. My mother, afraid, demanding to be taken home, sometimes in tears, as I played with Joe just out of earshot. I thought of Anna, up at dawn to catch the train and come with me, my brother and sister-in-law restructuring their lives and work around my seeing Joe. So many people's lives.

It was as if Jay, using the cogs and wheels of the court, was now able to control and abuse, not just me, but everyone close to me. The court machinery carried out his every wish so willingly as he dragged so many lives into his empire. Like a great spider in the midst of a web, he pulled strings and was more in control than ever.

"You might even be able to have staying overnight contact," the barrister said, gently.

The outcome of the criminal court case, the barrister in the family court told me, would make no difference to what happened in the family court – which was something of a surprise. A lot of Jay's lies had come out in the criminal court – surely that showed something about what had happened and what he was really like?

The barrister explained that the family court operated on 'a different level of proof' – in other words, they didn't need to agree with the verdict of the criminal court.

I wondered if they would have agreed with it if I'd been found guilty.

Given the amount of evidence which was inadmissible in the criminal court – the statements by the exes, the second-hand witness accounts, the letters – it was a wonder that the jury had found me not guilty, given that the prosecution had had photographs of Jay's injuries and I had had nothing at all except some photos of a smashed-up car interior and a diary.

Jay's team had made such a generous, sensible offer: They had read the transcript and had suddenly had an idea: why not come to an agreement with the issues in the Finding of Fact –forego the hearing and use the time instead to discuss possible changes in contact? This sounded too good to be true but my team were enthusiastic and enthused that it would work better for me.

At this time I still believed my social work training about how the family courts operate: that everyone there suspends all other considerations, all other thoughts and they all work together for the sole purpose of protecting the best interests of the child. The great minds which are employed in the family court, all of them, from judge to usher and all the barristers and solicitors, all bend their mighty power to the one ambition to secure: the safety and best outcome for the vulnerable: Joe.

Obviously, I thought, they had realised from the criminal court evidence the truth about Jay so now they wanted to get Joe back to me as soon as possible – and that meant they could bypass the formality of the Fact-Finding hearing, also saving Jay from having to go through this again – having all his secrets picked over once more.

They said that Jay was ready to accept that I had hit him out of fear.

This was such a huge and sudden change in his attitude, and apparently in theirs, I burst into tears. I realised that they knew at last the truth. Now Joe would be safe, I believed that Jay had finally realised the harm he had done and acknowledged that I had been afraid. I thought this was almost too good to be true. At last he was admitting his own behaviour.

So if we, Jay and I, could agree a 'compromise agreement', they said, we could dispense with the Finding of Fact Hearing and I'd be allowed to have unsupervised contact AND take Joe home for overnight stays starting the following weekend!

Shaking with disbelief, I read the compromise agreement the two barristers had drawn up. We both had to sign it. I needed to agree that I'd hit him – which I'd never denied. I said I didn't think it was clearly enough worded that I had done so out of fear but my concern was brushed aside by my barrister as 'too pernickety' as the judge 'knew all about domestic abuse' and would know what was meant.

Further, the agreement was that neither Jay nor I would ever again refer to the two events for which I was charged in any further hearings to do with Joe – the whole criminal court stuff was to be put behind us and we all focus on Joe's wellbeing. We wouldn't have the Fact Finding, we wouldn't need it.

I asked about whether the judge needed to see all the evidence to be sure about me and I was told, by my barrister, 'it will be on the file'.

I signed.

I then rang Ruby and Anna and told them the hearing was off and why, I told them I'd no longer need to be supervised. Anna said that sounded good – that at last the court were beginning to understand.

The barristers came up with a plan for contact. That weekend Joe would come back with me and stay overnight. I was delirious with disbelief and joy. After all Jay's lying and making me out to be violent, my mother being dragged up the motorway, my father struggling to cope with an anxious woman with dementia who was scared and didn't know why she had to be in these strange places, Anna travelling by train to meet me in the frosty mornings and give up her days to make sure I could see my son, my brother taking time off work, my sister-in-law rearranging her life for months and months and Joe, my little Joe, anxious and crying and not knowing why I always left, Joe being taken away from my care by lies and deceit – all now had suddenly been acknowledged as completely unnecessary. I was no risk to my son, I had never been a risk to my son – Jay had lied and lied again to cover up his own guilt. He had now acknowledged it.

I agreed to sign. There was a problem with the wording which seemed ambiguous about whether I'd hit him in self-defence or not but my barrister assured me it was only a detail and wouldn't matter in the wide scheme of things.

The barristers flitted back and forth like well-tailored attendees in designer gear at a fresh corpse on the African plain and brought me a piece of paper. I read it and signed it.

It felt like a war had been won.

Within minutes I was signing another piece of paper saying I no longer needed to be supervised when with my little boy and another that he was coming back to my house for an overnight stay that weekend.

Tears of relief flowed and sobs racked, my hand shaking and tears falling on the small piece of paper, while the barristers looked on slightly embarrassed and rather shocked.

The Fact-Finding Hearing was cancelled. A new arrangement around my seeing Joe was begun. The

Compromise Agreement was signed. All the barristers seemed pleased.

Joe was now nearly five years old. Our first trip out together is etched in my mind. We had not been alone together for two years. His early life had always been, after his dad got fed up with coming with us, trips out in the car with me. Now we were doing a trip out together, alone, for the first time in two years.

All my friends and relatives who had buoyed me up and come with me to stop that precious thread between my son and me from being broken were given release from duty. Joe got in the car with me when I picked him up at the lay-by and we drove off to explore our world again.

I have a particularly precious photo of him. He is standing in a stream in his wellies waving a little fishing net. It was in a place we had found on the map, when Anna was with us, where the stream was not cordoned off for private use and we could play in the stream like any normal family. This photo is special to me as it was the first time after two years when we could be together without an escort.

When I picked him up, he asked, "Who's with us today?"

I said, "Nobody today, just us," and we went to a stream and a pond nearby where we could wade in the stream and catch 'dragon fish' in his little net and feed the ducks.

It felt normal.

That weekend he came home for an overnight stay. We chatted and played word games all the way home. I stayed off the motorway for safety's sake.

When we turned into the drive of my parents' and now my home Joe cheered. Maybe because he remembered it but also maybe because of the long drives. But he ran around the house checking everything and greeting his grandparents – my mum and dad.

The evening and the next morning flew by in games and being together without that awful two-hour time limit ticking away. Putting him to bed in his own room for the first time for so long felt like something so long lost had at last returned. He was so happy to be there. When I had told him he was coming to stay 'the whole night' he had cheered and had kept checking with me that it was true; it was happening.

Marianne brought his oldest friend Archie over to play and they carried on as if there had been no time lost to their friendship.

The filthy, corrosive lie that I might be a threat to my beloved child was finally lifted. It had hung over me for so long. Jay had put that lie there and kept it there. I had come within inches of not being able to see my son, I had been prevented from seeing him for an entire month – but thanks to Anna, and my brother, and my mum and dad and Carol, I had kept some of my promises.

How many other children are there who do not see their loving mother or father because there aren't such good friends to hand? How long do they wait before they give up? How much damage does this do to the growing child? How much pain does it cause – to be betrayed by the one we love first?

The fact that Jay had told this lie – to make out that I was mad and that he was innocent of doing anything that might have frightened me into hitting him, seemed to pass everyone by. I was told the judge 'wouldn't be interested' in that point.

That became our new pattern – I'd drive up three times a week to pick him up after nursery one week and on the Friday, fortnightly, I'd bring him home overnight. Then at the next hearing the judge agreed that going back and forth for a one night stay was not reasonable or sustainable so, joy of joys, Joe was able to come with me home on the Friday and stay until I had to return him on the Sunday evening.

Now CAFCASS could get involved at last to do the long-awaited assessment.

My little one would cry on having to leave and state quite clearly that he did not want to go back after the weekend. I knew if I did not get him to return I'd probably be arrested or it would be claimed I was putting him up to it as it all had to be decided in the family court final hearing, so I'd persuade and comfort and promise it would all be okay and persuade him into the car and chat and play stories and word games until he fell asleep on the way back.

I knew that, if I broke the court order defining the terms of my contact with him, I'd be arrested for breach of court order and he'd be taken from me again and I'd be stopped from being able to bring him home – maybe from seeing him unsupervised at all. I had to get him back to his father's. So every Sunday afternoon I'd be persuading an angry, upset four-year-old to get in the car as he cried and insisted he did not want to 'go back'. And so I betrayed him again and again.

As I closed the car door on his cries and went around to get in the driver's seat I called on God to hear him and to show some mercy and to help us. I rang the CAFCASS officer who had been assigned to the case to ask her for help and to tell her of Joe's distress. She blandly said that I seemed to be coping as well as could be expected but the assessment would have to wait until nearer the time for the court.

I cursed God then and dropped any belief or faith I had begun to have as he seemed deaf to a child's cries.

I phoned the CAFCASS officer again and told her I felt I was abusing my own child and asked if somebody could at least witness his distress or advise me how to help him – but the 'assessment' was in the queue and I was told I needed to conform to the court order. She told me I was 'probably dealing with it as best you can'. She didn't seem to consider how Joe was 'dealing with it' and how this was damaging him. She had no advice to give except that the assessment would be going ahead 'soon'.

He'd wake up halfway through the journey back and sit quietly, not wanting to join in any chat. On arrival at the car park where we were to 'handover' his grief would surface. As I undid his seatbelt he would cry and climb into the front seat and bury his head in my front. Putting my arms around him, I could feel his whole body shaking. My words of comfort felt like the phoney betrayals they were.

On his father's appearance, he'd push further into me and repeat, "I don't want to go. I don't want to go," and his cries would go up a notch.

Fighting back my own tears, I'd urge him to go,

telling him, "It'll be alright, it'll be alright. We have to. You have to."

He'd get out of the car, still crying loudly and trembling all over as he walked across to his father who'd smile and say, "Hello there, are you a bit sleepy? Sleepy boy." Jay had never been good at getting other people's emotional realities if they were inconvenient to himself, but how could even he mistake, or even pretend to mistake, this distressed, desperate child with one who had just woken up was beyond me.

He'd take Joe's hand and start to walk back to the house he lived in. They had to pass a wall and Joe would stand on it to 'wave goodbye'. Joe didn't wave. He'd stand on the walk and cry loudly, mouth wide open, his face all creased up as he watched me, his mother, and drive away again. Why did I always drive away? I obviously didn't love him.

That summer he was allowed to stay with me for a whole two weeks. At the end when we were in the car park he cried, ran up to the car again and hung onto the window ledge, stating loudly, "No, no!" His father murmured to him about 'being sleepy', as if a child is roused to such extremis of distress by being sleepy.

It was unbearable. My whole body was racked with pain and grief. I'd asked my social work friends what I could do but the understanding was that if I broke the agreement of the court order – to return him to his dad's at the set time, I'd be arrested and he'd be taken from me by force.

I'd ring them blubbering and unable to drive home to ask for help – they tried to help – told me of various horror stories of children being placed with known sexual abusers – the mother unbelieved by the court. Mothers then 'kidnapping' their own children and hiding them with trusted friends in other countries and then going to prison for contempt of court rather than leave their child with the abuser.

Could I do that? Should I do that? Where the hell could I take him? I knew nobody abroad. Wherever I went in this country he'd be spotted and identified as soon as he went to school or nursery – and not to go to school would be a terrible isolated life for him. Since realising the truth about Jay's 'temper' I no longer had reason to fear he'd actually kill or harm Joe physically. Mentally the damage would be, as it had been with me, not being allowed to be himself, being scared all the time of that temper, not being allowed friends, being controlled. Having to meet his father's needs instead of the other way around. Becoming his father's carer – looking after the greedy, bad-tempered bully.

When I phoned him up during the week he seemed okay – not cheerful or chatty but okay. Resigned.

I didn't know what to do. So I did my best. If this was going to damage Joe emotionally the best I could do was do everything I could to make him resilient. For every hour spent in trauma and crying at not being (apparently) listened to by his mum, he'd have three hours of play and fun and total attention. I also made it clear that I did not take him 'back' because I wanted to – but because I had to. Children his age think their parents are omnipotent – then comes the shock of realisation in puberty as they see the same parents for the powerless mortals they are: Joe had to cope with this shock aged four and a half.

So what would he see when he looked back at his childhood? Would he see a murky dross of storm and grief and injustice? A mother who abandoned him and then kept right on abandoning him? Lied to him? Pretended to love but then left him – and kept on leaving him?

Or could we instead build a different view – one that would overshadow all the grief? I made it my plan – and my coping mechanism – that, instead of being able to be with him and ensure a good childhood I would use what time I had to make him good memories, memories that would outshine all the negatives.

The doubts he may have as to my regard for him were to be outshone by proving in any way I could that he was loved, he was regarded: my decision was that I would 'make him diamonds' and making diamonds – memories that were bright enough to last forever and outshine the bad memories – became what I did. I couldn't do anything about the present situation with the court and its queuing and waiting and endless assessments – but I could build us a future where Joe could look back and see some things good shining amongst the grey.

I knew only too well what low self-esteem does to a child and to an adult: belief that we are unloved or not important tears away at the person. What had happened so far would have damaged Joe's self-esteem and it was my fault: my fault for not leaving Jay the first time he'd ranted at me and showed his temper and cruelty; my fault for falling into a relationship, agreeing to live with someone whom I'd only known for a few months; my fault for being so arrogant, so self-assured and so blind that I believed I could 'help' Jay – even 'cure' him; and my fault for not realising what was happening earlier and finding a way out .

My fault for not trusting people and asking them for help – people who now were only too eager to help. All this had not impacted on me – I was safe, I was living at my parents' – it had impacted on Joe who was now trapped with a father who was unpredictable and frightening and who had to be obeyed at all times. This, when Joe's own personality was in its tender years and needed room to grow.

The evidence was all on file, the letters from Jay's exes, the neighbours' statements, my colleagues' accounts of what I'd told them – all I had to do was wait and help Joe cope with what we had to do meanwhile.

I had been going to the local church around this time. The local chapel was a place I could find help. People there were very kind. I had told them about my situation and we had prayed together and they had wrapped me in kindness. When Joe began visiting he'd come with me and play with the other children at the Sunday school.

I began again to believe in the possibility of God. There was comfort in believing that some force or energy protected Joe.

But I could only believe in it if I ignored all the other children who were so obviously not being protected. This was explained as being due to them not being in the right church. I decided that any God so bigoted was not worth the worshipping and quit going to church. Joe had been learning in Sunday school that the Noah story was the actual true historical event – but he reckoned it couldn't be true as 'what about the dinosaurs?' Bright lad: an expert of dinosaurs and the whole wonder of evolution and meteor-triggered extinctions, and a child who knew what an aye-aye was, where it lived, what it ate and the whole vista of the wondrous variety of the natural world: no-one was going to tell him we all got on a boat.

Instead I clung to the idea that prayer somehow affected outcomes, maybe there were spirits or angels who helped? Or forces beyond what physics had yet discovered? I had to believe in something other than bored solicitors and barristers in designer suits and sports cars.

Many of the people who helped were of one religion or another and they would attribute their kindness to God 'working through them'. But I think a more accurate explanation is that people are naturally kind but need a kind of 'excuse' to express the full generosity of human nature at its best. At its worst we are monsters indeed but in this system it is the greed and the selfishness which get rewarded – we are inundated with lessons on how we must 'get ahead' put others down and be ferocious – so our kindness is something we almost need to be ashamed of and explain away: It's God – he made me do it!

In any sane system, kindness and sharing would be the norm and the greedy, materialistic narcissist in his Ferrari would be an object of pity not a role model held up to us all:

"Oh look, here he comes now, yes very nice dear, *very* nice, lovely car/suit/gold watch/big house – makes you look *very* important, yes dear. (Aside: Poor love, thinks owning stuff means something. Poor duck, got dropped on his head when a kid I expect.) Yes dear, we've all seen it, hurry along now. Sad, really."

The only real diamonds worth having are memories. Towards making diamonds, Joe and I played hide and seek in the car and in the library. I don't know what we would have done without the little libraries in the area. Little public spaces we could go to read together and play quiet games of hide and seek around the shelves. We found parks and played at being gibbons or sloths in the bushes and trees. At Christmas time I decorated the car and brought Christmas to him – as he was not with me that weekend. Then we had another Christmas when he was at home – a treasure hunt of small presents around the house and a trip to the beach to play among caves with other families.

At weekends, we met up with other families and went on outings where there were other kids. I knew this would not be part of his life with his dad – and sure enough, Joe always told of going to town with his dad or to his auntie's house – never to see other kids except for annual visits to cousins. We drove over to stay at his old friends at last, Ed and Archie, and they met up and carried on as before and we stayed over – Joe in the bunk bed with his pals or top-toeing – and me downstairs on the couch.

Eventually the Sunday afternoon distress at having to go back had receded into an unhappy silence of getting in the car and we used story CDs and false cheerfulness to cover up what was happening. We had become experts once more.

The CAFCASS officer then did her assessment. She was brisk and efficient and matter-of-fact and she visited Joe at both of his parents' houses and observed him there, and spent time with Joe on his own – I took him to the office and left him with her for an hour.

CAFCASS came to our house in a weekend Joe when was with me. I was frantic before she arrived. Cleaning unnecessarily. Wanting my mother to look her best – irrelevantly. People with Alzheimer's become free of earthly concerns like what to wear and, after years spent in front of the mirror, honing her natural beauty to devastating results, my mum was having a holiday. I was anxious my dad would answer all the questions appropriately. Never verbose, I was worried CAFCASS would misinterpret his short answers as being to do with lack of interest.

Joe played in the garden. She asked him to show her around the house and he refused. I was anxious she'd think I was not a good parent as I could not even persuade my son to show her around the house. But she pointed out, "He doesn't want to be with me, does he?" and I realised, of course, he wanted to be with me and didn't want to go off with her. I liked her then –she really was understanding Joe and looking at things from his point of view. So we all went around the house together in a convoy with Joe's little friend who was visiting.

The summer drew to a close. The CAFCASS officer went to visit Joe at his dad's.

There had still been no crisis, no report of Jay 'losing it' or causing any affray with his family. Almost daily, early on, I had expected a phone call. A police officer... there'd been an incident... Jay had been arrested... an affray... He was being sectioned... someone had been hurt... Jay hadn't been present but could I come and get him now? ...He was quite safe at his auntie's... It never came. Now I knew it would not come – as Jay was very much in control of when he 'lost' his temper and with whom. I'd imagined scenarios where Jay, Joe always safely in school, had 'lost it' with his sister – who had then rung the police and had him arrested, in fear of her life. It never happened. If this had been a film, it would have done. If God had existed, and intervened, it would have done.

All the times when I'd been terrified by his rage and abuse, it had always been behind closed doors – never at large in public. He never lost his temper with men or with anyone in authority. Still I prayed. Prayed for the truth to come out about Joe's situation. Joe had told me a few things and I wrote them down with the date and where we were when he told me; that's all I knew to do. Joe had no-one else to tell. I told him to tell the nursery workers when 'Daddy's been shouting' or when 'Daddy was scary' but Joe said, "No I won't," so he just told me. I knew SSD would not be interested unless there were bruises or cuts.

"Daddy shouts and I run upstairs and hide under the bed," was one report. It was said in quiet distress with a pale face and downturned mouth. I told him that was the right thing to do – hide under the bed, and that he was a clever boy. I urged him to tell the nursery nurses but he wouldn't.

Another time we were out walking by the ponds we had found and a man on the other side was yelling at his dog, loud and callous and sounding a little drunk. Joe walked closer to me and looked over to the shouting. I reassured him saying, "It's okay darling, it's just somebody shouting – everybody shouts sometimes."

Joe replied, "The only person I know who shouts like that is my daddy!" and he wasn't laughing. I changed the subject and got out the bread to feed the ducks and watched the man and his dog head away from us back to the village. I'd already changed plans not to go over to that side of the pond and checked to see the man was not heading our way.

The Family Court Final Hearing was at last set for November – it had been postponed from July due to things not being ready. Joe was due to start 'proper' school in September – leaving the Reception class. He was starting school again in a strange new place. Not the school with his old friends he'd known since he was a year old. I knew that if he was settled in school there was much less chance of him being returned to my care.

The CAFCASS report arrived at my solicitors. I was up on the moors by the house. I'd been there all afternoon, praying for a good result and for the strength to cope if it wasn't good, praying for protection for my little one and for CAFCASS to see clear, to see past the deception by Jay. The solicitor had told me that the judge nearly always follows the guidance of the CAFCASS report.

The report told of Joe describing how he saw me and how he saw his dad – he'd picked out two Mister Men cards – his dad was Mr Grumpy and I was Sunshine. I'd smiled at that but my throat caught at the 'grumpy' – his dad always describing his rages as being 'grumpy': I'd learned from Women's Aid of abusers usually diminishing what they did, describing it as a 'slap' when broken bones had resulted, and Jay's description of his rages as being 'grumpy' had had the same effect – minimising and making me doubt my own senses.

Joe had chosen me to accompany him on his imaginary trip up the Amazon – not his dad, as then there would be 'no rows'. I was sad again at my son thinking what happened between his dad and me were ordinary 'rows' – but glad he was clear about where they came from.

The recommendation, stunningly, despite his being at school, despite his two years at his father's house, was for Joe to be returned to me 'as soon as possible'.

On my knees on the moor, I thanked God the angels and anyone else who may be interested.

Choking with relief, I went home and told my dad.

"Of course," he said.

He had never had any doubt of the system doing the right thing eventually.

Chapter 11

The Final Hearing came closer. The world relied on that. At the Final Hearing the Psychologist, Dr Grey, was to be cross-questioned by Jay's barrister. Many of Dr Grey's findings were the basis for the CAFCASS officer's findings – as the CAFCASS officer had frequently referred to them in her report. So, the CAFCASS report could not be accepted until Jay had had the right to have the psychologist cross-questioned in the dock – and that can only happen at a Final Hearing.

The psychologist, Dr Grey, had listened to me describing life with Jay; she had described it in her report as 'mental torture' and as 'psychological abuse'.

I realised then that holding prisoners in a permanent state of fear is a recognised form of torture as it breaks a person down – and that was what had happened to me. The victim of this kind of domestic abuse often does not recognise it is happening as the effect is so slow and corrosive.

It is not an event – it's a process. Emotional or psychological abuse is hard to spot and very hard to prove. There are no bruises except on the inside. Of all the types of abuse it is the aspect of abuse which takes longest to heal. Long after the bruises are gone, the effects of the emotional side of all kinds of abuse still remain. Emotional abuse, even when it occurs without any other kind, is the most insidious and damaging as it corrodes a person's very self. This is what had happened to me.

Meanwhile the investigation by my employer was going ahead. As a registered social worker, I was charged with behaviour not acceptable to someone of my profession and therefore I was due to be struck off if found guilty. A life of penury stretched ahead for me and Joe if I was struck off. I might never work again. Also, if I was struck off, that would almost certainly count against me when the judge was considering where to place Joe.

An ex-colleague was leading the investigation and looked at me with cold eyes as I answered the questions about my 'behaviour'. We met in rooms near my old workplace. My suspension was still in place so I couldn't talk to any of my colleagues – except Anna.

The trade union rep, Gary, a kind man who seemed to know exactly why my employers were being so vindictive and unhelpful, sat with me and sympathised with my plight. "They don't seem to know about domestic abuse," he said. He had copied and provided them with the evidence. They hadn't seemed to have read it.

They'd picked on the fact that many of my answers 'were contradictory' in that sometimes I'd said I was afraid for Jay killing himself and sometimes I was afraid of him as he'd threatened me, other times that I thought it was getting better. Surely this was evidence that I was lying? Surely truth is clear and uncomplicated?

Yes, that is what they believed: that truth is clear and uncomplicated.

One of the effects of abuse is that the mind compartmentalises itself; separates the parts of its reality – this helps the organism to survive, at least in part. Another effect is that the mind recalls, in patches – not an even, well-knit series of events – but a mess. This is because, during stress, the body does not prioritise the mind – it prioritises survival with blood and energy going to the muscles to run, escape, survive. So the mind, afterwards, has only incoherent glimpses. I'd been in survival mode for years. They fired sharp questions at me and wanted sharp answers – and I produced, instead, contradictory incoherence.

But, as social workers, didn't they know about abuse and what it does?

How many abused kids have been or are being disbelieved because they could not tell a clear, well-remembered story?

Also they found it suspicious that I'd not confided in any of my current friends but had said I might have confided in previous, older friends in the place I'd lived before – for twenty years. Surely, they thought, that was nonsense. If I could speak to my old friends, why not my new ones? Also, as a shop steward I had, surely, been part of the working group which had met and developed the Domestic Abuse policy of the employer – so I would have known how to get help, wouldn't I? Someone, a manager, had told them I was a shop steward so must have been part of the working group. They put that and more in their report which was very damning.

The part about the working party mystified me in particular as I had no recall of any such working group or any such policy. Was my memory failing me again? But how could I have attended it? I had quit as a steward and never went to any meetings after work as that would mean I would be late to pick up Joe.

And they were right – I hadn't told my manager anything of my home life – which social workers are required to do if there is anything happening at home which might impact on our work. And they were right – I had given lots of contradictory answers to their questions which made no sense when I read the summary.

I was very sad at not being able to be a social worker again as it was an important part of my identity and I'd always tried to be a good one. My family hadn't wanted me to become a social worker so I had trained in teaching – but I am too naturally inclined to be nosey about kids' problems and to try and do something about them, rather than give them marks out of ten, not to be a social worker, so I'd re-trained. Now nearly thirty years of my life's work was due to be written off as I was going to be struck off.

It wasn't as important as what was happening with Joe. Joe didn't need me to be a social worker but it felt as if Jay was also destroying this part of my life – which I had kept safe from his abuse for years. It had been my haven, my sanctuary, the place where I could still be me and experience myself as an effective, competent person away from his berating rants, criticism and put-downs. I wanted to protect it.

All my colleagues and friends had written character references and set them to the solicitor to be filed and used in whichever part of the case seemed appropriate. The cold-eyed investigator asked to see them and I contacted my solicitor, Ms Pane, and left a message asking her to send the references and I gave the address of the investigator. I left a message with the receptionist to be given to Ms Pane.

Like the family court process the work investigation had had to wait until the criminal court case was over but now they were meeting with me every few weeks and asking questions. The investigation was being led by a young, up-and-coming social worker with whom I had little to do beforehand as he'd been in a different team and had only recently arrived at the authority. He was on a fast track to become a manager and was very confident and assured in his suit. He had been briefed by Anastasia and her sidekick, Dan.

My union rep, Gary, came with me on these meetings. I was so glad of his support. I had been suspended 'without prejudice' officially, but the prejudice of the investigators was so tangible you could almost taste it: cold stares prevailed and I was looked at as if I was a substance they would rather not tread in. The questions were like the ones the first assessor asked: why hadn't I left? Didn't I realise that children were upset by stress between parents? Why hadn't I told my manager? I was required by social work code of practice to tell my manager anything which was happening in my private life which might impact on my working practice – and I had obviously had things going on in my life which came into this category. Therefore, I should be struck off as a social worker – did I not agree?

Around this time, in what there was of my life away from courts and investigations, I had become used to people I met drawing back if I told them anything of my circumstances: I had become used to the subtle shock of them realising that I was one of those people they had read about in newspapers and no longer one of those people things like this never happen to, could not happen to. I had learned not to speak of it. Sometimes I'd blunder and mention I had a child – and then I'd have to leave as my reality lurched into the delicate topiary of polite conversation like a chainsaw. I had learned to avoid all talk of family or children so as to deflect such questions. I avoided people; otherwise I had to again, and again, explain myself. My throat would close up and I'd be unable to speak. It wasn't until after that I found, when I did explain to people what had happened, how many others had been through similar – or knew someone who had. Some people judged me and did not want to know me and would not let their children play with Joe. Others understood. I couldn't risk Joe being ostracised so I kept quiet. But during the hearing, I had to talk about what had happened. Again. And again.

The fact that my home life had not affected my work, I was sure of. Work was a safe place and separate from my home life. With Joe in nursery I had had no worries. I'd used my annual leave time to make Mondays as short as possible – and I'd only started working on Mondays before Christmas.

But my employers asserted that, if being abused at home hadn't affected my work – then the abuse could not have been happening. Therefore, I must have hit Jay with no good reason – as, if he had been bullying me at home, then I could not have carried on in my work as well as I had.

So, I needed to prove, again, that the abuse had happened.

The point about my not telling my manager seemed a lost cause as there was no way I could claim that I had – as I hadn't. Gary was encouraging that it was still worth fighting it as they had got it wrong.

People like Gary are amazing. They work in unions, unsung, unrewarded except for a wage and carry on the daily war of attrition against the powers that be which threaten to flatten all our lives. The Head of Service was rude to him, tried to dismiss the evidence he presented and he quietly and calmly explained her own investigation process to her while I sat and quaked. He was not impressed with the young investigator for all his brash aggression or his suit.

"He doesn't know anything about domestic abuse," Gary told me.

I had realised by now that I didn't either.

My supervision notes were scrutinised to find any problem. There was a session when I had been in tears during supervision – but this was to do with frustration at young clients not being helped and it was during the time I was in conflict with Anastasia and her deputy in particular trying to get such resources. No-one seemed to spot the problem that it was these two, with whom I'd been in conflict before, who had been assigned to assess me – 'without prejudice' when they came to Esme's house and manipulated my child away from me with half-truths and lies.

The best evidence I could get about my work not being affected were statements from my colleagues as we worked closely as a team. They had all written character references in an attempt to help me as soon as they had known of my arrest. These had been sent to my criminal and family solicitor's offices for safe keeping pending when they might be useful in court or wherever. Some had been used in the criminal court to give the jury an idea of who I was. Could they now be used in the inquiry at work? I had asked Ms Pane to send the references to the investigator.

The next time we met, a month later, the investigator sneered at me and told me he hadn't received any such references when I asked about them and asked, sarcastically, if I was I sure they'd been written.

On the phone again to Ms Pane's office I emphasised why they were needed. My future work, income and career depended on this investigation and I was relying on the references. Yes, they would be sent, I was promised – again. Obviously, most importantly, the outcome of this might impact on how the family court saw me – if I was still registered and able to work surely that would help my case for Joe to come back to me?

The following month they had still not arrived. Back home after another session of questions and sneers I phoned again. This time I was quite assertive – without actually being angry – and I was again promised that the character references would be sent. I asked why they hadn't been sent before – I was afraid that whatever had gone wrong then would go wrong again – I was reassured all would be well and they would definitely be sent this time.

In the meantime, my application for Legal Aid was turned down. When the architect's report on the house had arrived, listing the reasons why it could not be sold, it ran to several pages of details about 'works done to the house' which broke building regulations and rendered it disqualified for any building certificate. This made it ineligible for any mortgage and therefore unable to be sold. I told my solicitor this as it would mean I could not sell it or remortgage it to get further funds to pay my legal fees. She had sent me an application form for Legal Aid. Now this had been refused because, even though I could not sell the house to raise funds it was still mine: I owned a house: Therefore, I was not eligible for Legal Aid. I could not use the house to raise funds, nor could I sell it – but owning it meant I couldn't get Legal Aid either. Neat.

A week later I received an email from my solicitor. She said I was 'advised to seek legal advice elsewhere' as our 'relationship had broken down'. Nothing else. No reason given – just that. Our relationship had broken down. No evidence. The Final Hearing was set for a couple of weeks away. A few weeks from the final hearing, she set me adrift without legal representation. A few weeks, coincidentally, after my application for Legal Aid had been turned down. Also, she would not forward 'the file' – all the papers on the case about Joe so far, unless I settled the latest bill – the latest bill of three thousand pounds. (This was what I was paying every few weeks.)

I did this with the suspended full pay I was still receiving and went touring solicitors' offices. No-one was interested. The issue of payment was a problem. I made appointments with solicitors but was met by secretaries who 'took down details'. Was it about contact? What did I want? The court was a long distance away. How much money did I have? I was planning to borrow whatever it took using my house as security. They made notes about the case as I struggled to put it into a coherent summary. I told them about the CAFCASS assessment, the mental health assessment, Dr Grey the psychologist's assessment and the earlier social services assessment – none of which had found any reason for Joe to have been removed from my care and one of which, CAFCASS, concluded he needed to be returned to me asap.

After I'd visited about ten offices, a solicitor, Mark, agreed to take the case. He sent off for 'the file' – an ungainly pile of papers and files. He believed it would all rest on what the 'experts' – CAFCASS – said. He was sympathetic. I assumed Ms Pane had provided a legally coherent summary of the case as the pile of papers and files would take a month just for someone to read and the Final Hearing was ten days away. In my own job, social work, when we pass on a case to a colleague we write a coherent summary so the next person has a chance of understanding the salient points without having to trawl through a mountain of files. This is called 'good practice' and is expression of the 'duty of care' towards clients.

We swung again into Autumn. Joe had now started school.

Collecting my little boy from the school was a wrench. It was the wrong school. He had to wear a uniform. It was the school on this strange village where he had come to live 'for a few weeks while the assessment is done'.

He came out that first day I picked him up looking unhappy and lonely. His face brightened when he saw me and he came running over. It seared at my heart – the echo of his running to me the last time I'd picked him up after his first day at that other school. I could not tell him what was going to happen – that in a few short weeks this agony would be over and he'd be home with me again forever. It would not have meant anything to him – a few months, he'd think I meant tomorrow and he'd say something to his dad and I'd be seen as manipulating him so I said nothing. I had written to the local schools near me, on the strength of the CAFCASS report, and secured a place after visiting them and checking what they were like He'd be in classes where at least he knew some of the other children. I'd be taking him to school and picking him up like a normal mum again and he'd be home.

The CAFCASS report had recommended I be able to see him three times a week now, so three times a week I drove the 100+ miles each way. On a Wednesday, I picked him up from school and we spent a precious two hours in each other's company. We'd go to a library or to a local park or just sit and read in the car or play hide and seek – still his favourite – in the churchyard. It took five hours to travel to see him for two. Then on Friday I'd collect him to come and stay for the weekend. Then the following weekend we'd have a day together on the Sunday.

It was during one of these journeys to see Joe – on the Wednesday, a week before the crucial long awaited Final Hearing – that the solicitor, Mark, rang me. It was on my mobile and I pulled over onto the motorway hard- shoulder to answer it.

He told me, quite matter-of-factly and as if he was telling me that it might rain later on, that the Final Hearing would not go ahead. It was postponed – again.

The reason for this was that the psychologist, Dr Grey, had had an accident, had fallen from her horse and was in hospital. The hearing could absolutely not go ahead without her as Jay had a right to have her cross questioned – it was his right. The hearing would be 'at some time in the new year' as Dr Grey would take some months to be better. And that was that. This was because Jay had the absolute right to cross-question her on her report on me and this could only happen at a Final Hearing. She had fallen off her horse so now this could not happen. I asked if she was badly hurt. She was in traction, he said. I was horrified for her; I knew what horse riding injuries can do.

Cars raced past the window like a heart beating too slowly. My own was racing in distress. Mark ended the phone call having passed on the message and I resumed my journey in a kind of cold daze. I'd ascertained that Dr Grey was okay and had no permanent damage and was conscious and would live. But the Final Hearing, awaited so very long, would be postponed as it could in no way go ahead without her. More months of Joe being with his dad – stretched even thinner the reasons for returning him to me. CAFCASS had made it quite clear that, even taking into account his being at the school now, so any move would disrupt his schooling, he must still be returned to me – but if he was at school for months would she still say that? I still trusted that everyone wanted the best for Joe and now understood Jay's nature so Joe would be returned to my care – but would the judge see it that way?

We played for our two allotted hours. I played football and chase and tree climbing with Joe then drove back after leaving him at the door of his dad's house.

I did all I could to hide the despair. I had for many weeks felt new hope and conviction we'd be back together again and my son safe once more.

On my return home I rang my solicitor, Mark – to ask if a video conference link could be set up from the court so the psychologist could answer questions from her bed. He said that it probably could. I asked what normally happened – in my own job someone would stand in and explain the report but this apparently was not an option with this. There was no way the judge would agree to go ahead with the hearing unless Dr Grey could be there. Couldn't her colleague stand in for her? Couldn't her manager? Couldn't her report be presented by someone else? Mark said 'no' to most of these and said he'd 'look into' the video conferencing idea. He estimated the hearing would be postponed 'some months'. Instead of the three-day Final Hearing they would be having a one-day 'Directions hearing' – which are hearings held to let everyone communicate and check we are all agreed on what is happening, what's needed etc.

Nothing to worry about.

I had told Joe that Mummy and Daddy were asking the judge, who was a very wise man, if he should live with me or his dad and that we were meeting with the judge soon. Joe had said to me that his daddy had said he would 'cry and cry and cry if he, Joe, went to live with Mummy'. Jay was obviously manipulating Joe the same way he had me. That wasn't a problem though – CAFCASS had done the assessment and knew Joe was safer with me and more attached to me. She had seen this by visiting us at home and asking Joe questions which a small child can answer.

Dr Grey's assessment was quite clear that I'd suffered years of mental abuse – she'd met with both Jay and me and also read the statements by witnesses to corroborate her findings. She'd had telephone conversations with some of them.

But at the Directions hearing – put in place of the postponed Final Hearing – Jay's team grabbed their chance. But it didn't look like that at the time. The pattern in any kaleidoscope, complicated and intricate, with one tiny flex either way, changes and gives a completely altered pattern. It doesn't need truth or justice or integrity – just a change.

When I arrived at the court there was another barrister from Mark and the CAFCASS officer and Jay's team had a proposal: they said Dr Grey's assessment needed an update as it was now ten months old and would be a year old by the time a new final hearing date was set.

I didn't see how it could be 'updated': the information she had unearthed would not stop being true in a few months, would it? They also thought the CAFCASS assessment of Joe was inadequate and needed supplementing – by 'a proper psychiatrist'. I felt that Joe had been assessed enough. My barrister, whom I hadn't met before, said the judge would look askance at me if I refused to have the report updated and refused to have Joe assessed by 'a proper psychiatrist'. The CAFCASS officer also said I was always worried about Joe's emotional state so here was a chance to have it looked at: the psychiatrist would meet with me and assess me, and Jay and Joe – fair and square.

It was like this at the family court: every hearing would have a new set of barristers or CAFCASS officers, new to the case, new to me.

I'd also noticed a strange phenomenon: eyes did not see me any more. Eyes have evolved to see things so the mind can make sense of them. When the mind is already made up – the eyes are redundant. Justice is portrayed as blind – maybe because of this effect. I'd have the strange sensation of talking to people and them not hearing me or seeing me. Of eyes not working, glazed, and looking through me.

When I tried to explain the details of the situation they would be impatient and cut me short – generalisations were quite sufficient, it seemed, to get the job done. Details were not needed. Like a domino effect, each person I met who was involved with the case, already had had a summary about me and Joe given to them – so they did not need to know more – or check if the summary was true.

Again, I trusted qualified people who were more articulate than me. Again, I handed my child over to the care of professionals who professed they had his interest at heart. I was also scared of looking like a bad parent to any of them.

I walked into the trap.

In the hearing, Jay's team put it to the judge that this update was needed – and that they had just the right psychiatrist who was, by a wonderful chance, immediately available to start the assessment – she was waiting in the wings.

Her name, Dr Felicity, was the same as the name of the child I sponsored in Africa and I saw this as a good omen. This was November, she could do the assessment and we could have the final hearing in March. It still meant Joe was with his dad and at school for another six months but what could I do but accept? I'd been told that to do otherwise would 'upset the judge'. 'Upsetting the judge', I had learned, was the equivalent of taking an axe to the Holy Grail. Or worse.

The assessment by the psychiatrist, Dr Felicity, would start within a week, the hearing would happen in March. What could possibly go wrong?

I drove home and awaited Dr Felicity's phone call. It didn't come. I assumed she was assessing Jay first.

Three months later, in February, after trying to contact Mark by phone about a dozen times by phone and letter and still not having heard from him or the psychiatrist, I went to see Mark. He was surprised to see me and invited me into his room which was laden with beige files, spilling lives. He was in a hurry, he said, as he had to get to an important meeting.

Then he told me that he'd 'heard' that **Dr** Felicity would probably not be available 'until the summer' so the Final Hearing would probably now be postponed 'until September'. Nearly a year away. He told me this as if telling me about a new brand of margarine he thought was nice. Then he ushered me out and left the building.

As I stood in the reception area, staring at the wall and trembling with disbelief and crying pathetically as the world crashed around me once more, the receptionist asked if I'd like a glass of water.

Later that day, I remembered something of court procedure – and didn't we have to have a hearing – the directions sort – before another postponing was accepted? I rang Mark – he agreed. I wondered, as I put down the phone, whether that phone call would be charged at the usual rate or if I'd get a concession.

My wonderful dad had pointed out to me that it is in solicitors' interests to be hopeless – as then there is more need for phone calls, letters, delays, postponements – for which the client pays. A useless solicitor is a rich one. Ms Pane was also well to-do: she'd fleeced me of over twenty-thousand pounds before turning me loose when it had looked as though the money would stop flowing. I was now living off the loan on the house which Marianne had arranged for me – it, too, was running out fast.

There is no need for any conspiracy for the way things are done – only for people who have the same mindset to be making the decisions. They do not need to confer as they all have the same priority: making as much money as possible for as little effort and inconvenience. Fordism was applied to the making of cars – in the courts it is applied to the destroying of lives: each life a bundle on the production line to be processed, prodded, stamped and discarded.

At the Directions hearing – which Mark did eventually call for, to confirm the new arrangements, the new (again) barrister showed me copies of a letter. Jay's team had sent this letter to Mark the very day after the last hearing in November, when the decision was made to instruct the psychiatrist, telling him that Dr Felicity, was not 'immediately available' after all.

In other words, Jay's team had lied at the hearing to the court, pretending it was all set to go, then 'found' she was not available – knowing full well this would postpone the Final Hearing still further, making Jay's case stronger. And Mark had filed the letter.

Winning was all.

Not the child.

And sure as hell not the truth.

Process.

So, as they had obviously lied to the court or at least misled it, why were they not charged with contempt? Or perverting the course of justice for that matter?

The judge seemed to have some awareness of the trick that had been pulled on him as he seemed wider awake than usual and slightly irritable. His jowls trembled as he expressed his displeasure. He admonished the Skull, my nickname for Jay's main barrister, for her 'mistake' of telling the court the assessment would happen immediately. I was reminded of a teacher admonishing a favourite pupil for flicking an ink pellet. He said the Final Hearing would happen in May, whether or not Dr Grey was well enough and that Dr Felicity would have to have completed her assessment by then too.

There it was again – one time we could not possibly proceed without Dr Grey being there or Hell would open and consume us all – so her horse accident had stopped the Great Final Hearing we'd all been waiting two years for, allowing Jay's gang to play their neat parlour trick and evoke the spirit of the yet unseen Dr Felicity and browbeat me into accepting this. But now the Final Hearing *could* go ahead without Dr Grey after all, no problem. It was all so arbitrary as if being made up as they went along.

So I drove home and waited for Dr Felicity's phone call and another hard month slipped by.

Chapter 12

My weekends with Joe, meanwhile, were like bright sunlight falling on dark water.

That winter I'd collected Joe from his father's house one snow-bright morning, Joe close to tears as I admired the new boots he was wearing. He told me they hurt. I took them off as soon as we reached the car in the car. His feet had white patches where the boots pressed on his feet; the size was clearly marked inside. They were two sizes too small. His father had insisted he wear them. I asked Joe if he'd told his father they hurt. "He doesn't listen," Joe said, tears running silently down his cheeks as I gently rubbed his feet to bring back the circulation. It was Christmas Eve, there were no offices open. Who would respond to a mad woman wittering about tight boots? I wrote to Mark telling him of this incident – evidence of Jay's parenting – and Joe's fear of him. No answer. It was down to the experts.

Other symptoms of Joe's home life with his dad had become apparent now our time together was more domestic. He had become distressed if I suggested he cleaned his own teeth. He shouted, quite suddenly, "I can't! I can't! I always get it wrong! I can't do it!" And he'd refuse to try. The same applied to other aspects of self-care. It was as if he had tried to do these things for himself – as children do – but then had excited adult anger when he didn't get them right first time or do them the way a certain adult insisted they were done. I could see in my mind's eye Jay ranting and instructing, crushing Joe's confidence.

I knew exactly what that felt like as Jay's rage descended as I hadn't cooked or cleaned or spoken the right way or said or done the right thing at the required time. Or when I'd said or done something which reminded Jay of his mother or his father or some other aspect of his lousy life. Now my child was afraid to get things wrong. You can't learn if you are afraid to get things wrong.

So I'd get it wrong deliberately and spray toothpaste out of my mouth and splutter the toothbrush as if it was a stuck in my teeth and he would laugh, all fear forgotten. Then I'd clean his teeth or wipe his bottom and reassure him that everyone gets it wrong and he'd be calm and smile. It's true that laughter takes fear away.

A little bit at a time he'd agree to do a little – we had a bargain that he would clean one tooth – then I'd do the rest. Then two. Then none. Then he could clean my teeth for me. Then he could do two of his own, then three – then the whole front row. It was a game. And he'd wipe once and check and I'd 'finish off', praising his efforts. And eventually the fear receded and he began to know he could do these mysteries. We only had alternate weekends to do all this and everything else – but we did.

I was concerned when he told me he couldn't toilet himself – with the same upset and conviction of failure as teeth cleaning. How did he manage at school?

He told me that he didn't go to the toilet 'Number two's' at school but 'kept it in' until he got home so Daddy could 'do it'. I told him he mustn't do this, that it could make him ill, and we practised more so he could see to himself and I told him getting it wrong was not important but going to the toilet was – for his body. We made a game of seeing how many 'wipes' were needed each time for the paper to come clean. He smiled at the praise at his efforts. He learned. We talked a bit about how the body gets rid of waste and that this is important – far more important than wiping bottoms 'properly'. He told me he'd try to wipe his bottom at his dad's house and then his dad would 'inspect' to see if he had got it right. Nobody needs to be that intrusive.

Another ruse had solved another problem. He had also shouted, "I can't do it!" when I had suggested a game of cricket one afternoon. He was unpersuadable. He got angry at me when I asked why not. "I can't do it! I get it wrong!" So I dropped the subject. I thought about it. I could guess what had happened. Same as the teeth cleaning and toileting – pressure, unreasonable demands, anger when he couldn't meet them. Too much instruction, too many rules. How many kids give up when they are not allowed to find out for themselves at their own pace but are tested and pressured to meet a certain standard? Isn't giving up less painful than feeling a failure? Isn't this how our education system of tests and more tests wrecks young dreams?

Jay would love 'his son' to be the great sportsman. He hated anyone doing things differently from himself – or 'getting things wrong' – which meant the same thing in his book. In his world, there was only ever one way to do anything – his way. There was no gradual build up or finding your own way or trial and error. He'd have introduced cricket with full adult rules and instructed five-year-old Joe in how to hold the bat – the 'right way' – with no allowance for Joe having a different physique or inclination – and interrupted with 'no, like this' with increasing annoyance after every effort until his temper was lost. The safest strategy for Joe was to avoid trying at all – to avoid failure or disappointing his father. I'd met children who threw books across the room and disrupted classes to distract from the threat of failure – and now Joe was on the same road. I puzzled over how to cut the knot of playing being tied in with fear of failure, of having to 'get it right'.

And that's how Joe and I found 'Tree cricket'. The game was invented. I said to Joe after breakfast, "C'mon, let's go and play tree cricket."

"What's that?" he said. So I showed him. I straddled the lowest branch of a tree, holding onto the toy cricket bat. He threw the ball towards me and I swiped at it clumsily. In a few moments, he was laughing and running about and wanting to have a turn in the tree. We swapped. The little plastic bat carried no weight or threat to his balance. He hit the ball. I wore myself out chasing it around. We were both laughing at the nonsense. Cricket was fun again. Did those who invented cricket also fall about at the ridiculousness of it all? I'd like to think so. The tree was in the garden. It was a weeping willow. Unusually, its lowest branch was only about a foot off the ground and perfect for Joe to sit in and play this daft game. My mum had planted it sixteen years ago, pushing a weeping willow twig into the ground. Even then, it had had this forked branch in miniature. I remembered her pointing it out to me on the young sapling as we worked in the garden. Of all the weeping willow twigs she had planted that day, this one had survived and grown. It was now thirty feet tall. And it was the one my son needed now – laughing and swiping at the ball, giggling, all fear gone.

It was our private game. Then we went to a garden party with some other 'lefties' – others who don't think organising the world into one big hierarchy is the meaning of life, or that competition has to be the heartbeat of the world. They'd got together a haphazard game of cricket in the early dusk of a summer's day.

They invited Joe to play. He declined.

We watched. The 'teams' were all ages. I told some of the others (quietly) that he was worried about 'getting things wrong'. They put the word round. They then fumbled the ball and missed easy hits and fell over. Big men and women and much older boys and girls – getting it wrong! And laughing! Not cursing or yelling! The first time someone fumbled and dropped the bat, I noticed Joe's face fell and his eyes fastened, wide in alarm, on the tallest male present.

But that man laughed, good naturedly. Along with the others. The miscreant picked up his bat and had another go, hitting the ball. Joe watched it all in something like wonderment.

I went to play. I too floundered about and missed and was encouraged to 'try again'. Then they asked him to play. He shook his head. No. They beseeched him. One young man said, "Oh come on Joe, we all get it wrong, it doesn't matter." They were all smiling, encouraging. Not a raised voice anywhere. No frowns.

It is etched in my heart forever. The sight of my little boy, lit by the evening sun of that summer day, teetering on the edge of the cricket pitch. Torn between love of playing, of wanting to learn this new game and be part of this big, friendly group – and fear of failure, fear of that anger. And then stepping forward, picking up the proffered bat.

He missed the first few times, and he hunched and went to put the bat down, shamefaced, anxious-looking – but when the response was cheers for effort and encouragement and another chance his face changed into a smile, then a grin. His whole body relaxed around that cricket bat. Then he swung it again, relaxed this time, and the ball sailed across the garden and into the rough. Cheers went up. After that he was hitting the ball all over the garden his face an open grin as he entered this strange new world.

So we enjoyed our times together.

But every day that ticked by while Joe lived with his dad, was making it more and more necessary for Joe not to depend on me, not to want to be with me, to make a distance and adjust completely to his present circumstances and put away any wanting of anything different.

Then I got another note. The psychiatrist, Doctor Felicity, would contact me soon.

She did. I was given a time and place to meet her for my assessment. She would also meet and assess Jay and Joe, Joe with me and Joe with Jay.

Weeks went by. It was now well over two years since Joe had been 'placed' with Jay, since I'd reacted in fear and been arrested and accused by Jay of being a mad woman who had hit him for no reason. Two years since I'd agreed for Joe to live with Jay and his auntie while the assessment was done – 'just a few weeks.'

Joe had been three, now he was five. He was at school. He had spent months telling his mum he didn't want to live at his dad's. I'd been returning him there for a year after 'staying contact' was agreed, despite his protestations. He had made it clear to one CAFCASS worker where he wanted to be. But nothing had changed. His mummy kept telling him 'everything will be alright'. But every Sunday she returned him to where he didn't want to be and walked away ignoring his cries. She drove away as he stood on the wall and cried to the sky. She came to see him, they had lovely times. He did his best to make her love him again but then she left. This had gone on for over two years.

The moment when I knew Joe had changed towards me was a Friday. I was waiting outside the school. It was in the wait after the hearing which spoke of the need for an 'updated report' – the hearing which should have been the Final Hearing – which should have put an end to the pain. Usually he ran out, eyes focussed on mine from the moment he could see me, all else lost in the periphery of our being together again. But this morning he was not the first out. This morning he didn't look at me as he came out. He was still pleased to see me but something had happened. There was a distance. I was still waiting to hear from the new psychiatrist who had been 'immediately available'.

When you are in great pain there is a way out. You can make the decision to die and find a way out – if you are able to access the means. But apart from that, when the body is in pain or when the mind is in pain, it can cut off a part of itself. It can kill off the sense of pain by numbing the connection. Frostbite is one example of when part of the body 'dies' in order that the rest of the body can go on living. You feel part of yourself dying but it does mean you can carry on functioning.

I no longer spent every minute of every day and every night in agony about being separated from my child. I could not have survived that. Eventually a numbness sets in which alleviates the pain. You feel the death of something – but the relief of pain is like a balm. And the numbness means you can go on – most of you can survive. When the body is wounded it forms scar tissue. This is less sensitive than ordinary flesh and skin. It's tough and it helps the body survive. But the feeling is gone. The saying is that 'time heals' – I don't think it does – but it numbs – in order to make it possible for life to go on.

There was now scar tissue between Joe and me. In our phone calls I'd learned not to tell him of my day or about what I was doing as he'd say, "Can I come and do that with you?" So I'd learned to tell him stories – I'd find stories which were ten minutes long and intelligible without the pictures and read them to him. I'd make up stories – often about characters having to struggle through difficulties or of losing wonderful things and then finding them again after lots of adventures. We could be together without it hurting him.

Our parting at the end of our sessions together had become well-oiled routine lubricated by time until there were no tears. He had learned there was no point in tears. He was five. We always spoke of 'next time' and what we would do and when I would ring and we'd tell each other of love in pretty ways. His favourite was 'I love you big as all the sky' – and 'see you next time' was our scar tissue which lay over the pain and kept us alive.

I always told him to go and look after 'Henry' – the big dog belonging to his auntie who was a particular friend. Routine was our morphine.

And so we awaited the new assessment by Dr Felicity.

Dr Felicity and I met in March. My solicitor told me that Dr Felicity had read all the papers to do with the case and knew all the background to the case, which was reassuring. Someone with her qualifications and expertise would understand the territory.

She was a young woman. Early middle aged, I guessed. Smartly dressed, of Asian origin and friendly, she was carrying big boxes. I helped her with the door. Here was the person who would understand Joe and what was happening to us. Here was the person who knew all about the subtle effects of the court procedure and emotional dynamics, and of coping strategies. Here was the person who had been waiting in the wings to do this assessment in November and was now able to make a start – in March.

She asked me if she could record the session of me with Joe on video 'in case it's needed in court' and I gave assent and signed a form. The plan was she would see me alone, then with Joe, then Jay alone, then Jay with Joe. It would all happen on the same day and in the same room.

The solicitor, Mark, had told me she would have used the time before meeting me or Jay to read all the paperwork and familiarise herself with all aspects of the case – so I knew she'd know all the background to the case, the outcome of court, the previous assessments, Jay's mental health history and convictions, anger problems.

We would meet, he'd said, in the library of the community centre, so I'd anticipated a children's section full of Joe and my favourite playthings – books – with cushions and windows and room to play. The room which was 'the library' in this building, however, was a bare, small room with a few shelves with ancient tomes on them. Fortunately, and 'just in case' I'd brought along some drawing to do together and a few children's books.

First I sat with Dr F and answered her questions. She asked me about my childhood and I told her how good it had been and the good memories I had. She didn't seem particularly interested and didn't ask for details. Her pen remained still. She then asked if my parents had ever had 'rows'. Now I had read all the statements made by Jay's family and one sister had said that maybe, as I had been raised 'gently' that I wasn't used to 'rows' – and so I 'overreacted' to Jay's behaviour. (This sister had never lived with the adult Jay so never knew what it was like when he was targeting you with his out of control rage so I'd forgiven her for this misapprehension.)

I immediately thought, when Dr F asked me this question, that Dr F had also read this statement and was exploring this aspect – was my 'too gentle' childhood the cause of my 'not being able to cope' with the abuse? The 'rows'?

I was keen to scotch this line of thought and to make the distinction between 'rows' – two people arguing or shouting as equals, neither afraid of the other – and abuse – one giving vent and the other cowering or tiptoeing about in fear of upsetting. I explained that yes there had been rows when I was a child, between my parents – but no abuse. I made that clear so she would see the difference. I wanted her to know I had not been brought up too 'gently' to cope with ordinary 'rows'. Dr F wrote things down with her pen. She asked me more questions and I answered her as fully as I could. Sometimes she wrote things down as I spoke, sometimes her pen stayed still.

Joe arrived, brought by his auntie at the set time and we ran together. He was watchful of Dr F but after a while he relaxed and we got on with our visit. Dr F held a cine-camera to film our time together. We drew pictures and read stories. Joe sat in my lap some of the time and next to me at others. We chatted as always, all the time. We played 'Hide and Seek' – his idea – around the sparsely furnished room, Joe giggling as I pretended to not be able to find him under the only table.

Dr F sat with the video recorder in front of her face and recorded all of it. I was glad she was making the video because if the judge saw how we interacted, our humour and our eye contact and how I parented him, he would know the quality of our relationship. If he also saw the video of Jay and Joe he would see Joe being more cautious, Jay being false, and Joe having to be a parent to his father. Jay being gushy and sentimental or irritable by turns. He wouldn't lose his temper on film – that was too much to hope for – but the judge would notice the difference in Joe: the relaxed child with me and the careful child with his dad.

I'd asked Dr F to let me know when I had fifteen minutes left. I always prepared Joe for our parting – to smooth the way for him. I talked of 'next time' as usual and about the fun time we'd had today. Joe's face went serious – he knew what was coming but was used to this. I said we only had a bit more time so what would he like to do with it? He nominated a close, sitting-together cuddle and a hand massage, and we did this. I talked of next time – which was actually only the next day as the assessment had fallen on the day before my usual day of the week when I saw him, and we celebrated that we'd had this extra time and that I'd be seeing him tomorrow. I always tried to leave him cheerful and looking forward to our next time and it was easier this day because we would meet again tomorrow.

Joe whispered, "I love you as big as all the sky," and I said this back to him. I'll never know why he whispered it but it was loud enough, in the silent room, for Dr F to hear. She had stopped recording and was putting her recorder away but she must have heard him. He had glanced her way during the hour and was obviously wondering what was up. I had no idea what his dad had told him.

I left. We had a hug at the door and I reminded him I'd see him tomorrow and told him where we were going for the day and left. Jay was just on his way in to the building.

When I saw Joe the next day I asked how the rest of the day had gone with 'the lady' and he said Jay had met with the doctor 'for a long time' and he had played outside with the auntie. He said he and his dad had then played two board games which his dad had brought, while Dr F had watched. Then Joe had seen 'the lady' on his own and she had asked him to make up some stories with some animals. I knew the test she'd used – the start of stories is provided, using figures and model animals – and the child has to provide the endings to the stories. The way he or she develops the story is then analysed to show the child's mental state.

The problem with it is, if the patterns made by the stories are not looked at in context, like anything else, they can be meaningless or interpreted any which way. I was dying to ask more but changed the subject as I did not want to interrogate him. It was all done now anyway.

I did wonder at the wisdom of having Joe aware of his dad meeting, with 'the lady' while Joe sat outside for an hour. This so obviously established Dr F as a 'friend' of his dad's. Wouldn't it have been fairer on Joe for him to meet someone who at least appeared 'neutral' and not such a big friend of his dad's? How about her meeting with me for an hour while Joe waited outside?

We went pond-dipping. I decided I needed to have a bit more faith in the professionals.

*

The strength of the 'Story stem' assessment, as it is called, is that it is meant to be 'objective'. But no assessment can work out of context. No aspect of human behaviour can be understood out of context. Cut a section out of any pattern – in a carpet or a pattern of behaviour – and you can draw another pattern around it which would seem to fit the piece you have isolated.

Select only pieces of a whole environment, draw causal connections between any items in the landscape, and you can make anything at all mean anything else. Newspapers thrive on the basis of this practice. Politicians too. This Causes That – no need to prove any connection, just to assert it. Advertisers do this – the laughing smiling family and the product, prominent in their lives. Causal connection so subtly implied. Hitler probably scored the highest result with this practice: recession/Jews and other undesirables = ten million gassed.

Hitler had his motivations – world domination, power, control, racism, working out some complex or other and pleasing his paymasters. Fascism is all about lies. Truth becomes a commodity when it is for sale – and it stays on the shelf when lies come cheaper or the truth is inconvenient to those with power.

Can an assessment of a child's life be just another commodity? Maybe it is when the person doing it is looking for work and future, further employment. Isn't it pragmatic, if looking for work, to please your pay masters? Dr F was engaged for the court by Jay's team of solicitors. I wondered how much work they had put her way over the years and how she maintained objectivity? Of course, filming the meetings would help do that.

I got a bill of a few thousand for the assessment and awaited the outcome.

In the meantime, I was sent copies of letters confirming the appointments with Dr F. Jay's solicitor had mentioned in his letter advice to Jay to take along some games to use during the hour with Joe. I hadn't even had that advice. I had almost gone to the interview believing it to be in a well-stocked library. We'd have managed anyway but it would have been harder. Dr F had asked me, "Have you brought anything to do with Joe during the assessment?" and I had. But all I had been told was that it was in a library and had almost not brought anything. Again, if felt like Jay was being looked after and provided for while I was not.

The CAFCASS officer had visited my house as well as Jay's and had concluded Joe should return to my care asap – despite the change in schools, despite the upheaval – she saw he was more relaxed and more himself and wanting to be with me.

She was due to update her report by visiting again but a week after the Dr F assessment she phoned to cancel her visit. She said it would no longer be necessary. She said she had read Dr F's report and would say no more.

I got a copy a few days later. I read it twice in disbelief. She had written down everything Jay had told her – about his 'average' childhood, with 'no particular issues in the home' his 'distant' relationship with his father, his unhappiness at his marriage ending, his love for his children.

Had it not even crossed her mind that she was being lied to? Had she never come across deceit before? She hadn't asked him about 'rows' between his parents – but no doubt he would not have told her about his mother getting beaten up regularly. Nor had she asked him if his sisters got abused or whether he has been systematically abused, physically and emotionally for years. He'd had a chance to talk about his past with a psychiatrist and all he had done was lie.

But she was a psychiatrist. Almost by definition she was used to working with people who come to her precisely because they need to tell the truth and get help with understanding it – to divulge and tell all and get an expert's help with unravelling the pain.

How could she possibly have the first clue about dealing with someone who was hell bent on hiding the truth?

My solicitor had said to me 'she'll have read all the papers – all the statements'. This was given to me as a reason why we had waited for four months before the assessments could start. I only found out after the assessment that she had read nothing whatsoever. I sent her an email to clarify something I'd said in the interview and referred her to an earlier statement to illustrate. She replied that she had not read any of the statements – that it was her policy not to read anything but just go with what she was told on the day. I had spoken to her in the belief that she knew the case – she had known nothing.

So she had no way of knowing if anything she was told fitted with what had been told before. There was no context for any of the information. Jay could sing like a bird all the merry songs she wished to hear without any risk of being caught out.

For my report, she had not even referred to my concerns about Jay's behaviour or mental stability or his past abuse, his unpredictable rages, throwing things, threats and hitting things, his long-term depression. I had read recently of another case of a parent with depression killing themselves and taking the children with him. At these times in the interview her pen had grown still and I'd thought at the time she would summarise it in her own words. I did not think she would leave it out completely. She had also taken my 'admission' that my parents had had 'rows' when I was a child and drew from this the reasoning that I therefore was not able to 'cope with Jay'!

So it was my fault then. And Jay's tirades of abuse at me over the years had just been, to use his word, 'rows'?

She had done in her report the trick which keeps conjurors and mystics, politicians and newspapers in business. She had taken one factor in the environment and drawn a straight line of causal connection between it and another factor and called, "Ta da!" It's so easy – anyone can play. Try it at home. Think of a thing – anything you like – then think up another thing – then make a line between them as one causing the other. (This only works if it's taken out of reality and this she had certainly done.)

Of millions of people across the world there must be only a handful who would answer 'no' when asked if their parents ever had rows in their childhood. I had been quite clear that there was a difference between these and abusive events. She had asked me that question almost certain of the answer – in order that she could pull her party trick – so was it a foregone conclusion? Why would someone insult her own discipline in this way? Why would someone reduce something which is supposed to be a science to a game of trickery and supposition?

She had set everything I had said in a context of her own making. She had made no effort to understand the context and therefore the meaning of anything which had been said to her. Jay had lied to her for all but half an hour of his interview. For that half hour, he'd chatted to her about the world's religious beliefs. Her report referred to him as 'thoughtful' and 'widely read'.

She was of Asian ethnicity – I could just see him in my mind's eye, the chameleon Jay changing his colours to fit the circumstance – pulling out the file in his head marked 'Asian' and charming her with his knowledge of religions of Bali, of India, of the food or anything else. His knowledge was superficial of course but sufficient to the day's purpose. If she had been Scottish or a Londoner or American or Welsh – he would have pulled the same trick. It was the trick he had pulled with me when we had met. He was good at it – and she didn't have a clue at the web he had spun and into which she had, so willingly, walked.

But would she have wanted to spot it? Her paymasters certainly wouldn't have wanted her to spot he was a liar. Through her, like a spider pulling threads, he was back in control once again – not of me, but of the whole court process.

So I did my best. I went through the report and picked out the parts which, when cross referenced with other statements, by Jay or by his family, could be seen to be totally awry or at least ill founded. It took two days to do this. I typed out the result so it was as clear as day. I was due to have yet another new barrister – the fifth so far in the case – for the Final Hearing. I knew he or she would not be able to get even a slight grip on the case in the time allotted. So I went through Dr F's report and cross-referenced it and prepared questions I knew would help her see what she had missed – questions which, in the Final Hearing would take her, and the court, to the relevant places in Jay's earlier statements or mine or his family's or the police reports or the medical reports – all of which showed him to be a liar again, and again, and again – and what he had told Dr F to be a tissue of lies. After two days and nights of reading and writing and cross referencing and listing I was exhausted but felt ready.

I had an appointment with the new barrister. He was twenty-eight years old. Sharply dressed. He had a tight-fitting brown suit, very designer, very becoming. He didn't want to listen to what I had to say – about Joe, about the psychiatrist, about the work I'd done on the report. He told me the judge would rely on the 'experts' so it was all down to what they said as witnesses. It was all down to the psychologist – Dr Grey – who had listened to what I'd said about the abuse – who had been appointed by my solicitor –

and the psychiatrist, Dr F, who hadn't listened and who had been appointed by Jay's team.

This solicitor, so young, so confident, had very prominent dark eyes which he obviously knew were his best feature in a handsome face. He practiced them on me. I got the strong impression he was used to women being perhaps overwhelmed with his beauty and simpering at him as he gave his instructions. I repeated my concerns and asked him if he would please do his best to dismantle Dr F's report – as, if, we did not do this, the case was lost. He repeated the judge would go with what the 'experts' said and there was little he, or anyone else, could do about it. I tried to talk about my concerns about how Dr F had ignored much of what I had told her and misunderstood others but he interrupted me to repeat, patiently with a hint of sarcasm this time, that the judge would listen to the experts.

I reminded him, as he hadn't mentioned it, about the recording of the interview and that it would make things clear to the court. He agreed it would. He looked annoyed. I decided I did not like his eyes. After our meeting he left, sleek in his well-fitting brown suit, disappearing into the revolving glass doors, smoothly.

'What the experts say.'

And that's what it boils down to. As we allow justice itself to be commodified, we create businesses who pitch not to find out or to expose the truth, or to protect children – but to win. They go all-out to win. And Truth lies bleeding on the battlefield as Mamon rides away triumphant. Evidence is buried or denied or allowed to go 'missing'. Companies in turn employ 'experts' to use as weapons in the war to win – and they in their turn employ the most malleable of weapons to twist, elude and camouflage: they use words.

I told friends about the report and they assured me that the court would look at the recorded tape and see the truth. In her report, for one example, she had said 'during the reading and drawing activity they sat apart'. Joe and I had actually sat next to each other by the paper as we drew – and sat and snuggled as usual when we were reading. She gave the impression – by the use of the word 'apart' – that we had sat at opposite ends of the room or that there was not the closeness between us. She noticeably, to me, had said nothing at all about the seating arrangements between Joe and his father. They had played two board games during the session so presumably had sat 'apart' throughout but this was not deemed worthy of mention.

This, I felt would become clear once the court saw the recording of the sessions. The video would show how her words varied from the truth.

Of the story-stem tests she didn't say much as there was not much to say other than Joe's story endings were not pathological or outside of normal in any way. There was nothing to say –but she had said plenty. She had stated the story-stem results showed nothing unusual – but then went on to hint and elaborate on supposition that 'most children find moving distressing and the court would need to consider this'. As if the court hadn't thought of that!

Of my efforts to make life easier for Joe, of preparing him for departure, of helping him look forward to our next time, of the routine we had both developed to help cope with being apart which had been our reality now for two whole years, all she said was, 'when they parted there were no tears'.

Did she really expect tears as if we were parting for our first 200 times? Did she not see the work we both did to make the parting less painful? Of Joe's earnest whispered statement, said well within her hearing, as we parted, 'I love you big as all the sky' – she said nothing at all.

A friend sent me an article. It was about a psychiatrist having been found guilty, recently, in Britain, of falsifying reports on parents in order that their children were taken from them and put up for adoption. It had been found he had had financial benefit from this. I was glad he had been caught. I did not know how he had been exposed. I do not know what his sentence was or if he had even received one for this gross inhumanity. I cried for the mothers and fathers of those children and for those children. I cried for myself. But at least I wasn't at risk in that way. I had the recorded tapes – they would reveal all.

In desperation I had recorded, on a dictaphone, Joe crying at the end of one weekend – as we went through the hell of parting after two days together. "I don't want to go back! I don't want to go back! I want to go home!" His whole body shaking as he clung onto me. Then me persuading him it would be okay, it would be alright, he had to go back. I had no choice. I had rung CAFCASS and asked for help and been told there was nothing we can do until the assessments. The assessment took place during my visits to Joe after school – Joe being quite used to the brief two hours we had together – but CAFCASS were never there on the Sundays. So I recorded it. I had prayed for help and the idea came to me so clearly as what I needed to do I thought it was a message from God. Many of the people who were supporting me at this time had deep religious conviction and told me how they had had help and told me to put my faith in God and pray for help. So I did.

I went to the IT shop with my dad and he bought me a dictaphone and the next Sunday I switched it on as we pulled into the car park where the 'handover' had to happen as usual. I had the tape with me when I met the new barrister in his tight suit.

But at the meeting, the barrister, in another smart designer suit in a slightly different shade of brown, probably chosen especially to match his eyes, wasn't interested. He told me the judge would think I'd told Joe frightening things about what Daddy was going to do in order to scare him into being upset. The recording was useless.

He wasn't much interested in the questions I'd written – fourteen of them – to be put by him to the psychiatrist to pull apart her report. He said the judge wouldn't be much interested in them either.

That was another recurring theme: what was and was not of interest to the judge at any one time. It was as if the judge was this sleeping morass of lethargy who could only be sparked into wakefulness by dramatic antics and fireworks otherwise all the subtleties of life, of abuse, of pain, of a child's life, was just one big massive bore to which it was tiresome to pay attention. The case seemed less about discovering reality and more about striving to catch the judge's attention and keep him awake.

Like a Rip Van Winkle of the law he dozed, waking occasionally into a world he struggled to recognise. I did meet, in one lesser hearing, a judge who listened and seemed to know something about domestic abuse: he actually challenged Jay's barrister on some points and referred to something he'd actually read in a statement! I was so amazed at this unprecedented event, I told Anna about it. We speculated that his Yorkshire – sounding name hinted at a life maybe less deafened by comfort, less blinded by its own privilege. It had only been one of the Directions Hearings and my usual hero of the law had been elsewhere but I had seen that not all judges are the same.

During the endless hearings, where I'd sit at the back of the court while others discussed our lives, I had sunk into the habit of a spectator – I was never required to speak – and I couldn't help, as we'd all rise to show respect as the judge entered in his gown, the tones of 10cc sounding in my head or, worse, 'here comes the judge, here comes the judge'. I wondered if the others in the court, the sycophants in suits, had the same problem.

When everything you care about or which gives meaning to you and your life and the rest of reality is stripped away or forced from you – there is a reaction. It is not possible to go on in the same way. It is not possible to carry on believing in things you once believed in. I had spent twenty years of my life working for social services. I believed I was part of a force for good – for helping folk in trouble.

That belief had been shattered into a million pieces by two callous liars who were out for revenge or so blinded by their own arrogance and prejudice they could not see or hear. I had believed in the justice system – to some degree. Yes, it had its faults but it was full of people who meant well and who did their best, I was sure. I had believed in myself. I had believed I was helping Jay, that he could not help the dreadful rages and temper tantrums and that he had blackouts which caused him to behave in dangerous, hateful ways over which he had no control.

When I read the psychiatrist and psychologist's reports, I encountered a different Jay – the real one. Cold-bloodedly, calculatingly lying – about his life, about me, about Joe. And my belief, as I saw how Dr F had cherry picked what I had said to slant the report to damn me, and had believed verbatim everything Jay had fed her – my belief in the system dissolved utterly. There was nothing for me to stand on anymore.

The image I'd had of myself, as a capable, intelligent, strong, loving and caring person, also lay bleeding.

Instead, I'd spent the best part of my adult life as part of a crass machine which took children from loving parents and placed them with abusers. I was an idiotic doormat who had been taken in completely by a two-bit conman out for sex and an easy life of no work and plenty of money who had just spotted the weakness of his 'mark' and used them. He must have been laughing up his sleeve as he pretended to have 'blackouts' and 'rages' and watched me cowering and obeying his every whim.

Instead of the caring, helpful woman, I was left knowing I was nothing but a shallow, easily tricked, naïve pushover who was also arrogant enough to think I could 'help' such a person as Jay. Me! Teams of mental health workers, as he'd told me (although that might be another lie), and therapists, he'd told me, had failed but I, I would be able to help because 'my love was so strong'?

I loathed myself. I thought I had known loneliness before but when you no longer have yourself in your own life – that is loneliness indeed.

The human brain has a function to compensate for our lack of claws and strength – it is to make sense of our environment and feed back to the brain to instigate action. But when our environment does not make sense, when we are surrounded by lies and the feedback to the brain can produce no action to rectify the situation – because the person is powerless – there is no longer any function for the mind. The feedback loops back on itself as the person cannot respond or act – there is nothing which can be done. The function of the mind begins to become useless and, as did the appendix, when we no longer needed to digest leaves and twigs as we swung down from the trees, begins to atrophy as it is no longer needed. I felt myself teetering on the edge. Each morning I'd wake up at the bottom of the pit of snakes, spend the day dragging myself up to the rim, teetering around it and falling back in as night fell.

Suicide was not an option although it had beckoned for a while. Joe would grow up and one day would want to know why his mother had abandoned him. If I killed myself he wouldn't even have the precious short times of being able to play and laugh and not be afraid of his dad's temper. No doubt Jay liked controlling Joe as much as he'd enjoyed controlling me.

I've never been religious. Not as an adult. As a child I'd thought Jesus was an ideal to live up to – the giving, loving ideal who looked after others. But in later life this was just what I saw in people – some people. It didn't have to be religion. It was just human nature at its best. It was also human nature despite the pressures of this system to be greedy, fixated on material things and aggressive. Capital needs those things – greed, materialism, aggression – to further its markets – but people don't. People turn to religion because they want the world to be fairer – and that want, like hunger telling us there is such a thing as food, tells us that human nature's needs are not met in a world of injustice and cruelty.

But with all my beliefs smashed, I had nothing to cling onto. Friends assured me that God was watching and that all would be well. They gave me examples of when God had intervened directly in their lives and brought them safely home. He had left a message or given a sign which they had followed and all had turned out well. All I needed was faith.

I prayed fervently, hoping to hear from God, any god, to help me, to help Joe. But, of all the gods we have invented, is there one who sits in the celestial corner and shrugs?

I started going to church trying to find something to make sense of what was happening to me. I prayed regularly for Joe to be protected. I still believed that the dictaphone would help in some way. A friend assured me that the judge would want to hear it and would be interested if I had enough faith and asked him.

But the barrister assured me I'd be done for contempt of court if I didn't follow court procedure.

Maybe that was why Jesus, according to the Bible, kept schtum in the court of Pontius Pilate. We'd had hearing after hearing where I was not required to speak. The barristers in their designer suits would exchange words and simper at the judge and sit down again and a decision would be made and we'd all leave. I'd written reams of statements but hadn't heard any of them referred to by anybody. It didn't seem to matter whether I spoke or not.

I'd got used to sitting at the back of the court watching it all as if it was nothing to do with me at all. My mind would wander. I speculated on how the little, spikey-looking, hairy wigs they all wore got washed. Were they washing-machine proof? Wool cycle maybe? I wondered when the tradition had started for the judge to wear the flamboyant, big red cape? Unbidden, tunes would play in my head and I'd hum them under my breath: irreverent tunes: 10cc's 'Good morning Judge how are you today?' and 'here comes the judge, here comes the judge, look out everybody cos here comes the judge!'

I had originally felt concern at the judge's health – he was too florid so I felt he should stay off the claret and take more exercise. I hoped he didn't have emotional problems which weighed on his heart – as shiatsu teaches emotional problems often do.

But too many hearings had eroded away any such

concern. He had little enough concern for Joe, after all, and none for me. When we are concerned about something, we take an interest, we want to know, we are curious – we stay awake.

Chapter 13

---·+··❈··+·---

The Final Hearing was in the same court as all the hearings thus far had been: a bland red room in wood and velvet high up inside the court building so outside the windows were the tops of other buildings.

No-one could see in. Clever architect.

The experts gave evidence first. Dr Grey was to speak. I had high hopes of her sticking to her analysis of my having been the target of mental torture for some years and that this would give the judge a clue about the risks to Joe. But she seemed to have changed her mind.

My twenty-eight-year-old hero in his tight-fitting suit and big eyes, asked her two or three questions about Jay's depression affecting his care of Joe. Jay was flummoxed by this and floundered for an answer. His barrister, smiling like a skull, stepped in graciously and prompted him to say he would, of course, take Joe to his sister's should a depression attack arrive. I had thought that leading questions were not allowed in the court or that lawyers and barristers were not allowed to tell clients the answers but the judge did not object, nor did My Hero who sat, apparently pondering deeper matters.

The judge slumbered peacefully on.

One of the worst aspects of depression is that many people suffering from it do not get 'oh I'm suffering from depression' insight – unless they have a lot of insight into their illness. Jay had already said, "I probably won't get depressed any more," which showed he had no such insight at all. I reminded Lizard of this but he just shushed me and smiled apologetically at the judge.

I wasn't very worried as I knew that the statements from all the witnesses who had seen what he was like when in a rage were on the file and the judge had already read them. The transcript from the criminal trial, with Jay telling obvious lies about kicking the car was on there too. So were the letters from two of his previous partners – neither of them strong on its own but together they told the true story of what Jay was like.

Dr Felicity answered blandly about the possible risks to Joe. I'd told my barrister that Jay had been lying to her for all but half an hour of his time with Dr Felicity. He'd misunderstood me and accused her of only meeting with him for half an hour. He turned to me looking annoyed when she disagreed with this. He looked like a sleek predator rounding on a possible prey. I had to agree the meeting had been for two hours – it wasn't until later I remembered why the 'two hours' worth of information' was a fallacy. Of the fifteen questions I'd asked my sleek hero in brown to ask Dr Felicity, to pull apart her report, he asked three.

I wondered when he was going to ask for the video to be showed so the judge could see for himself the difference between what she had said and what had actually happened in the little library that day.

CAFCASS also seemed to have changed her tune – from supporting Joe being returned to me asap, now, after Dr F's magical report, this was no longer seen as necessary.

Jay gave evidence. My hero had spent time looking through Jay's statements and matching up all the lies and contradictions in nearly everything he had said – and he took Jay and the court through these. I was so pleased at this tactic – he was showing the court that Jay was a habitual, abject liar – this would be seen as undermining everything he had told the 'experts'. The judge would surely realise nothing Jay had told the 'experts' could be relied on.

In the break I thanked my barrister, my hero for doing this – but then he grimaced and said he didn't think it was enough to convince the judge. He was quite complacent when he said this. Then he licked his lips and looked at me with half-lidded eyes, his hands resting on the table, drumming his fingers. The sun shone through the window behind him – shining down yellow highlights on his tight-fitting brown suit. He licked his lips and smiled at me again with his thin lips. He looked all the world like a sleek lizard which had just swallowed a nice juicy mayfly.

So why spend your time on a strategy that isn't going to work? He explained that 'cases like this' always rest on what the 'expert' witnesses say. I said, "But what about when the experts have been told things which aren't true? Or when they are saying things which aren't true? What about when experts are basing their analyses on lies – when they don't know it? And when is the video going to be shown?"

He looked impatient. "They won't let us do that." He said it as if the question was an annoying and inedible insect which had buzzed into the room.

Later when I remembered why the 'two-hour interview' was a fallacy I went to find him – we were in another break. He came out of the room where he was reading and interrupted my hurried explanation with a nastily patient repetition of, "This case will be, as I have tried to explain, decided by what the experts say. I'm working on another case now as there's nothing else I can do about this one." He went back into the room, his long legs flicking behind him through the door like a tail.

So, the entire court was being controlled by the abuser. Jay met with 'experts' and charmed and lied to them the same way he charmed and lied to his other victims. The legal teams were in their turn beholden and in awe of these duped 'experts' – or comfortable about leaving them to do the work – and let their repetition or 'analyses' of the abuser's lies permeate the court and carry the day, while the judge watched.

We live so naively, believing the people in charge are able and competent. The depressing thing is, when you meet them, they are depressingly ignorant – and arrogant in their comfortable ignorance. The mistakes they make do not mess up their lives.

In the criminal court, fingerprint tests, tests for chemicals, photographs, identity parades – all could be taken out of context. The results of scientific tests can be taken as applying where they do not apply – and innocent people imprisoned for years. In the family court, assessments of deliberate liars, analyses of their lies – does the same job.

The Birmingham Six spent many, many years in prison because results to a test which were ambiguous were reported as not being ambiguous. Ditto Guildford Four and probably countless others.

Dr F was instructed by the legal team representing Jay to do her assessment. No doubt they supplied her with a lot of work and a regular income. Her status carried a lot of weight with the other professionals – is a CAFCASS officer going to argue with a psychiatrist? Is a psychologist?

Do any of them have a chance in the hands of a real expert like a Jay? Jay played them all like a puppet-master plays his toys. And the judge danced along with it all.

All Dr F had said was that the 'Story Stem' tests had not shown anything significant about Joe – that was all she had to say – but then she had gone on to say, in her report, that the court 'would have to consider the possibility of Joe being upset at leaving his school' – as if no-one else had thought of that – and made other bland generalisations about children needing security –none of which anyone could argue with.

She didn't need to prove that any of this applied to Joe – she just needed to imply that it did. Like the head of a media empire out to destroy a reputation – she didn't need to prove it – she just needed to print it.

Her report was a tide of general vague statements which swept any detail or specific evidence away – and this was allowed because she was an 'expert'. 'This is true sometimes – therefore it must be true now.'

The scientist whose evidence put the Birmingham Six away for the best part of their lives was also played like this by the prosecution – using this approach and misuse of science. This one took Joe's childhood away.

The theory of the survival of the fittest tells us that in any given environment, the creature most fit to that environment will be the one to survive and to dominate. On the savannah, we get the ultimate beauty of the cheetah and the wonder of our own origins. Unfortunately, in the filth and slime environment of pond life, we get the horse-leech – which slithers its way through life, swallowing baby frogs whole and sucking the blood of other creatures.

In the environment of the family court, we get Dr F.

My turn came to give evidence. I noticed Jay's barrister was asking him to change his seat. I realised why when I reached the witness stand. Looking at the barrister who was to question me, I had to look directly at Jay, just over her shoulder. No doubt she knew that and how difficult it is to face our abusers. I tried to ignore the fact he was there. Image of his past treatment of me kept coming to mind.

And where in that court were my peers – the ordinary people who knew what it was like to be scared? I was surrounded by people who were in the 'intelligence' trap – they believed in the concept of 'intelligence' and, as intelligent people, they therefore believed that everything they thought was true as they passed judgement on a world they knew nothing of. That arrogance, believing themselves to know better, blinded them to understanding someone else's world, another life beyond their ken. Once, one of the barristers had said to me, "You must have been very scared – after he smashed the car up." This was the one solitary time I felt any of them had shown any intelligence about what had happened to me. She was only there for one hearing. The others constantly referred to my being 'angry' or of having 'a long fuse' – they were getting their information from somewhere but it wasn't from me. I did talk to them but saw dull, switched-off eyes and closed faces. Again and again I had explained and told what had happened – and received blank looks. Eyes are redundant when they do not need to see as the mind is already made up. We cannot see what we cannot comprehend. People who gain their eyesight after a lifetime of blindness have to learn how to use it to make sense of their world. The barristers did not need to learn or to see – they knew it all.

Jay's barrister, the Skull I had dubbed her because she looked like one – especially when she bared her teeth in what she obviously thought to be a smile, led me in the 'bundle' to a statement I hadn't seen before. It was by Sophie, Chloe's mother, Jay's ex-partner in the north-west. It spoke glowingly of Jay as a wonderful partner and philosophical person. I could see, in my mind's eye, Jay standing and dictating it to her, probably sitting at the same table where I'd sat and begged for help.

"But surely this contradicted the letter she sent me?" I asked the judge.

"What letter?" he said, looking even blanker than usual – itself, something of an achievement.

I explained about the letter Sophie had sent – one of two letters from Jay's previous partners – that were on file. Jay's legal team objected. The bundle was gone through. No letter. The CAFCASS officer found a copy I'd given her and the judge read it: it didn't say anything of what she had told me when we had met – but it mentioned her leaving Jay and going to Women's Aid for refuge. There was no copy of Wendy's letter to help it along. That was missing too. I became aware my breathing had become difficult.

The Skull and Jay had a whispered consultation and then Jay eventually said that Sophie had only gone to Women's Aid to get help with finding a new house when they had split up. I said the other letters would show the full meaning of this one. But no-one could find the other letters.

I wanted to object – as Women's Aid don't provide a rehousing service and Sophie had hinted enough in her letter that she didn't go there for this reason but because she was needing to get away from Jay urgently – but Lizard told me the judge wasn't interested He said, "The judge knows Women's Aid will believe anything a woman tells them." He said this with a sneer. As he turned away, I couldn't swear he hadn't just licked his eyes.

The statement by Chloe also told the court how I had said 'sorry' to her – and Skull explained how that was evidence that I had done wrong. I tried to explain how I'd said sorry that they had been told about Jay being nearly dead when he hadn't been anything of the sort – the judge ignored me. No-one else paid any attention to what I'd just said.

I looked at Lizard: twenty-eight years old, rich, complacent, stagnant in his belief in his own universal intelligence – and he didn't have a clue. In his comfy little world, people who are abused are all liars.

Lizard had spent the last afternoon muttering, "We're running out of time," which only added to the anxiety I had before I had to give evidence. There was so much I had to say to challenge what had gone before I didn't know where to begin. I'd spent the night before trying to write it all down so I wouldn't forget any of it – to no avail. When I was called into the box and tried to explain – the judge insisted that I only respond to questions. Much was made of my mother being ill with dementia and Skull told me that this was traumatic for Joe. I was confused as Joe took my mum's illness in his stride – he was bemused at her being sleepy all the time but not traumatised – but because Skull asserted this so confidently I was thrown into doubt. Was he traumatised? Wouldn't I have noticed that? Why weren't they concerned about him being traumatised by being frightened and bullied by his dad?

Were these people wanting to help Joe or not?

Dr F's report of what Joe had said to her was reported: what he had said earlier to CAFCASS somehow never saw daylight. She had asked him three wishes – and he had said about dinosaurs.

As a practitioner, I knew that children can stay in

'play mode' during an interview. To let them know that this is a serious business, the interviewer needs to tell them something like 'now this is serious now, and I need to know what you really think'. This helps to engage the 'adult' and 'serious thinking' of the child as distinct from 'play mode'.

There was no evidence she had done this – she had just asked what he'd like to change in three wishes, in the middle of playfully chatting about his hobbies and games he liked. Fun, fun, fun! She had given him no hint that they had moved from play mode to 'serious' or important mode. For his wishes, he talked of live dinosaurs he'd like to see – and this was taken as evidence that he would not want to move back to live with his mother.

Well played, Dr F. Hope your pay-packet had a bonus for that one. I wonder how many times she had used that tactic to silence the children given over to her care; how many children had played with 'the nice lady' and laughed with her and never been given the chance to tell what really mattered to them. Well played, Dr F.

And may you burn in Hell.

Her use of science was like that of Erich von Daniken, who, in the 70s had misled an entire public by cherry-picking details from old sculptures and pictures and making them fit his thesis: that aliens had landed and led ancient civilisations. Fortunately, others had later looked at the evidence and found that the pictures did not represent extra-terrestrial astronauts or airfields. But no-one looked at Dr F's work.

The Skull, Jay's barrister, had gone through all my statements and now put them to good use: the Lizard challenged none of this as, new to the case and disinclined to put too many hours into it, he didn't spot the deceits. She quoted part-sentences to misrepresent what I had said in previous statements: my reassurance to the court, for example, that I would stay in the same village and Joe would stay at the same school even if my parents died and I needed to move (which I had explained to address any concerns about Joe having to move school again should he move back with me), she re-interpreted as meaning I was 'already planning to move'.

No-one could possibly have misunderstood my meaning from reading the statement – she achieved this by quoting out of context and leaving out the other halves of the sentences she thus lifted. Eh voila – for my next trick! Anything taken out of context can be made to mean anything else – and this she did. This was how she made her living. She carried on doing it. Everything I had written was twisted to mean its opposite. It was a disgusting spectacle.

By the time I got into the dock there were too many points to come back on. Lizard asked me two or three questions then sat down and said nothing as Skull took over.

Skull prompted Jay about the statements I'd made of what Joe had said to me – about running upstairs and hiding under the bed when his daddy 'was shouting' – and Jay was able to tell the court that Joe was only talking of playing a game they had invented where Jay 'shouted like a dinosaur'. As if Joe could not tell the difference between shouting and a dinosaur roaring. As if I could not tell when he was upset and when he was describing a game. But the judge nodded as if this all made perfect sense.

One line of attack was that I couldn't be afraid of Jay as I came into the area where he lived in order to see Joe. This woman, a barrister in the family courts did not, apparently, know what Domestic Abuse was – i.e. it's **domestic**. It happens *inside* houses – not on the streets – that's why it's called DOMESTIC: the clue is in the name. I looked at my barrister to point this out but he was looking elsewhere.

She seemed to think it was the same as fighting in the street or a riot. I had always felt safe in the streets and where there were other people around as Jay rarely got angry and then only slightly, when there were others about. She did not seem to know this or to consider that, to see my child, I would have gone anywhere and done anything.

I tried to explain all this but the judge was nodding in agreement with what she was saying. I couldn't think why the judge, knowing what he knew, would nod at what she was saying. I guessed he was showing encouragement and listening to both sides.

Basically, the family court seemed to think that the three-day trial by the criminal court had all been a mistake.

"She never got an injunction. No restraining order – nothing," said the barrister, the one I thought of as the Skull, as I stood in the dock, the judge nodding. This was evidently proof. One can always rely on a piece of paper to protect you from someone. Especially when that someone is an SAS-trained exsquaddie who has lived outside the law most of his life, despises the police and all they do, is familiar with violence in general and killing on occasion. Especially when that person gets in a bout of a rage and doesn't always know what he is doing – especially when people leave him or otherwise fail to meet his needs. Needs that were never met.

I looked at the barrister and wondered if she'd ever needed help from the police? Had she ever been scared?

There were reasons I hadn't looked for their help: the memories came to me:

I was living in a flat at the top of a house which had been converted into flats. It was gloomy and pigeon crap occasionally fell in through the kitchen roof, but it was home. The landlord occasionally sent round his drunk cousin to fix gas leaks, or whatever repairs we had told him about, but we usually managed to keep him out and then make our own arrangements to get things mended. It was safer. The house had been glamorous in its day in the last century.

On the ground floor, there were two small flats next door to each other. One was occupied by a white guy, Will, who was always drunk, and the other by a black guy, Cliff, who was always sober. Once, Will had had his electricity cut off for not paying the bills. I came home to see a long, white, plastic-coated extension lead threading out of the window of Cliff's flat – delivering electricity into Will's place. A few days later the police were there and it seemed Cliff was getting arrested. I heard Cliff protest, "His power's cut off! The man's gotta live!!"

That remained with me as the basic statement of life versus the greed of a system which always puts money first – "The man's gotta live!"

Anyway, things were made legal once more and life went on as before. Cliff, apparently, had had a few run-ins with the police in his life. He was the only black guy in the house of flats.

A student moved into the room below mine in the flat on the next floor down. He took to playing his television very, very loud at all hours of the night and in the early hours. Sometimes this was not a problem as I was sleeping over in my work in the children's homes at the time. Sometimes it was a problem as I'd be turned out of much needed sleep at 3am by the latest blockbuster on at full blast. Even my flatmates in the other rooms, not directly above his, were woken up at times and wondered what we could do.

As I was the one directly above it seemed I had the most to complain about so I did. I went downstairs the next day, knocked on the door and, when he answered it, told him he played his television too loud at night and could he please keep it down? He looked bored and insulted as if listening to petty requests were way beneath him. He closed the door in my face after saying, "I like it loud."

My flatmates took turns to go and complain on subsequent nights with similar, and ruder, responses from him.

I took to going downstairs to complain when I'd been woken up thinking maybe this would prompt his flatmates into asking him to keep it down. No response. I left notes. I asked again, less politely. I explained about work, shifts, the need to sleep. The work I did. The fact that I was often awake all night at work. He smirked – and closed the door.

The best I could do then was to thump, pathetically, on the floor, when I was woken in the early hours by film dialogue echoing around my room, hoping this would at least interfere with whatever crap he was watching at two in the morning. He turned it up. I still kept thumping on the floor – for the sake of doing something rather than expecting any good result. I started looking around for another flat. I started looking at his car, parked in the front, and wondering what you would get for puncturing all four tyres.

One night, it happened again, really loud television, on what must have been full volume and I woke up and thumped on the floor in annoyance. The next thing was, he came charging out of the flat downstairs, stamped up the short stairway, kicked the door to our flat open, breaking the lock, and kicked open the door of my room.

He shouted abuse and said he'd hit me over the head with the television if I ever banged on his ceiling again Then he banged out of the flat, a pane of glass broke in the door as he passed and he went back down to his own flat. I think he had the whole flat to himself as we never saw any other people there. My three flatmates all came out of their rooms and were shocked – as I was. They all suggested I call the police. I said no as that might make the situation worse. They all said that no, it wouldn't, and that what he had just done was breaking and entering and threatening violence and he shouldn't get away with it. It was appalling the way he carried on keeping us all awake and it was time something was done. My friend dialled the number.

I spoke to the police and explained that the guy who lives downstairs had just threatened me with violence and kicked in the door of our flat. There were three other witnesses beside myself. The police asked for the address and seemed very interested. I went downstairs to meet them, surprised at how quickly they had come out to respond to the call.

There were two of them and they were very keen. Their eyes were shining with enthusiasm. I was impressed and ashamed of my earlier cynicism. They said they knew this house and had been here before and it was the guy on the ground floor, wasn't it?

"We'll arrest him – breaking and entering, wasn't it? Breach of the peace. Threatening behaviour. Oh yes!"

I corrected them – no, it wasn't the guy on the ground floor – it was the guy on the middle floor.

They hesitated in the doorway to the house. They looked at each other uncertainly then back to me. Which flat? I repeated – the one on the first floor. My room was on the second floor – his room was below mine. The light went out in their eyes.

"It isn't that Cliff then?"

It was like I'd taken away all their toys at Christmas, for being naughty.

"And what does he look like?" asked one of them, and the penny dropped.

I described the student – he had light brown wavy

hair, about six foot, slim build. They completely lost interest.

They looked me up and down, in my dressing gown as I was, with something like contempt. Somehow, the fact that the guy who had done this had 'brown hair' changed the situation completely. Black people don't have light brown hair.

"Okay," they said, "we'll have a word with him."

A word? What had happened to 'breaking and entering and breach of the peace'? What happened to 'we'll arrest him'?

I went back to the flat and my flatmates and we all leaned over the banisters to hear what the police said to the thug downstairs. We heard them knock and he answered and we heard a quiet, very respectful murmuring. Then they said, "Goodnight sir," (sir!) and then they came back up to our flat. We all piled back into the kitchen ahead of them.

The police came in – they looked me up and down again and said, "So he's your boyfriend then?" I gaped and said no! And my flatmates shouted this down, one repeating the scenario which had happened that night and asked, weren't they going to arrest him? The police looked bored and said that that would not be necessary and left. The sneers never left their mouths. They were suddenly fed up at having been called out to no purpose.

We talked, desultorily. My flatmates were as disappointed as I was. I told them what they had been like on arrival – keen, bit between teeth, intent on arrest, reeling off charges. We all knew, if it had been Cliff – the only black guy in the house – who had been so rude and threatening, he would have been dragged off and charged. Because the thug was a white guy with the right accent – he was immune. He probably knew this and would know it all his bullying life.

Another time I'd called the police…

A shift at the children's home. Everyone placed there was fourteen plus, and the maximum age for anyone placed there was eighteen. Over eighteens had to be placed in the adult prison system – a police cell or remand. Most of the children I helped to look after were scared teenagers with a lot of bravado and acting tough as their lives so far had made it necessary for them to be.

They would swear and yell and steal stuff and fight each other and threaten worse. They looked out for each other. They appreciated kindness and not being lied to or talked down to. They had all been badly let down by the world they were born to. Many were on their way to court so were placed with us after being arrested. The adult world was a scary, dangerous, threatening place and they would have to be part of it soon.

Then part of it came to stay a while.

It was a ruse among some criminals to give a false date of birth so as to appear to be under eighteen – that way, instead of being placed in a cell or remand centre the police had to place you in a children's home or children's remand centre – which were easier to escape from, until they could verify your identity. And one who had pulled this stunt arrived at our place.

He looked like serious trouble the minute he arrived. Any idiot could see the adult musculature in his face and hands, the heavy build, the beer belly – you can't get a beer belly in your teens – the five o'clock shadow. The other kids – or, I should say, the kids, took one look and most of them left the building. He emanated violence. He had a cold stare with dead eyes. Our youngsters may try and emulate that stare in their efforts to cope but theirs was ersatz – his was real.

He started to chat to two of the young girls in the home and offer them cigarettes. Nervously they played up to him. He told one of the young lads to 'fuck off'. Bravely, this lad gave it back and the big guy went for him. He pushed me out of the way as if I wasn't there. I was used to bravado and mutual 'ragging' between them, especially when somebody new arrived and they all needed to show they weren't afraid – but this was different. The young lad ran into a cupboard on the landing and the guy, the adult male, went after him twisting the handle out of shape in an attempt to break it open.

I told him to get away from it or I'd call the police. He smirked at me and went through into the lounge. I didn't feel we could protect our young people as he was bigger than any of us and seemed used to violence. It was also creepy that he was chatting up the girls who were obviously underage and vulnerable teenagers. My colleague went to call the police to ask for him to be removed as he had already attacked one of the other residents. He seemed out to impress the young teenage girls who kept safe by staying on his good side, smiling. But one of them asked me, out of his earshot, "How are you going to stop him getting into our rooms tonight?"

They were not naïve. Life had already robbed them of that.

He went for one of the teenage lads – maybe to show us all how tough he was – maybe to frighten the girls. He held him up by the collar against the wall and threatened him. The lad was terrified. He gave him what money he had and all his cigarettes and the man dropped him. Man? He was a man by age but not in any other way. He was just a big bully. A big, dangerous bully. Real men don't frighten children.

The police arrived. Four of them. He was upstairs in his allocated room. We told them what he had done so far and what our fears were. They asked for the names of the boys he had threatened. We told them. The police then relaxed and smiled and asked to speak to him. I realised they were not going to remove him. He came downstairs, offered them all cigarettes and they accepted and they all stood and chatted, all pals together.

The boys' names we had given, the ones whom he had attacked – were all Asian, Moslem, black Afro-Caribbean, or white kids who were well known to the police. That was why they did not want to remove him. They found it amusing that a big white guy would frighten them and chat up underage girls. He was white so they wouldn't touch him. If he'd been black he'd've been dragged out of there and probably had his picture in the papers by morning.

As the police were leaving, the big guy smirking round at us, I put the word round that I was offering an outing in the minibus and all could come who wanted to – I didn't have to say – 'but don't tell him' – no-one did. Minutes later, the minibus was full without a single kid left behind. The two girls did one better – they invited him upstairs and then ran around the maze of corridors and down and out into the minibus – leaving him blundering about upstairs.

'Quick, Cathy, step on it!'' – and we pulled away before anyone had their belts on – looking out of the back window to see if he was in pursuit – elated by our escape A colleague came with me and off we drove.

We went for miles to the nearest beach and hung out there, chatting. The kids were shaken and so was I and we all did our best to hide it and reassure each other. I phoned the 'unit' and was told he'd got bored and disappeared out into the night. We came back and locked the door and I made them all cocoa.

Human beings are one of the few species who can bond with youngsters not biologically ours as much as we bond with 'our own'. It was years before I learned that on a training course but, working with these youngsters, I'd known it to be true long before.

And, another time…

The Nazis had set up a bookshop. It was in the part of London where Stephen Lawrence had been murdered a few months previously. The bookshop gave the Nazis confidence – it gave them a base. Fascists accepted onto council property! So we marched. It took weeks to arrange the delegations and agree the route and sell tickets for the coaches. The police blocked the route. One of the march's leaders had blood running down her face as she addressed the crowd, having been truncheoned. As we retreated, to regroup another day, police pushed us over the fence. We had to climb over a low fence to get clear of the area. As we balanced at the top, the police would push us, grinning inside their riot helmets. They then charged the stragglers and many were hurt.

And...

A friend was being attacked in her flat by her ex-partner. To be exact, he was coming through the door with an axe. She rang the police and they asked her, "Do you know him?" and she'd said yes. They then told her, "We don't get involved in domestics," and rang off. Her neighbours got her – and her baby – out of the flat, via the window before he was able to hack his way through the door frame.

But also...

More recently than any of the above, I'd been attending meetings at work with police and other agencies about protection plans around people on the run from their partners. One had gone wrong – she was dead. Where would we put the children?

And other meetings at work about a guy who had broken the restriction imposed on him by a restraining order and who was now at large in the area where his ex-partner now lived. He had served his sentence for attacking her and had said he wanted revenge. She was trying to find somewhere safe to go to. The police had told him to stay away but he had been sighted in the area.

But also...

I was at an anti-poll-tax demo outside the town hall with hundreds of other people chanting, "No poll tax!" but not hurting anybody. Police charged the crowd with batons drawn. Three piled onto a young black man near to me and he's on the ground choking. I try to push the top police officer off the pile, to reduce the weight piled on the young man underneath – and he swipes at me with a truncheon. They get up, arresting him. He's done nothing more than what we are all doing. Some of us run to sit in front of the van to stop the people inside being taken away but we're not organised enough and the van hurtles away.

And before that…

It was the early eighties. A friend returns from Wapping – they had been trying to stop the mass loss of jobs. She is shaken by what she saw there. Police charging repeatedly, attacking folk. Grown men in tears of shock, having believed in the police force all their lives, unable to believe what they were now seeing.

And before that…

Mid-eighties. Miners' villages under uniformed occupation. Striking miners fighting for their livelihoods and those of their children. Policemen waving wads of overtime under their noses and laughing and truncheoning them to the ground. The female photographer as she stands defenceless against the charging mounted policeman raising his riot stick high as he charges at her.

So… the barrister asked rhetorically, why hadn't I gone to the police if I was scared? It was not my time to speak as the reasons crowded through my mind.

…People like judges and barristers don't know

that their system doesn't work. They don't know that, because it works, so well, for them. They don't live in houses which are overcrowded or with thin walls. They don't go on marches to try and stop Nazis organising in an area and preparing to kill young men at bus stops. They don't use bus stops and nor do their sons. They don't live behind doors which break after one kick or in areas where police don't arrive for weeks, or where insurance companies refuse to provide cover. They hardly ever have black skin or friends with black skin and so don't draw the attention of racists – in or out of uniform. They never, ever have to fight to defend their working conditions or their jobs.

They are well fed by the system they serve. They do not know its underbelly reality, only its sleek, well-groomed upper façade.

So they could not understand why someone would not run to the police if they felt in danger. They had no idea that, to many, the police do not seem a safe haven but quite the reverse. I was judged on not seeing them as able and willing to protect me and this was presented as evidence that I had not been afraid. No-one asked me why I had not gone to them for help or for a piece of paper to keep Jay in awe. They all took it as evidence that Jay had never frightened or threatened me. If I had gone to the police, what would have happened? Would they have believed me? Would there have been any evidence? How easily would he have charmed them round? And where would they have put Joe and me where we would be safe?

Would a piece of paper have kept us safe?

I'd learned something of the forces of law and

order. Jay knew more plus he had learned a thing or two about the army.

Jay had trained in the army for eight years. Part of his training was in 'Intelligence' – particularly how to cope under interrogation. The training showed the different techniques used by interrogators.

He found this training about intelligence methods very useful in his later life. After leaving the army and embarking on a life of drug-dealing he would sometimes be arrested. He would then be questioned. Jay quite enjoyed these times as he would watch the police use the various techniques and be amused to see that the police did not realise that he knew what they were doing.

He liked to play them at their own game. He liked to let them think he was falling for the 'good cop, bad cop' routine or whichever they used. Then he would lay a false trail. He would apparently let slip a piece of information or give a hint, as if unintentionally, about something they wanted to know – as if unaware of the significance of what he had said. Then he'd laugh to himself to see the police conferring, excitedly, and one leave to follow up this 'lead' while the other one offered tea or cleverly changed the subject so as not to let the naïve prisoner realise that he had given them a clue.

One time, for example, when he was apprehended and taken in for questioning and searched, in his pocket were the keys to the car, which was parked elsewhere in the city with the takings hidden within. The police questioned him about a lot of things. But, Jay noticed, they didn't ask about the car. He left the police station and knew not to go back to the car.

They had given him his keys back and waved him off, smiling.

He had lead the plainclothes 'tail' they'd put on him on a two-hundred-mile false trail by bus and train – for the fun of it. He'd passed on the keys to an accomplice who had emptied the car boot but had left the car where it was in case it had been reported. As far as he knew, it was still there. He didn't know when he'd stopped being tailed. Most people would have felt relieved and smug at coming through the questioning and being released without charge and gone back to the car – and been arrested with significant amounts of money or drugs – I forget which – found in their possession. But not Jay.

Just one time he had come close to being caught – through being careless. He had hired a car to take some 'supplies' across the country. This was normal practice and served to hide the trail if ever a car was stopped and searched. It was normal practice among the drug-running fraternity to use a false ID when hiring a car and to give a false name, etc. He delivered the drugs and returned the car to the car-hire office – but the police had been called and were waiting for him.

There had been something wrong with the passport he had used and the car-hire office worker had been suspicious of something about it, called the police and found it had been reported as stolen. Jay was arrested and charged with using false documents and found guilty. The police never knew why the car was hired or the extent of the trafficking operation he was involved in. All he had on his record was 'fraud'. One slight conviction for many years of crime and deceit. But it should have given them a clue. When asked about it he said something which was so obviously a lie, that he'd used the false passport on a whim, as a kind of joke – and the Skull worked hard to make this sound credible. No jury would have swallowed that – but the judge did. Was he actually the Skull's father, I wondered?

Jay smuggled and grew drugs for years across borders in Europe and around Britain. He worked growing houses in various towns. He took carloads of marijuana and other substances across the borders in Europe when he lived there. He carried loads of the stuff around between towns in his van or on his motorbike. Once a greenhouse-full was found which he was growing in the garden and he was charged and convicted of possession. The police did not complete their search of the garden or they'd've found another greenhouse-full around the next hedge. In those days everyone believed, or pretended to believe, that drug dealers were black, which probably helped Jay stay uncaught. What he was growing at home was nothing compared to what he had growing at three other addresses in the town which they never found.

So Jay was not in awe of the police or their methods. He wasn't in awe of the army either. So would Jay be in awe of a piece of paper – a 'restraining order'? Would that make him stay away from me? Would a 'restraining order' have kept me safe? What would he be afraid of that hadn't already been done to him? What would they do which he wouldn't be able to outwit?

But the fact I had never applied for an 'injunction' to protect me from Jay and had never called the police – was here taken as evidence that I had never been afraid of him.

I tried to answer and explain how asking the police had never helped before and I was afraid of making things worse, but it was as if I had said nothing.

My barrister could not stand and watch me being ignored and rubbished in this way – so he sat and watched instead. He didn't know the case well enough to know the background.

The Skull carried on, her jaw working, chewing on the words, spitting out truth in mashed-up gobs, unrecognisable and twisted.

The fact I'd lived abroad for some years in my twenties, when there was no work in the UK for newly qualified teachers, was also used against me – cited as proof of my 'flighty' character. The fact I'd not been out of work all my adult life while Jay drank and smoked his way through the years was passed over.

Dr F had actually described me as 'a woman who has never been married'. It was like something out of another century. As if it was a crime or a failure on my part not to reach this pinnacle, and surely the only possible, achievement in a female life. The fact I don't believe in the state or church sanctioning relationships was somehow a count against me.

I was bewildered at why the Skull, or Dr F, would do this. Why would a woman, or any person, deliberately lie, deceive, and help to hide the true nature of an abuser to win a case? For money? For a sense of victory? For a sense of control? Alienated workers the world over go through the motions of the processes by which they earn a living and so it was here. Jaded and bored, immunised by repetition against any sensitivity to the complexity of the lives they processed and the pain therein, they did the minimum.

Fordism was here – how much money could be made out of each bag of pain being processed? How could each 'case' be processed as speedily as possible with the maximum profit outcome, minimum input, minimum use of labour? Ms Pane seemed to have calculated she could get no more money from me – as she didn't understand about Buy to Let mortgages – so sacked me and Lizard had worked out just how much he had to do to cover his tracks, but no more, to get this 'case' over with. My life and Joe's – on the production line.

They all earned money by pleasing whoever it was who had supplied them with the work. They were each a private business, after all, in a privatised service, competing for profits in a tight market. They were all instructed by people who were out to win the case – not to find the truth. 'The one who pays the piper calls the tune' - and they all played so very well. The psychiatrist, the barristers, the judge and psychologist must have known what narcissism is, must have known they were being lied to by Jay: they could not have believed his stories and evasions and bluffs and the gaping holes within them but, like true professionals, they pretended they did. The psychiatrist knew she was lying or being very misleading about what had happened in that library, for example, but she still lied. All the evidence I had paid to have included in the file had somehow evaporated away between Payne's office and the court. The Fact Finding Hearing I might have had where witnesses were called, I had signed away - believing the promises I was made of the judge being shown this evidence and for the bribe of Joe having overnight stays. They hadn't wanted any facts to be found or witnesses called .Jay had for years taken advantage of my trusting innocence and that of others he had conned - but he could have learned a lot from these artists.

The figure of Justice, like a proud angel, is often depicted as blind – but it is not meant to be a blindness to reality. Instead of an angel, I found her to be a blinded warrior, mad with power, slashing generally and with the blunt instruments of generalisations and prejudice – with these her servants, obsequious and dishonest, creeping around in her shadow – foraging for fallen scraps of money. A fractal of a wider, insane, blind system – sick with its own power. And, educated as they were, they were so easily, so willingly deceived by Jay.

By insisting on the mental health assessment of me at the very beginning, Jay had successfully turned the whole focus of the case away from domestic abuse and towards mental health – so successive assessments had been all about finding out which of us was nuts. The experts buzzed along in the wake of this, all of them cross-pollinating each other's ignorance Believing Jay's assertions of having depression, as I had for years; I had addressed this in my statements, thinking depression underlay his behaviour.

Skull surprised me by pulling out Jay's medical records as if brandishing an Olympic Torch which would light us all to the promised land: there was no history of depression. No diagnosis of depression. Nothing. My last belief in anything he had ever told me fell. He had even lied about that. And of course, now it looked as if it had been me – that I'd been lying about his having depression.

Jay's sisters gave evidence – all about how wonderful he was. One part of what one sister said hit me hard. She described Joe arriving at her house with Jay two years ago after being taken from my care. She described Joe as having been distressed on his arrival and hiding from them all under the table and crying. So Joe had not been 'okay' on his arrival at his aunt's house after all. I remembered her phone call, for which I'd been so grateful at the time, telling me he was okay. But he hadn't been. He had shown all the distress at being suddenly among strangers and separated from his main carer which a child does show – and that reassurance to me had been a lie. He had been distressed and afraid and hidden under the table – unless this was a lie too.

But now it was presented as him being distressed after the incident for which I'd been arrested – despite the fact that it had been two days earlier and Joe had been living with me, happily at Esme's house and at school and nursery for two whole days before going to live with Jay and hiding under the table distressed. But this fact was not regarded or even known. There was no-one in that court apart from me and the judge who would have read the chronology, but he probably wouldn't recall such a detail.

The nursery had given me a statement about Joe at the nursery – it was clear if he was going to be distressed by anything I'd done that day it would be then – not two days later. Out of context, anything can be made to mean anything else. This same sister had told the social worker, Anastasia, that, no, Joe wasn't missing his mother, he was quite happy – the lies had started even then. So the family court heard of Joe's distress as being evidence of his having witnessed his mother doing something dreadful, not evidence of his distress at being parted from her. No-one looked at the dates. My barrister certainly didn't.

I asked, from the dock, for the nursery report to be looked at – again, it couldn't be found on the file but I'd given a copy to CAFCASS and she produced it. Skull rubbished it, saying the nursery workers had obviously been friends of mine.

Somewhere it is written, in the rules of custody battles, that the material wealth of each side is not allowed to be part of the points considered. Despite this, the auntie's big house and the swimming pool were mentioned four times across the three days of the hearing. Wicked mummy I was, wanting to take my child from such delights! What was not mentioned was that it had no shallow end and Joe was too scared to go near it.

We, Jay and I, had each been asked to make a statement about our plans for Joe's schooling. Jay had put in that he wanted Joe to pass the entrance exam and get to one of the prep schools in the area. The judge read out the name of the local school I had chosen from among the ones I had visited: he swirled the word 'comprehensive' around his mouth. He could not keep the sneer from out of his voice. He did not even try. It was obvious the contempt he felt for any who went to comprehensive schools – and their parents.

I asked, again, for the video made by Dr F to be shown. I knew this would speak for itself –they'd see how Joe was with me and more importantly, see how the reality varied from how she had reported it.

It was as if I had said nothing. I asked again. There was an embarrassed silence and the judge asked Lizard or Skull about something else. I got the very strong impression that they had not heard me or my voice was audible only to myself.

I never saw that video. Later I asked Mark to write and obtain a copy. Dr F wrote back that it had been destroyed. I wonder if the camcorder had even been switched on. I know medical records have to be kept for six years before they can be legally destroyed so similar restraints must protect legal evidence – but no-one was listening, nobody cared.

If a jury had been there – the judge and the barristers could not have got away with this. As it was, Lizard was just intent on not upsetting the judge and I was the only one there who knew that what was happening was a gross distortion of truth.

Sophie's letter was perused by the judge who said, in his bored drawl that it showed no evidence of abuse. Lizard said 'the judge knows Women's Aid believe anything women tell them'.

Not 'thinks' or 'believes' – but 'knows'!

Why was he in charge of a case about abuse if that was his worldview?? Why was Lizard if he also saw the world that way – 'oh these bloody women, you know – what liars they are!'

I remembered the fifteen-year-old Jane – telling of her abuse and being sneered at, by Anastasia and Dan – 'old enough to know what she was doing'. The taser marks on her arm by her 'lover' were described as 'apparently self-inflicted'. I had always had an idea of how she must have felt to be spoken to in that way by powerful, ignorant people. Now I knew exactly.

Skull also made much of the fact that Jay had no car – so, if Joe came to live with me, how could he possibly see his father? I'd written how I would take Joe to see him at wherever venue was decided on but the judge kept referring to the 'no car' situation. Skull also used the fact I had been travelling the 200+ round trip miles three times a week for some months as evidence that I could keep doing this indefinitely and the judge agreed. Jay was presented as someone who couldn't possibly be expected to be able to travel to visit his son and the fact that I did was used as another reason to keep him at his dad's.

The conclusion by the judge was that Joe should stay where he was – with his father.

By now my body and mind knew exactly what to do and the ice had formed long, long before the judge had finished speaking. as he droned over the summing-up statement and Lizard sat and looked out of the window, probably perusing his next case, or, more likely, his next car.

I managed to ask for and get agreement for an extra phone call in the week as the legal teams, led by the Skull, busied about details and forms. I sat quite still in my frozen cocoon.

I noticed something about the Skull: I had not

seen her so animated before. Now she was flushed, her eyes dilated, a manic smile on her thin face. I realised that this was probably as close to being alive as she ever got. Winning the case! What higher glory in her life could there possibly be?

In one of the breaks I'd overheard her telling another barrister that her father was a judge. I thought that might explain a lot. I'd wondered how and why anyone could lie, deceive, twist truth and play word games just to win a case – knowing the result will be a child living with an abuser. Surely it just couldn't be the money? I looked at her and pictured her hurrying to telephone Daddy and tell him she had won again and maybe getting a pat on the head. She was at least fifty years old but she twisted truth, hid abuse, lied and bullied an innocent woman and left a child with an abuser – just to shine, once more, in Daddy's eyes.

After the issue of the letters a suspicion had begun to form. When the judge had crawled back into his cave I went to Lizard's table and opened the file. I looked all through it – looking for the letters, the transcript from court, the statements from friends and the nursery about mine and Jay's behaviour towards Joe over the years they had observed us, the statements from the neighbours who had been raged at by Jay, the statements from mothers of Jay's friends and from my friends at work who had met Jay and noticed oddities in his behaviour, blatant rudeness to themselves, observations on my parenting by professionals in the field , even the chronology – in other words I looked in the file for the evidence.

None were there.

In a sort of daze, I pointed this out to Lizard. All he said was, "That's not my responsibility, I wasn't on the case when the file was made." I was reminded of a two-year-old denying he'd nicked the biscuits. He was absolutely not concerned at what had happened or curious to know why.

There was a scrap of paper on the file – the 'compromise agreement' Jay and I had signed – agreeing not to mention the incidents and my arrest – in exchange for the Finding of Facts hearing being cancelled. This was on file – but all the evidence which was due to be looked at in that hearing was nowhere.

Well played. No set of gangsters could have played it better. No other set of gangsters. I saw then that they were, morally, on a par with the kind of scum who had gathered around Jay's dad and cheered him on as he emotionally abused his son. Actually, they were worse. Like the scum, the barristers watched the evidence of abuse – and not only did they do nothing to stop it, like the scum, they actually worked to hide it so the abuse can continue. And were paid, well, for doing so. The commodification of justice has consequences, as she holds aloft the illuminating torch of truth – while close behind, her servants grub after pennies in the slime.

Skull and the others on Jay's team had made me that offer, of overnight stays, of unsupervised contact as a ploy, a trick, a clever strategy to hide the evidence from the judge and thereby win the case for Jay.

Clever, clever people. How right that they should be able to practice out of sight of common eyes. Maybe they each had similar problems to Jay – maybe being taken and put into public schools and bullied, estranged from their families had all damaged them the same way. Jay had no known mental illness — the Skull had proved that, but isn't the need to control others an illness by definition? Isn't the lack of ability to empathise an illness? Isn't the ability to knowingly and without conscience, distort what you know is the truth to boost your own bank balance, also some kind of disorder?

Illnesses come in many shapes and sizes — maybe there are some not yet recognised?

There is a virus, for example, which has killed millions, called HIV. It changes its shape and so cannot be found by the immune system of the body it has invaded. Clever, clever virus. Jay also changed his shape and hid his true self. Maybe all abusers do. While the immune system, which is meant to keep us safe, provides it with extra cover.

When we the left court, Lizard told me there were no grounds for appeal, bade me farewell and slithered into his Porsche. In silhouette, against the evening sun, he looked just like a well-fed lizard crawling back under its rock.

Driving home, once I had recovered enough to be able to do so, I realised washing barristers' spikey wigs was probably no problem — no self-respecting bacteria would go anywhere near them. And the judge's robe was probably compulsory wear to save the court from having to rise and clear each time he awoke and broke wind.

I drove home.

Chapter 14

For the next three days, I dug a pond in the garden: it was the most strenuous and creative thing I could think of doing with which to numb the pain. I felt as if I'd been punched all over, repeatedly, by a sneering mob, Jay at their head calling the shots, directing them where and how to hit. A smartly dressed, articulate mob. The bruise, all that was left of me, was all I had. To survive, I couldn't look at what had happened or why. I must not think about it or recall it.

When we are in pain we cry out for home – for safety, for a time when we felt normal, maybe even happy. People in extremis wander back to places of their childhood or a place where once they felt safe. My childhood had always included wildlife, countryside, frogs and toads, being in the garden with my mum and dad, 'helping' them as children do, feeding the birds, watching the hedgehog climb the link-wire fence and snuffle across the postage-stamp lawn. As an adult, I'd worked as a volunteer gardener in the city, helped haul car parts out of ditches and clear rhododendrons as part of a conservation group – just an excuse to do a kind of gardening when I had none of my own.

So I dug a pond.

Lifting the weed-ridden turfs and setting them aside; keeping any flat stones I came across; digging out the brown soil in a roughly oval shape; scouring the sides to make sure there were no sharp edges anywhere which might puncture the lining; driving to the garden centre and buying a piece of rubber lining, prevaricating over the type and size to make it matter, seem important, discussing the type of pond I was making with the assistant, my voice sounding far away as if it belonged to somebody else and I was just overhearing this banal, idiotic conversation.

The cold, damp, gritty soil in my hands as I pushed it away, the cold wooden handle of the spade, were solid connections with the world while the rest of me hid away inside a numb, stricken shell. I checked the pond was two feet deep at one end – so the creatures that might come to live there may have somewhere to hibernate – and borrowed my dad's spirit-level to make sure the sides were even. My dad offered help but I politely turned him down as I needed this task to not be too easy. It helped to be in the garden alongside him as he pushed the lawnmower over the grass. It helped to have this to talk about and not look at that dark place which threatened to overwhelm me.

When the pond was dug and the liner was in, that part of the garden looked like a mud swamp or a battle ground. I filled it with water, put the turfs back, using the lining to make a shallow 'marshy area' around the edges for bog plants. I edged the pond with flat stones, resting them here and there over little caverns where creatures could hide or sleep. I put soil in the pond and waited for it to settle then put in plants to aerate the water.

It was spring – the time of year when life and hope return to the earth. I was trying to find my spring which had been snatched away. There didn't seem to be any point in doing anything really. I had to keep going, for Joe's sake. I needed a plan. Ahead lay a desert. I had to find some way of crossing it, of keeping going.

When he looked back on his childhood – what would he see?

Would he see just a barren, wasteland – or would he see diamonds glinting there? I knew I had to make sure he saw at least some diamonds which would last forever and which he could take with him into his own future.

I couldn't give him the childhood I wanted to give him – Jay and the court had seen to that – but I could give him as much as I possibly could – of normality, of friends, of the right to be himself, of feeling loved unconditionally, of being nurtured and kept safe – not controlled, not manipulated. He would have at least one parent who would not use tears, lies and aggression to control him.

I planted the iris which Anna had given me at the shallow end of the pond. Mud swirled and settled. A week later the flower blossomed. A single deep purple star reflected in the water.

After the war of the family court, the minor skirmishes, the 'clearing-up operation' could go ahead for the rest of my life. I carried on the 200-mile round trips, making weekend magic.

The hearing about my job and registration was now due to go ahead: it had been put on hold while the criminal case and then the family court case had gone ahead and now came its turn.

How could I care about my job when my child had been taken away? I had thought it was important – thought that having a decent income would at least help me compete with the millionaire sister and the swimming pool.

But it did matter: "You take my life when you take the means whereby I live," said Shylock, as Portia's 'mercy' rained down on him with utmost cruelty and hypocrisy. I had to fund my 200-mile trips to see Joe. I had to be able to replace the cars as they wore out. I had to be able to be a parent as far as I could.

It was odd people saying to me, "Oh I couldn't do what you do, you're amazing." As if people who suffer, volunteer for it.

I was accused, and my job and my professional registration were under scrutiny and due to be taken away from me on two counts: I was accused of breaking the social work code by a) not telling my manager of circumstances at home which might affect my work and b) of conducting myself in a way which might bring the reputation of social work into disrepute. My friends had howled at the accusation. One said, "If they can take Joe, none of our kids is safe." All of them felt they could never turn to social workers for help if Anastasia and Dan were typical.

Gary, the trade-unionist who was dealing with my case, had already accompanied me on several visits and meetings with my employers and with the panel representing the professional body with which I was registered. I was supposedly suspended 'without prejudice' and had been for the past two years while the court cases had dragged themselves along.

The social worker, another manager, who was conducting the enquiry into my job, couldn't look at me without sneering. The manager who met with Gary and I was as rude as she could be without breaking the rules. They had asked the two social workers, Dan and Anastasia, for their accounts and lots of documents had been produced. They had met with me and written down my answers to their questions.

They had all expressed the view that I couldn't possibly have been in an abusive relationship as I was 'a professional woman' so would have known how to get out of the situation and, further, I had sat on a working committee as a trade unionist which had worked on the employer's policy about domestic – abuse – so I would have known exactly what to do to get help. I also had had a lot of people around me, including my manager, to whom I could have confided at any time – but I had not. By not telling my manager I had broken the rules – but probably because I had nothing to tell – was the gist of where they were coming from.

I didn't see how they could not win the case. I had lost the most important battle by evidence stacked against me. Witnesses would not come forward now any more than they would before. The two social work managers had had the ear of my employer. I certainly hadn't told my manager or anyone at work the full extent of what was happening with Jay for the same reasons I had not told anyone else.

The criminal court had found I was not guilty of the acts of which I had been accused by Jay – after a three-day hearing – but the assumption here seemed to be that this was a mistake on the part of the court and if only the two social workers had been allowed to give evidence, I would have been convicted. It seemed a hopeless case.

Gary was brilliant. He was used to representing people who were being investigated by employers or accused of various misdemeanours. He listened as I told him about Jay. But he would not represent me at the hearing as he felt a legally qualified person would be best. My union would pay for a legal representative to support me through the hearing. I accepted this as being a sign that it was a hopeless case. I looked forward to meeting another Lizard-eyes or another bored Suit.

But, instead, I met Sharon.

We had had telephone conversations before we met. Gary had explained the need to postpone the hearing until all my other court cases were over and thankfully this had been accepted by my accusers. Now my weekly routine was going to see Joe, bringing him back for a weekend each fortnight, ringing him during the week, working at the hot wash or as a gardener or cleaner – and going to hearings. Sharon telephoned me to introduce herself when Gary told me he needed to pass the case on.

I started to outline the case and what had happened and why I was in this mess. It was becoming an automatic recital as I had repeated it so often to so many people.

But Sharon already knew.

She cut across my robotic recital and explained what the charges were. Then she explained why they were ridiculous charges and only showed how backward things were in understanding domestic abuse. This was something I'd not heard before and a tone of voice which had been missing awhile. I explained that they were right, however; I had not told anyone what was happening.

She said, "Well of course not – you were being abused – it had become normalised – what do they expect?" She sounded angry – but not with me. Normalised?

She went on to explain why the registration body had got completely the wrong end of the stick and obviously hadn't read my statements or anything else on the subject of emotional abuse and were completely out of line accusing me of these charges. She had read my statements, all of them, all the records of the case and of my accusers. She had spotted inconsistencies in their accounts, all of them, where they contradicted each other's accounts and other areas where they seemed to be admitting prejudice or unsupportable assumptions about me and the case and plain, unadulterated ignorance about how abuse works.

That was just the start.

They had not checked their prejudices; they had not consulted other professionals or communicated with other agencies involved, they had not questioned their own assumptions, they had ignored several very basic factors about how abuse works... As I listened, I was hearing, for the first time, my own confusion about what people were saying and thinking about me expressed in someone else's voice – but not as confusion, but as articulate, intelligent analysis. The reason it was so confusing was not because I was idiotic – but because it was wrong. Horribly wrong.

In her voice, brisk and matter-of-fact, was understanding, compassion, intelligence – and anger. Quiet, calm, perfectly rational and contained, but very real anger. And not at me. Sharon understood what was happening to me, what had happened to me – and she wasn't pleased. She didn't tell me that other women put up with much worse; she didn't tell me that the judge might not be interested in this or that fact; she didn't keep telling me that Jay had not hit me.

The effect on me of this phone call was quite powerful.

Up until then, solicitors were people who looked bored, made inaccurate notes and sent you bills. Or got irritated if you tried to disagree with them. Or rather, those who worked in the family court had been like that. Richard had immediately recognised that I was duped by Jay and had been manipulated and abused by him for years and the criminal court team he headed all seemed to know about how people like Jay operate. But the family court team simply hadn't had a clue. Or they had had clues – but had worked hard to bury them.

I didn't meet Sharon for a while. We met at the union office via video-conference link and talked. I was amazed at how she had read all about my case. I realised that no-one else had in all this time. They had 'read as much as I needed to' (Ms Pane) or 'none at all' (Dr F) or 'the main points' (Lizard). Everyone had cherry picked, 'got the gist' and found enough to stick a label on my 'case' and process it accordingly, with minimum effort. She had read the lot.

She explained to me what she was going to argue and that she was also going to get, 'to educate the hearing', an expert to talk about emotional domestic abuse to help them understand what had happened to me – to put it in context. I didn't like the sound of another expert. I'd met experts before.

I didn't see how she was going to win this one though – I was accused of not telling anyone – and I hadn't. I was accused of having a personal life which had factors which *might* have affected my work. I was pretty sure it hadn't – I had kept it so separate – but it *might* have done – if it had carried on. How can you prove something might have done something at some point? Possibly the stress might have broken me at some point and caused me to break down at work or go off sick? It might have done.

Compared to losing care of Joe this was minor but the fact of losing thirty years of my career and such a major part of my identity was still huge. What else could I do? I'd always been a social worker. I didn't know how to do anything else except help people sort stuff out – or wash dishes. Ironic given my total failure to sort my own stuff out but hey, we can't be good at everything.

The hearing was at smart-ish hotel in town. My dad dropped me off, my mum in the car, not sure of what was happening but happy with what we told her. I waited in a little room on the ground floor for

Sharon to arrive.

Because of her force of personality and the clarity with which she spoke I had envisaged Sharon as being about nine feet tall – or at least six. She had been sitting down during our video-conferences so when she walked in I was surprised. She was less than five feet tall, petite, very good looking and on crutches. I'm white, she was black – her parents were from Jamaica. I was so very glad they had come to Britain. She had grown up on a council estate in the 60s and 70s. The local racists had attacked her brothers and put dog mess through the door. She had grown up knowing the world was not a fair or a just place.

She was a fighter in a way I would never be – sharp, fully aware of how horrible people can be and very articulate – without my uncertainties and second thoughts and maybes, and looking at it from all angles, and getting lost in other people's points of view, and losing my own. She knew that what had happened to me was wrong and she was going to prove it.

In her job, she was nearly always the only person under five foot in the room, frequently the only black person in the room, and often the only woman. Standing up, using her crutches, she would stand and speak out in rooms full of tall, white guys in suits, employers and their legal teams, who were gunning for her or her clients, and fight for the rights of employees using words, truth, sheer intelligence and ability.

I asked if the crutches were permanent. They were. She had been a sporty girl but a lorry had driven over her as she rode her bike in London. She had nearly died on the spot and had spent eighteen months in hospital knocking on Death's door and getting skin grafts. The crutches were permanent and so was the pain. During our talks, she would often get up and move about the room and I realised this was part of her pain management. She'd been studying to be a barrister but this accident had stopped that plan. Now she worked for the union as a legal adviser.

In the hearing, there was: the panel from my accusers – five people, who were to act as a kind of jury but also able to ask questions in the enquiry; the guy with the case against me; his legal adviser; Sharon and me. There was a table and chair for witnesses to sit.

Sharon introduced herself briefly. I couldn't help noticing the tiniest of what looked like smirks on my accusers' faces as she did so. Was it pity? Was it acknowledgment that this was probably the best I could find to defend me? Was it tolerance? Was it irritation at having this nuisance get slightly in the way of the inevitable conclusion – me being struck off?

I realised than that every day of her working life Sharon had to walk into rooms full of little smirks like that – the barely veiled contempt because she was black, tiny, a woman, on crutches and a union rep. How could she, the smirk said, possibly contend against the 'real' professionals? These grown-ups?

Over the next three days, I was privileged to watch Sharon carefully, completely and utterly, but very politely – wipe the floor with them, their accusations, and their smirks, as I sat next to her – as close to her as I could get without actually falling off my chair. I realised I hadn't felt safe for a very long time.

A lot of the time in the hearing I had my eyes closed to listen all the harder as she told my story. The sensation was one of a marvellous ointment being poured on open wounds which softened the hurt like honey softens on the tongue. She had read the evidence – all of it – she had understood the details – all of them – and she knew how domestic abuse worked; what was normal, how a person responds to abuse, how the mind of an abuser works and, more importantly, what happens to the mind of someone abused – why we don't think rationally, why we don't 'just leave', why our answers are often contradictory – as our reality in which we live is a mess of contradictions and why we don't, ever, ever – even when our lives are at risk and we are scared out of our wits – 'just tell someone'.

She included accounts, in case the panel weren't getting the point, of what had happened to women who *had* told – how the act of telling had escalated the abuse – as I had always feared it would, as Jay had warned me it would.

The family court judge, I'd been told, would not be interested in the behaviour of the two social work managers, Anastasia and Dan. I had had no chance of questioning them or of putting before the court who they were and how they knew me before that dreadful day. I had had no chance of asking them about the assumptions they had made or the lies they had told.

Anastasia and Dan had told the enquiry how they had not known me before that day – I had been in different teams and our paths had not crossed: Sharon established the long history that showed otherwise.

Sharon called Ruth as a witness who testified to the letter of complaint I had made to Dan the sidekick and the long conflict I had had with Anastasia over that one case in particular. Ruth had got the file out of archive and brought a copy of the letter for all to see. I found out later that Ruth had been threatened with disciplinary action if she attended the hearing and spoke up for me. She had come anyway. There are people like that in the world.

My supervision notes were brought out and showed the meeting with Anastasia, my manager and me when we had tried to resolve our differences.

So they were liars. It was proved. They had lied. They had both had long and acrimonious relationships with me (and we didn't need to talk about the other aspect of where we also clashed, as managers and union rep) long before they had ever walked into that caravan or elected themselves to carry out the investigation – or written their report.

Sharon had read their accounts and notes and pointed out how they had assumed things about me due to them being true in other cases – but which did not apply to me. This also was prejudice.

They had stated they did not believe me when I had said I would have confided in older friends, whom I had known in my previous city, but had not felt able to in my new area – saying this could not be true. Sharon pointed out they could not know the nature of my previous friendships so could not state this. An obvious point really, but no-one else had made it.

I had not been able to remember anything about

being part of a trade union group which had worked on the domestic abuse policy and was sure it couldn't have happened as 1) I hadn't been a steward in my new team, plus I had not gone to any meetings after work when Jay had become unhappy about my doing any such thing – so I could not have attended even if I had been a steward. Sharon had asked for minutes of the meetings to show if I had been there – but nobody ever produced them. A copy of the policy was produced – I was certain I'd never seen this document before. Again, an assumption had been made and included in the armoury against me – but not proved. Sharon showed this was another myth.

My accusers asserted that I could not be a victim of domestic abuse as my answers in the enquiry had been inconsistent; sometimes I'd said I hadn't left Jay for one reason – sometimes I'd referred to another. Further, they said I could not have maintained myself in my work if I had been being abused at home. Again, I had been the main bread winner – so had the control in the house. How could I have been abused? I had friends at work but I'd not told them of abuse.

Sharon explained to each of them very carefully, so they would understand and remember, that all they were demonstrating by these assertions was their complete ignorance of the dynamics of domestic abuse.

"That proves to me that you know nothing or very little at all about how domestic abuse works or its effects," she said.

This wasn't a question – it was a clear assertion. And just for a few seconds, maybe a minute, I was able to see the smug sneering confidence wiped off their faces. It wasn't much perhaps – not for all the pain and the months of agony and for my child's childhood being taken away from us both, for the fear, the self-hate and the ruin, my mother's distress in the car being dragged to 'supervise me' with my child, my father's grief, my child shaking with distress as I left him again and again with his father – but I closed my eyes and held on to the images of my persecutors, storing them away for future reference – each, momentarily, looking like two cheeks of the same slapped arse.

I also had to give evidence. I sat in the chair and answered the questions from the accuser and from Sharon. I realised I had not done this before: in the criminal court; they were only interested in the two events for which I'd been arrested: crime deals with events, not processes – and abuse is not an event – it is a process. I had written statements about the rest but not told it.

In the family court the first solicitor, Ms Pane, had been more interested in the outcome of the criminal trial which she had believed to be a foregone conclusion. She also, I now discovered, had had a long working relationship with the two social work managers, Dan and Anastasia, so maybe was swayed by them in what she believed rather than anything I'd tried to tell her sat in her office, verballing away. I wish I had known that. If I had known she was 'friends' with Anastasia I would have certainly gone elsewhere.

The Finding of Fact Hearing had been sidestepped – I had never been able to explain to the family court what living with Jay had been like and why I had been so scared of him and what he might do if provoked or 'triggered'.

I knew now that he had been acting the whole time as a way of controlling me – but I hadn't known that then. The legal team around Jay had obviously deliberately manoeuvred the court away from the Fact-Finding Hearing – wooing me with offers of 'unsupervised contact and weekend stays' in order to bury the evidence and win the case for Jay.

Once I started talking I didn't seem to be able to stop and I told them the lot. I told them all the details I knew of his having attacked the young man with a block of wood and his being nearly killed and his telling me I would often similarly push him to the edge by reminding him of his father as that young man had done.

I told them of the smashed plates and threats to snap my neck and the fact he'd traced his previous partners so I had nowhere to run. Of the threats of suicide, his tearfulness, his apparent remorse, his commitment to make thing better and get treatment; my worry for Joe losing his dad, of his being snatched, Jay's rage if he ever thought I'd been talking about him to anyone, my previous efforts to get help from the police which had failed so spectacularly, his army training, his skills and disdain for the law and all its efforts.

When I sat down I felt strangely lighter and cleaner than I had for a long time.

The accusers then stated that if it had been that bad there was no way I could have kept it a secret from either my colleagues or my friends – plus it must have affected my work.

Sharon had anticipated this – my work record and supervision notes were scrutinised and no word of concern about my practice was there. My manager was called as a witness to testify this was the case. The character references were read out – at last! (I had eventually been able to get copies from Richard's office having never heard from Ms Pane's office again). Each showed that I was a good colleague – they even included one from the student I had been supervising, saying how fair, helpful and nice I was to her in placement.

Sharon's case was that the conditions at home might not ever have affected my work – as they had showed no sign of ever doing so.

This tiny woman hadn't finished yet. She wanted the hearing, and also me, to be very, very clear about the reality of emotional or psychological abuse. She had asked the union, and they had agreed, to fund someone who had worked in the area of domestic abuse for many years to attend the hearing and tell us a little bit more about it.

This woman had received awards for her work in this area. She sat in the chair and calmly spoke to the hearing. She had notes in front of her but did not seem to need them as she was speaking from memory and the heart. These were experiences she could recollect clearly of people she had met and the lives they had led, helping us to understand what emotional abuse, or psychological abuse is.

She told us:

Of a judge who was very high up in her profession

and well respected. The abuse she was suffering at home only came to light after a car accident. It was found she owned no clothes of her own except for working clothes which were kept under lock and key and she had to ask her partner if she wanted to get an outfit or change of clothes. In hospital, the truth about her home life came out and Ms Henderson became involved in helping her to exit the relationship safely.

Of a successful businesswoman who had been spotted climbing into the boot of a car one day after close of business. The onlooker had reported it and a kidnapping was suspected. It was found that this was normal for her as her husband had convinced her she was so foul to be with and such a despicable personality that travelling with her could not be expected. Similar abuse and degradation had carried on at home and had become 'normalised'.

Of a successful career woman in medicine who, at home, was required to sit and eat separately from her partner and her children as, she had been convinced by her partner, she smelled foul, was a danger to her kids and did not deserve to sit with other people.

Of a policewoman whose partner had CCTV cameras mounted outside the house to ensure she did not leave the house except to go to work when he was away or have any visitors to the home. He would ring her daily to check she was at work and scrutinise her timesheets for any discrepancies, and interrogate her about where she had been and with whom while she was in work...

Also, she told us, people in the caring professions are especially susceptible to being controlled, believing themselves to be 'looking after' the abuser – as I had been – their empathic nature being especially easy for abusers to prey upon.

And on and on…

The cases she chose to tell us about were all of successful career people and all about women – as my accusers had asserted that this sort of thing 'cannot happen' to 'successful career women'. She acknowledged that men can also be victims and people all over the social scale – but she told us of examples to illustrate the context in which my circumstances had to be understood. None of these other women had ever told of their plight until chance had revealed them – like me. All of them had been controlled by use of temper, tears, and being convinced they were 'helping' their abuser – like me. None of them had been hit. Like me they had lived in fear; threatened, controlled, thinking they were helping their abuser and unable to leave for fear of the abuser being hurt or killing himself and/or coming after them.

Tears came to me with understanding. Not racking tears this time, but more gentle, as if some of the scar tissue was melting.

Also, she went on to give examples of how emotional abuse often escalates over time into physical abuse, how my experience with the house was not unique but was an example of financial abuse and for those reasons I had every reason to fear that Jay would use other means to control me if his rages ever became less effective in frightening me into compliance.

I knew then that I was not alone, and never had been. I knew then that if I had gone to find help, eventually, if I had kept looking, I would have found it. Jay had had me convinced that there was no help but here there was knowledge, a whole history, a culture, an understanding of how people like him operate and how people like me end up inside abusive relationships and don't even know what is happening to us.

The panel exited to discuss and I went to thank her. We talked awhile.

She mentioned that she had lost a child, her child had died. She didn't say in which circumstances but here again was someone who had gone through worse pain than I had, and, again, turned that pain into a force for helping others.

The two women who helped me in this hearing had worse to deal with than I had – Sharon in constant physical pain and the loss of the life she'd had before the lorry had done its work and Ms Henderson who had had to cope with the death of her child – both of them, turning their pain into a force for good. (Made my pond-digging look a bit poor.)

Sharon and I went into our room. I was high on the euphoria of finally being believed and meeting others who understood – and of seeing my tormentors who had caused Joe and I such pain, humiliated and seen for the ignorant, arrogant nothings they were. The outcome was not as important – I felt validated and real and connected to others.

I was intrigued by Sharon's 'tablet' and how it worked – being ignorant of such IT – and she said she could access 'anything' on it – we therefore discovered a mutual love of Richard Pryor and we spent the time when the panel were deliberating laughing hysterically over his gig about cheetahs on YouTube.

I was high at all the emotion and talk of such difficult times. I was slightly hysterical. It crossed my mind that Pryor could have taken my pain and made a good sketch out of it.

The panel came back: on the question of my having personal issues which might have affected my work they found me not guilty – as it hadn't, my work had remained exemplary as evidenced.

On the count of my failing to disclose they found me guilty: They only had to find me guilty of one count for me to be struck off for bad practice. They left again to consider if this did warrant bad practice on my part and we went back to Mr Pryor.

A few minutes later we reconvened again: even though I was guilty of not telling my manager of problems at home, they did not find that my failing to disclose my personal life constituted bad practice as my failure to disclose was due to the effects of domestic abuse – which normally silences its victims, so I could not be blamed for this. So, although guilty of silence, I was not guilty of bad practice. I was not going to be struck off.

My thirty years of practice as a social worker, this central part of my identity, could continue.

Tears came as the chair read out the conclusion,

but they were not tears of pain but of a kind of healing, the kind of healing which begins when we are accepted and understood. Gentle tears, not the racking sobs of grief. I caught up with the chairwoman in the hotel corridor outside and shook her hand and, chokily, expressed thanks. I was surprised to see she was tearful too and I wondered if she too had had experiences like mine. The accuser and his legal help had left the room on the verdict, in silence.

Sharon allowed herself to become less formal when the case was over. She expressed loudly, "The charges shouldn't have been brought in the first place!"

My dad gave her a lift to the train station and I never saw her again. On the way, I asked her if she would ever consider working in the family courts as her knowledge, her attitude, her ability is needed there so very, very much by so many, many kids and victims of abuse.

I would like to have seen her in action in that setting – wiping the complacency off those smug faces and tearing through the cobweb of lies woven by the many-legged, empty-headed monster within.

I was pretty sure she would rouse the judge to pay attention and take an interest in the lives spread out before him.

Chapter 15

———— ✦⋯❊⋯✦ ————

If this was a film, it would have a happy ending but, as it's a true story, we must make do.

In a film, Jay would long ago have 'lost it' in a public place and been witnessed by the CAFCASS officer, or even the judge. I had imagined these scenarios dozens of times – Jay 'losing it' with someone in his house and the judge or the CAFCASS officer just happening to be calling next door and recognising his voice, the plates shattering – the blinkers falling from their eyes as they rushed to put things right, realising at last, what Jay was like and what Joe was now living with. The judge or the CAFCASS officer cowering as Jay frothed and ranted, jaws clenched, fists raised… Sometimes the fantasy was of Jay 'losing it' with his family and them reporting him – in sudden realisation that I had been telling the truth. They'd ring me (after they'd had Jay arrested) we'd reconcile, they'd demand of the courts that Jay would be given professional help – and I would support that demand – and Joe would come home.

But domestic abuse is domestic abuse – its perpetrators don't appear in public except as compliant, charming and harmless.

At first I'd kept my phone on day and night, believing Jay would, in the first week of living at his sister's with Joe, 'lose it' and I would get a call, maybe in the middle of the night, that he had been arrested, and could I come and collect Joe? But the weeks and months had passed and I'd realised that Jay did not lose his temper uncontrollably and I'd found out why; it wasn't a 'loss' of temper at all, just a ploy to control me.

Later I fantasised about his 'losing it' with his sister, trying to control her, and being 'shopped' by her husband who had, unbeknown to Jay, been upstairs on a day off. That didn't happen either. Were they fantasies or were they prayers? Domestic abusers, often but not always, only abuse people in a domestic situation – their partners, parents or children out of the sight of prying eyes. Jay would no more be caught in public showing his true colours than he would be caught flying to the moon.

His own family, having spent their entire childhoods covering up for their paedophile father, were experts – at not noticing, at making excuses, at shutting out the world. If they had never reported the physical and sexual abuse of themselves, what hope of them reporting or even recognising emotional abuse of someone else?

So where is the happy ending? Where my victory? Where the healing?

Joe, like I had before him, has learned to tread carefully. He edits his personality around his father's preferences and whims. He doesn't take toys his dad doesn't like to his dad's house, where he still lives, or invites friends back or go to the local youth club or eat foods of which his dad does not approve, or express opinions.

But at my house, he has a drawer of clothes he likes, chooses and changes into, if he wants to, of which his father would not approve. He keeps toys in his room and in the car and is careful to leave them there when he has to go. He has sleepovers with local kids and we go camping out at theirs. We play vast games of hide and seek all over the house and football in the rain. Sometimes we have days together, just him and me, sometimes he wants a story read at bedtime and a cuddle, other times he is independent – like others his age.

He has met and chosen friends from out of the groups we joined and had a network of buddies with whom he can be all aspects of himself.

I did reapply through court: I'd hoped some parents would help me – Jay had lost his temper with their son who was the first, and only, child Joe had invited back to his dad's house as a treat for his sixth birthday: Their son was escorted back to his own house in tears and Joe told never to be friends with him again. His crime? Joe told me his friend, at six years old, had 'been too noisy going upstairs'. He was six years old and Jay and yelled at him until he was in tears.

I thought this would bring out what Joe was living with – especially being told not to be friends with another child. But they didn't come to court and later told me they had been 'too busy'. Jay was free to make out to the court that their son had been of 'very difficult character' and the judge had nodded sympathetically – as if not being able to manage a six-year-old was all perfectly understandable in a parent of a six-year-old. He looked no further – but he did make the point that Joe should be allowed to mix with other kids and since then Jay has allowed him to go to some children's parties, to visit some children of whom Jay does approve (those with rich parents) and to go to after-school clubs – which is better than nothing.

I drive to the school to watch any assemblies or plays which Joe is in – staying with Mike and Ian to enable me to get there in time. They have never met him but support my efforts to be a good parent by letting me sleep at their house rather than have to pay for a hotel – or drive in the small hours and darkness to reach the school on time – or miss these aspects of Joe's life. Jay, who had, of course, bought a car a few weeks after the final hearing, takes Joe climbing and pushes him up routes. Those weekends are spent with Jay's cronies with never another child in sight.

I use my time with my mother, she can no longer talk but we sit and hold hands, listen to music, watch telly. My dad looks after her most of the time and I help.

Joe is now ten years old. We see each other every weekend – one day in the area where his dad lives and the weekend in between he is at mine, at my parents' house. We are experts at car games because of all the 100+ mile journeys we share: we play I-spy at PhD level, and word games and alphabet games which would shame a laureate.

The weekends, every one a diamond, are packed

with 'quality time' – of youth clubs, of other friends, of films together and conversations which go anywhere – and there is my victory, my healing: it does not always come with trumpets and a fanfare; sometimes victory is in a child's smile, our delight in each other's company, in my child telling me of his life and his passions, disagreeing with me, negotiating, laughing, and, as far as I can tell, at least when he's with me, being himself. He still runs to me at times – sometimes he runs so fast the curl flies back off his forehead.

I work as a cleaner, a gardener, a volunteer in the local dementia ward. I cannot work in a regular job as the hours would always clash with time with Joe or being with him in the holidays. Plus, I help look after my mum who is now in Alzheimer's dreamland – contented and happy-looking but in a world of her own.

I found my music. Cleaning out the shed for new tenants at the repaired house – the repairs paid for by the bits of wages coming in over the years. As the house was healed I felt myself repair and Jay's power recede.

I found two cardboard boxes under some crates in the shed. They were crushed and damp had caused them to rot. Inside were the tapes and CDs I'd collected over the years of my life before Jay. The tapes I'd recorded, mixer tapes I'd been given. All my treasures. Mould and damp had got in and they were ruined. All my old friends; Aretha, Nina, Marc, Freddie, Dusty – and all the others: the pulse of my life, buried here. But I'm finding them again and they are back in my life, one by one as I find them again, online or in second-hand shops. I can now play them and sing along. And I'm painting again and do performance poems too.

I am getting back into my life.

I no longer have to think twice before speaking or live in dread of a temper. I revel in conversations with normal easy-going people.

And what about God? Or gods? Is he there? Are they? Obviously not. And yet…

Looking back, at so many points I received help when I most needed it. It wasn't always consistent help and not the help I wanted or had asked for – but it had kept me going at the time: when I was floundering out of Esme's kitchen and the phone rang – and it was Debbie telling me she could make a statement and tell the court about how Jay had frightened her and her family – that gave me hope when I needed it; the other promises from Jay's exes and from the neighbours – none of them fulfilled their promises or kept their word – but all of them gave me a stepping stone, a space to breathe, a light, from across the mire of despair when it was rising high around me.

And Anna, and Esme, and Sandra, and Richard, and Marianne and Carol, my dad, my brother, my mum, Ruth, Ruby, Gary, Sharon, Ian and Mike… so many – who had done everything they could. And other strangers who had been kind along the way – all of them kept me able to keep going. Remove any one of them and I might have gone under. Without any one of them, I could have been incarcerated, insane – or found guilty of attempted murder, as Jay had wanted.

What if Richard had not been on duty that day – what if the duty solicitor had been a Lizard, or a junior Skull – not believing in or understanding domestic abuse and what it does? I'd now be in prison.

And how many do go under; have gone under, because they do not have such friends as these?

Some of them were motivated by religious beliefs – but maybe religion is just a vehicle through which people express who they are; it gives them an excuse to be kind, permission to be bigger than they otherwise would be? All of them had helped: The unexpected phone calls, the offers of help – most of which bore no fruit but which had given me hope to keep going – and then – the weirdest of all: it was how I got back into court.

After the final hearing, after digging my pond and becoming numb in order to cope with what had happened, I had tried to find a way forward: I couldn't leave Joe at his dad's for the next ten years without trying again. I visited several solicitors' offices – I'd ring up to make an appointment and find the office and sit and wait in my best clothes, a photo of Joe in my hands to try and show the solicitor what this was about. Always, to be met, not by the solicitor with whom I thought I had an appointment, but with a junior in smart clothes, with heels, shoulder pads and an efficient manner, who made notes and asked me how I would pay, took the copy of the judge's summary from the final hearing and closed the meeting.

I would not hear from them again for months than I'd call and collect it and they said the judge hadn't made any legal mistakes so there was no ground for an appeal, so I had to start from square one and, further, all the evidence, which should have been at the final hearing, was now null and void, as it should have been seen then – even though it hadn't been.

I came to a dark place where I could see no way ahead:

Nights were full of visions of Joe having the childhood from hell – being isolated and kept as a little carer by his dad and manipulated as I had been into being his little doormat. I prayed for help and for guidance but none seemed to come. I scanned legal pages on the web and took out books on child law. I went through the farce of approaching yet other solicitors before realising the door was closed – on Joe, on me. There was no way forward. At weekends, I saw Joe and squashed love and fun and being a parent to him into those few hours. There was nothing I could do to stop the rest of his childhood being a round of pressure, criticism, fear – trapped in Jay's control.

Then, weirdly, I applied to go on a computer course to help with the search for work – I needed to improve and update my skills, I needed work to pay for all the petrol and keep the car on the road and generally be as good a parent as I could be: as a carer, to my mum, I could access a computer course at half price so I applied and got a place – at the university campus, one night a week. Even from the depths of my mum's dementia, which had progressed now to where she seldom spoke to us any more and had stopped walking, she was still looking after us.

I arrived at the campus in winter's pitch dark. I parked the car and went into the building at the entrance described in the confirming letter I had received. Corridors. A map of the site. Bright lights. I walked about half a mile down hollow corridors and up stairs. There didn't seem to be anybody else about. I found the room with the number on it. There were rows of desks and computers – all empty. Then I heard voices. A uniformed caretaker was walking towards the room from the other direction with a woman who was carrying a briefcase. When they arrived he explained that the computer course had been cancelled the previous week and that a letter had been sent out to all the fifty people who had places on the course.

The other woman and I were the only ones who had not received the letter. The caretaker left us in the room while he went to find out if the course had been given a new starting date. He was very apologetic.

When he had left the other woman and I got chatting. I told her I needed the course to help with my work and she said she did too. I asked what she did and she then said, "I advise judges in the family court when there are children involved."

She noticed the look on my face as I stared at her.

When I outlined my circumstances she told me, "You can self-represent – go to the court, get a form, pay 200 quid and reapply."

And that was it. That was how I got back into court.

I asked my only witness, the mother of the six-year-old child who had visited Joe and had been yelled at and reduced to tears by Jay. But she wouldn't make a statement or come to court – I had thought that might just give the judge a hint of what Joe was living with. Again, the witness I was relying on wouldn't come to court and I was left with no evidence, nothing to raise the alarm – all I could do was express my concerns about Joe never being allowed to go to other kids' parties, never, except that once, being allowed to have friends round or to visit others, only going to school, nowhere else.

At last the judge, waking eventually to the suspicion that maybe he and his court had possibly got it a bit wrong, instructed Jay to let Joe have friends, let him go to after-school clubs and birthday parties – so he must have at least suspected I might be telling the truth – and since that hearing things have been a lot better for Joe. 'Better' meaning more like normal.

By being with other kids and other families Joe would see more of 'normal' and know that adults don't have to be bullies, it isn't normal for women and children – or anyone – to be scared in their own home – and he is less likely to grow up accepting his father's ways as his own.

It was a tiny victory – but it made all the difference. Joe was safe.

Any of the solicitors I'd visited could have told me that I could self-represent – but they were gagged by money-interest, or maybe they thought I knew it?

So maybe gods, God, or the angels, or the universe, had arranged for fifty letters to go out cancelling people attending a computer course, arranged for it to be cancelled and that for only two letters to go astray – mine and this woman I so desperately needed to meet. If three people had been in that room we would not have had such a conversation. If either one of us had not turned up at that room I would not have found out how to get back into court.

Again, it didn't produce radical change or the outcome I so desperately wanted – but it took away the despair. Again, it provided a stepping stone when I was in a very grim place – it gave me strength to carry on and more hope – like Debbie's phone call, like the petition, like the statements that were promised but never written; like the CAFCASS report – the first one – like the advice from my mum; like stepping stones – they gave me hope, false or otherwise which enabled me to survive. Just.

Maybe, in its arbitrary blunderings, this clumsy universe, just occasionally, gets it right? The same universe allowed Anastasia and Dan to be the ones to come and 'assess' a situation they could no more understand than fly to the moon. Maybe things just sometimes go terribly right, and we think God is helping us, and at others they go terribly wrong – and we think he is testing us – when it's all just arbitrary quantum chaos.

When I heard, months later, that Dan was dying of cancer in hospital, I thought again, probably another arbitrary stroke – but this time of brilliance. I wait with mild curiosity what pit of her own venom awaits Anastasia's drowning.

Someone lent me the tape of the song: 'I Tasted Hate's Sweet Hanging Tree' and I played it over and over – and decided to step away from hate. Nelson Mandela said, of his captors, 'Resentment is like drinking poison and expecting it to hurt your enemies'. So I stepped away. But I had my flights of fancy first.

The judge, whose health I was originally concerned about, has no doubt choked on his own claret or died of gout and piles, or, better still, had a stroke and now lives dependant on those he despises for his comforts, all educated at comprehensive schools – and maybe he'll finally learn what matters in life. Either that or he has fallen into a cesspit at his own house and drowned – I cannot decide.

Dr F, of course, on an expensive holiday, paid for with her ill-gotten blood-money, has for certain, long been eaten by hyenas after running for hours, not years, through the undergrowth, desperate for help – discovering, for the first time, what it is to be scared.

I found myself wishing, when I heard of Dan's impending death, that all those who had played a part in my pain, would die. It took a moment to realise that, of course, they all will. I'll get that wish. There was no need to plot or resent – the best thing to do was get on with my life and leave them to their various self-made hells. Forgiveness? When you are being abused the act of forgiveness can lend you some sense of being in control and so take away some of the pain. So turning the other cheek, in Roman-occupied Palestine, could be an act of defiance as could 'going the extra mile' – defying your abusers' control over you, choosing the terms of your abuse. And when the odds are overwhelming and fighting back not an option, it can be a means of remaining sane. A rather wonderful vicar, Helen, took time out to explain this to me. She helped me understand that 'turning the other cheek' and 'forgiving an enemy' can be an act of defiance, of survival and of self-respect – not of defeat, of cowardice or of compliance in the abuse.

So I forgave them. I forgave them to hell.

I enjoy my time with Joe and count my blessings – and I wait. Joe is ten. The wonders of the teenage years are not far away – the years of questioning, of the adult brain arriving and no longer accepting whatever is handed out – the years of change. He lives with his father – but he also has a good life here – friends and a home he loves and where he can be himself – and one day, maybe, he'll make a choice of his own.

Whatever else happens to him, he has had a good childhood – or at least a childhood which has included many good things, good memories and good times, and maybe that is all we can ever give our children to take with them into the future. Whatever else happens to Joe and me, we have had some wonderful times and they add up to years and no court can take that away. The people who hurt us – Jay, Anastasia and Dan, the solicitors, the Judge van Winkle, the Skull, Ms Pane, the Lizard, Dr F – they will never be Joe's mum or know what that is like, so I feel sorry for them and wish them much joy of their money and their brilliant careers.

As for all those who dish out the hurt – I have this advantage over them: I have met the Annas, the Esmes, the Ruths, the Rubys, the Mariannes, the Garys and the Helens, the Sandras and the Richards of this world – and I'm on their team. And proud to be so. That is a choice we all have to make.

I tried to appeal: I wrote to every one of the institutions which are there to make sure this doesn't happen: the Minister of Justice wrote back to tell me how experts are appointed by the court and to describe the process I had written to him to express my concerns about; the social work body, which I'd written to explaining how Dan and Anastasia had behaved against all the codes of practice, did not write back but then insisted they had; the office which oversees the work of psychiatrists said they do not get involved with individual cases – never hinting at what the hell they do get involved in – and I wrote to the Children's Commissioner – who does not get involved in cases which have been to court.

The ombudsman spoke to Ms Pane – who then suddenly, amazingly, discovered I still owed her £3,000 – which was impossible for me to prove was untrue as they had never sent me detailed bills, only vague summaries – and offered to forget this amount if I dropped the complaint. The ombudsman advised me to accept this as the best offer I'd get even if the complaint was proved. I wondered how many times they had used that ploy and understood why the bills they had sent had always been so vague. Such respectable gangsters! The MP I went to see, to explain what happened in family courts about abuse, was kind and sympathetic and said he'd raise the issue – but not the case.

I had come to a fork in the road I was travelling.

I spoke to Anna, who had done more than anyone to keep me and Joe together, of my admiration for the Lawrence family who had moved heaven and earth to bring about change for the sake of the memory of their son, Stephen – murdered by racists. Could I, should I not do this for Joe? Should I not take on this battle life had brought me and strive to get things changed – fight for juries to be in family courts – fight for the use of 'experts' to be curtailed – for the antagonism between teams of barristers to be set aside and an investigative, cooperative approach adopted to get at the truth in cases – not compete to distort it to 'win'?

"Joe's still alive," Anna said.

So I had a choice.

I had reached a crossroads: either to go on battling trying to get something changed, trying to make someone accountable for the lies – or not. To use that energy instead to make Joe okay. To cope with the 200-mile round trips, to find work to pay keep me out of penury, to keep myself sane – especially the latter. Keeping sane is a struggle every day not to be consumed with grief and anger. Respect to all who struggle likewise and who don't go over the edge. Respect and sympathy to all who do.

To write the story down in the hope it might help others? I was tortured for a long time by 'what ifs' and 'why didn't I's?' but that way madness lies – now when thoughts like that threaten I think of otters playing and turn my mind away from what can only bring back pain. I could hate myself forever for getting it wrong in so many ways – but that will change nothing.

I found others had done similar: my hero, Austen, gave us Colonel Tilney – in Northangar Abbey – who had destroyed his wife, not with physical cruelty, the writer makes clear, but with emotional cruelty. Daphne Du Maurier gave us Josh, the landlord of Jamaica Inn, who bullied and terrorised his family and drove his wife out of her mind – but he never used physical force, only its threat and relentless anger. So Jay has literary precedents – and an ugly portrait gallery they are.

In ancient Africa and China, maybe in many more ancient societies now gone, whole villages would turn out and set on an abuser, sort them out. Hunter-gatherer tribes lived communally so any abuser could be spotted and driven out as a danger to the tribe. In any oppressive society, an oppressor will feel at home, even welcomed, and be seen as normal. Our society thinks injustice is normal and in our closeted world of the private nuclear family, the shadows are deep wherein abusers can hide as we turn to look the other way. Like viruses they hide in their holes, unseen.

At the cafe in Women's Aid I told another woman of my horror of finding the evidence not in the file. I expected her to be struck with horror and disbelief. She didn't even blink. She told me of the evidence from the hospital – of her broken ribs and blackened eyes – also having gone missing. I realised then, and after similar conversations, that this was not my story; it is our story. It is the story of thousands, maybe millions, who look to the courts for justice – and only find yet more abuse in hidden places.

I expressed horror at the behaviour of the legal teams in the family court: Richard explained, the family court in Britain, unlike those on the continent, use not an inquisitorial approach – where everyone is focussed on inquiring into the truth – but 'adversarial'. This means that the outcome rests on which legal team does 'best'.

And there it was. The context. Within those parameters, the respectable and bewigged tore truth apart to prove which was the winning team. Was their behaviour excused by the parameters within which they worked, the rules that were set? When did 'best' come to mean 'most ruthless', most unprincipled or most depraved? Is hiding or twisting evidence in a clever way something to be rewarded?

But courts in Europe don't do the 'adversarial approach'.

So, I meditated on the long way home, if Napoleon had won at Waterloo, and had unified Europe as was his intent, not only would we have gained a wonderful cuisine, a sexier language and WW1 would not have happened – there then being no separate national ruling classes to have that spat – but besides these heady rewards, we might also have got a family court system which is fit for purpose – and Joe, and heaven knows how many like him, would have come to live with the non-abusing parent. By Waterloo, of course, Napoleon had dwindled or warped from a revolutionary hero into a mere dictator and Wellington met only a half-hearted French army – disheartened and disillusioned with the revolution. They hadn't overthrown or abandoned Napoleon for the same reasons I hadn't abandoned or overthrown Jay – fear, confusion, lack of organisation and the remnants of love.

I've always known there is injustice and oppression woven into the fabric of the society in which we now live – but it had never hurt me so directly before. For there is something wrong with this world of ours: the family-court system, and domestic abuse itself, is rooted in that wrongness – as surely as is a dangerous, poisonous fungus rooted in a wider, overall and far-reaching rottenness, and it threatens to choke us all.

A woman's place is not in the kitchen or home – it's wherever she wants to be and, most of all, it is in the struggle for a better world. It was a victory for me to, again, go on protests against job cuts, racism, war and climate destruction without any fear of abuse on my return home. It was a victory to be able to ring friends and family and chat without looking over my shoulder and to visit them when invited without fear of repercussions. It was a victory to get back into my own life at last.

There was another, lesser victory: I got a job in a care home, looking after other mums with dementia. It was part-time, in between looking after my own mum, seeing Joe, being with my dad.

The first day there, one of the patients was in distress, needed someone to talk to – and suddenly, from nowhere – there it was: like the long note or the chorus from a long-forgotten, favourite song or like the face of a best friend you have not seen for a while, it came – unbidden: I felt a surge of empathy and compassion and was able to go and hold her hand and chat for a while until she was calm again – and I knew – there is nothing wrong with our empathic response to each other, nothing wrong with responding, one human to another, to another's pain.

It is so easy to imagine a world based on kindness and empathy – where these are rewarded instead of, as now, the violence, greed and worst aspects of our natures.

It was the best part of me – and it was still there. It was and is the best part of me, of all of us – the ability to respond to the pain of another. It wasn't something to hate in myself but something to value and protect and celebrate. What was wrong was the taking advantage of that – Jay's falseness and cruelty. Yet, despite all he had done, there it was and I could sit with this elderly lady and listen because I cared and he had not, could not, would never, with all the courts in the world, take that from me.

It was as natural as breath and sure proof that I was alive and still the person I had ever been.

So I have stopped hating myself. I have stopped blaming myself for being abused – and my heart is with all those who have that struggle: all those who are blamed for being hurt.

Afterword

One year after Deputy Dan died of cancer, Anastasia was escorted from her workplace and sacked — due to her malpractice coming to light — not about what she did to me but another 'case' — so someone else had spoken out and been heard.

Whoever you are, you unknown hero, I salute you and owe you thanks.

Change can happen if we make it.

Appendix

So how do you spot an abuser?

How can you tell if the person at the desk at work next to yours is in an abusive relationship? Either receiving the abuse or dishing it out?

How can you tell if you are?

Here's a checklist: it is not exhaustive.

Are you ever – ever- afraid of your partner?

Does your colleague or friend ever seem to be wary of them or careful around them? Ever? Domestic Abusers often behave quite differently in public so if you glimpse anything at all it will be a rare slip up on the abuser's part.

Does the person make excuses for their partner's behaviour?

Is the person unusually hesitant about having people to the house? Do they make excuses – even with people who are friends?

Do you change plans or keep friends away that your partner does not like?

Do you seem to trigger criticism in your partner about your clothes/body/beliefs/habits?

Do things which are precious to you get broken/lost/hidden?

Is it difficult for you to invite people around or to socialise how you used to?

Do you think your partner 'can't help it' or has an illness or some other reason for their unusual behaviour?

Do you edit your conversation and your personality in order not to 'upset' your partner – or another person you live with?

Do you tell yourself it's getting better – then it happens again?

Does your partner make it difficult for you to keep in touch with your friends or family?

Do you feel guilty when you do?

Does your partner punish you with temper or threats – or sulks – when you do or say something he or she doesn't like?

Does he or she reward you with shows of affection when you do what he or she wants you to?

Do you think your partner could hurt you physically? Do you sometimes think they are about to?

Do you think it's your fault when he or she loses his or her temper?

For 'partner', read 'someone in your private life' – it could be a parent, it could be your grown-up child – but it's most likely to be a partner.

What to do:

Tell someone. Either someone who is a friend – or someone who is a professional.

If they diminish or normalise your concerns they are not hearing you properly and have not understood. Tell them more, if they still can't hear it – tell someone else – there will be someone who knows what you mean and who can respond helpfully. Find that person.

A lot of people don't want to know about abuse.

Ring Women's Aid – they know. If you are a man who is being abused, ask them who to ring in your area.

There are organisations that could help you to get out – you can't do it on your own.

Tell your family – anyone who cares about you. You might have become convinced, via the abuse, that no-one does or could – give it a try. You'll be surprised.

If you are an abuser – there are organisations which can help you stop. Contact them. Stop manipulating and controlling people in your life.

If you think you might be being abused or if you know you are:

Tell your GP. If he or she diminishes what you have said, see a different GP.

Tell your union. Has your workplace got a policy?

Tell your colleagues and friends. Tell them what is happening, what you find difficult to cope with.

If they start to normalise it, tell them **listen** – normal rows are not the same as being abused – the difference is – **normal rows are mutual and nobody is afraid**.

If you suspect someone you know might be in a controlling relationship share with them what it was that makes you think that.

They might not even know or accept that they are being controlled – but let them hear your concerns, what you noticed. It might help them start to find a way out.

Emotional Abuse is now illegal – so keep a diary of 'events' it will help you see the pattern and realise what is happening to you – and may help as evidence.

Ask to speak to the police Domestic Abuse officers – they will know what you are talking about.

Finally.

If you can't relate to people except by wanting to control them, if you cannot return love with love, if you cannot be vulnerable and kind or close and respond to other's kindness and love only with an urge to control, to hurt – get help, professional help.

And if you can't be bothered to do that – go and buy a tee-shirt and get it printed with the words, 'I am an abuser – keep clear' in large orange letters on the front and put it on, very carefully.

And then go jump off a cliff.

THE END

Printed in Great Britain
by Amazon